THE DEVIL SHE KNOWS

I0525325

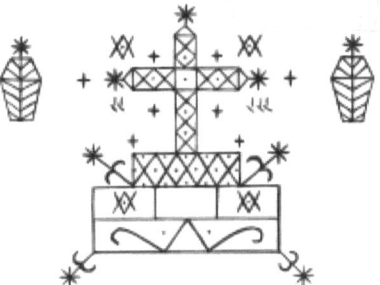

M.T. FALGOUST

Printed in the United States.
Wagging Tales Press
First Printing, 2025
ISBN: 978-1-962191-02-9

Dedication

For the lost, the fleeting, and the unforgettable.

To those whose lives brushed mine—some briefly, some profoundly, some only through stories and headlines.

You lingered long enough to leave an impression, and now you live again, in fragments and shadows, between these pages.

You are not forgotten.

Not here.

Prologue

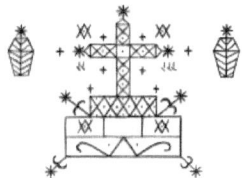

The scream strangled in her throat. Harmony willed her legs to flight. Her deadened limbs refused to respond.

She could see, though. And hear. She saw Death coming. Heard the thudding gallop of his skeletal steed. In moments, it would all be over.

The whip-like crack of the bonfire's flames snapped her back to reality. The pounding of hooves was the race of her own pulse, though now it grew steadily faint and thready, the echo of something dwindling into the distant past. Although—she struggled to form the thought— nineteen years wasn't all that past. But, until tonight, she had thought she was young enough to know it all.

She'd known enough not to cringe at her stepdaddy's sour beer breath when he pulled her close to him. She'd known enough not to talk back when he'd cuss at her in slurred syllables for burning his work shirt with the crappy flat iron they kept in the closet of the double-wide. Known enough not to whimper when his clumsy drunk fingers fumbled at the button of her cut-offs the nights Mama worked late at the Waffle House.

Known it all—at least until she'd known enough to crush a handful of Mama's nerve pills into his tall boy. By then she'd known enough to blow that ratty-ass Mississippi trailer park before the smoke had even dissolved off the cupcake candle on her sixteenth birthday.

She'd left with nothing but the clothes on her back and the crumpled wad of tens her stepdaddy kept in a fake beer can. She'd known that's where he kept his stash. It was the only can that survived longer than a day and a half in the fridge.

She'd hitched her way west and made it a full ninety miles across the state line. From there, it was just a line of cheap rental rooms and bad boyfriends as she struggled to make her way.

But she had.

Despite it all. Got a place. Got a job.

Screw 'em all. She was a survivor.

Right?

Perspiration beaded on her forehead. It trickled in tiny rivulets down along her hairline. A well of thick, slimy mucus welled at the corners of her dry, cracked lips and began a slow trail down her cheek. Her instinct was to wipe it away, but no part of her bowed to her command.

Resolve began to dissolve.

Her fractured memory jumbled together like so many puzzle parts.

How had she gotten here?

She tried desperately to remember. She'd finished her shift at the club. She'd asked Pete, the bartender, for a glass of water before she headed out. He'd offered her a ride home.

Not likely.

He'd been more pickled than the eggs bobbling in the murky, sediment-filled barrel jar on the scarred mahogany bar. She'd laughed at him, drank her water, and left.

Everything after that was murky as the egg water.

Her pupils dilated to pinpricks of black in orbs of Aegean blue. Shadowy wraiths danced in the firelight. They twirled in a macabre waltz against the banana leaves nearby. Her breath came in tattered rasps.

She heard a whimper. A timid mewling, like the cry of an infant.

Melody!

Sudden electric clarity coursed through her fogged brain.

Melody. The one decent thing ever to happen to her. Her eyes rolled wildly in their sockets as she searched for her baby girl.

Where was she? What had happened to her?

If—she succumbed to the hopeless possibility—if she didn't make it out of this, who would take care of her? She struggled to search, but the baby was nowhere to be found.

The mewling had come from her own lips.

Her heart hammered as waves of nausea cramped through her abdomen. Tremors vibrated through her. She could not tell if they were driven by fear or something worse.

The sudden, violent convulsions that wracked her body removed all doubt. Her lithe frame arced in twisted, gruesome pain. Unbidden tears streaked black.

In a cruel respite, her multi-studded ear picked up a strange, but familiar sound.

A rhythmic shush.

She couldn't quite place it. It unnerved her all the same. At least it was a sensory reminder she was still alive.

The sound ceased.

Thunder rolled, long and low. A storm was coming. It was coming, and it was bringing death.

Chapter One

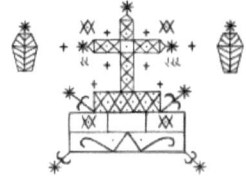

Rain was coming. He could smell it.

The prevailing wind brushed a whiff of charged ozone under his nose. It mingled with the loamy scent of freshly over-turned earth and something more dank and musty. He grinned like a mad skeleton. He was nearly there. He caught a snatch of newscast drifting from one of the neighborhood bars.

"The National Hurricane Center is monitoring an unnamed storm system approximately 350 miles south of the southern coast of Florida." The first fat, wet drop splatted the uneven street in front of him. He pedaled harder.

I am Rabbit. I'm faster than you. He challenged the falling water. Rabbit liked the rain. It washed away the grime and grit of the city. Bourbon Street, with its sticky red puddles of spilled Pat O'Brien Hurricanes. Conti with

sticky, red puddles of something darker and much more…
mortal.

He darted into the intersection at North Rampart. A
banshee wail screamed past the front fender of his rusted-
out Mongoose. He scudded out the path of the rocketing
police car and jumped the curb near the corner where St.
Louis Cemetery Number One met the Iberville Housing
Project.

I am Rabbit. I'm faster than you.

He chanted silently. The cruiser's revolving lights
splashed the scene in a kaleidoscopic wash of red and blue.
Rabbit skidded to a stop, sending loose pebbles skittering
across the cracked sidewalk. Sweat soaked the armpits of
his Grateful Dead t-shirt. He dragged a pale forearm across
his dripping hairline.

Yeah. He probably shouldn't be here. But Eugene
had been crazy insistent. Kept swearing he had something
Rabbit had to see. Rabbit straightened his shoulders and
concentrated on the wandering fissures under his feet as he
waited for his racing pulse to slow.

They look like veins.

Rabbit's heart thumped wildly in his chest. Not a
bad analogy.

New Orleans breathed. A living entity. Alive and
pulsing with activity at any hour. Even 3:AM. As if to
prove his point, a random snatch of trumpet floated on the
breeze from the direction of the French Quarter.

Laissez bon temps roulez.

Let the good times roll.

They certainly did here. Once upon a time, anyway.
He stared at the dark cluster of buildings that formed the

outer edge of the Iberville complex. Like a collection of eerie gingerbread houses. The whole thing had been revitalized in recent years—part of the nationwide gentrification initiative. This area, like so many New Orleans neighborhoods, had a rich, if colorful, history. It once boasted a booming red-light district called Storyville. Famous musicians like Louis Armstrong and Jelly Roll Morton plied their trade in the jazz halls that thrived in its streets and back alleys. More recently, Iberville was one of the first public housing units to reopen in New Orleans after the devastation of Hurricane Katrina, having suffered minimal structural damage.

Two pops echoed off the pastel siding.

Well, not all damage was cosmetic.

He brushed his long, unnaturally black bangs from his eyes with fingers tipped in chipped, black nail polish. An angry red gash interrupted the arch of his brow over his left eye. Rabbit winced a little as he prodded the fresh wound. He hadn't been quite fast enough this time.

The gritted teeth turned into a wry grin. Pop was a southpaw. Played in the minors. Too bad he couldn't stand straight long enough to piss, let alone pitch a baseball anymore. He might have made something of himself. If it hadn't been for Eugene, it could have gone a lot worse. Cracked Pop with an empty beer bottle.

Set him on his ass is what he did.

Not that Rabbit wasn't grateful to his buddy for intervening, but Rabbit knew he was the one who would pay for it later. And he hated going to the clinic time after time to have Doc Steele fix him up. Always having to come up with some damned excuse or other to explain away his injuries. But Ms. Sabine always insisted. Wouldn't let him work unless he got checked out every time.

Quit whining.

Rabbit admonished himself. Besides, Eugene was waiting.

An angry caw trumpeted over the stone wall behind him. Something had disturbed a large black crow. It took flight over the pale walls of the graveyard—a black, swooping shadow—then dissolved in the night.

An old decrepit cemetery probably wasn't the best meeting place, especially one where many of the graves had crumbled into anonymous piles of red brick and dusty mortar, but that was Eugene for you.

Every time he came here, Rabbit half expected one of the dead to stretch a decaying, bony hand from one of the dark holes and clutch for him, awakened by the tantalizing aroma of his fresh brain. Stupid, of course. A by-product of one too many late nights with TV host Morgus the Magnificent and his classic, cheesy B-horror flicks. He started to push his bike toward the shadows, but the old bike limped feebly forward.

What the hell? Rabbit looked down. The front tire frame resembled a half-baked pretzel. The damage must have occurred when he hopped the curb.

Awesome. He wasn't looking forward to the long walk home. He gave the damaged bike a well-placed kick. It collapsed in a useless, rusted metal heap.

Rabbit's ears suddenly pricked at an irregular, shuffling sound. He grabbed his wheeled pile of sourdough scrap and pressed against the whitewashed cemetery wall. He held his breath. A lazy spider peeked out from the recess where he had spun his web. He decided Rabbit was too large to make a suitable snack.

The shuffling got closer, only now it was joined by a guttural groan.

They're coming to get you, Rabbit. Images of Romero zombies flickered in Rabbit's brain. Tattered clothes. Dead-eye stares. Stiff arms reaching out for—

"Hey, kid. Got a light?" The vagrant that had been shuffling along the sidewalk startled the wide-eyed teen. Rabbit stared blankly at the toothless, grizzled face.

"Whatsamatter?" the drunk continued. "Marie Laveau put a zombie curse on ya?" The old man jabbed a crooked thumb to the walls behind Rabbit, toward St. Louis Number One. Reference to the famed voodoo queen jarred an awkward motor response from Rabbit. He patted his pockets and offered the lighter that always lived in the pocket of his torn jeans.

"Yeah. No. Sorry. Take it."

The man reached out his palsied hand and wrapped his long fingers around the lighter. "Mighty nice of ya. How's about a smoke?"

Aggravation stripped the last vestiges of uneasiness from Rabbit's nerves. He was running out of time. It wouldn't be long before his father slept off his Jack Daniel's nap. If Rabbit didn't make it home before he woke up—well, there were worse fates than having your brain eaten by a zombie.

He dug into his back pocket and shoved the entire pack of Lucky Strikes into the man's outstretched hand. He'd snaked them from Pop's bedside stand.

"Unfiltered? C'mon! Gimme a break!" the vagrant

groused as Rabbit melted into the darkness overshadowing Liberty Street. Rabbit left the old man grumbling and made a beeline for his secret entrance as the random splats of rain grew more insistent.

Good thing ramen didn't put a lot of meat on your bones, Rabbit thought as he pushed his skinny frame through the crumbled hole in the brick wall.

It puzzled him how his plump friend always managed to squeeze through the small opening. The cemetery didn't have twenty-four-hour security, but the iron gates were locked tight at 3:PM most days. Fortunately for Rabbit and Eugene, someone had tried to establish a drive-thru service, the front end of their vehicle creating an opening just large enough for two thrill-seeking sixteen-year-olds with nothing better to do on a Saturday night.

Rabbit thumped to a tumbled heap on an expanse of grassy plot. The unofficial entryway opened just over the Protestant section of the cemetery. This part of the graveyard was largely anonymous, with few markers identifying the sleeping interred. Rabbit picked himself up and dusted the graying dust from his legs. He looked up and caught sight of that which continued to amaze and bewilder countless visitors to the Crescent City

A city of the dead.

The unusually high water table in south Louisiana prevented standard interment in the ground. A good flood could raise long-gone ancestors to visit once more among the living. While Mom and Pop were sorely missed, it was a little disconcerting to have them bobble up to ten years after they had been buried.

So, like Père Lachaise in Paris, the dearly departed

were entombed in mausoleum cities, clusters of miniature marble, and stucco buildings along small brick and grass streets.

Rabbit navigated his way through the decaying city of death. Right. Then left. Five tombs down.

No Eugene. Rabbit checked the time on his cell. 3:15. Eugene should have been here.

That's when he heard it.

Chink. Chink. Chink.

The sound of metal biting into stone.

Rabbit ducked down behind a shabby, crumbling crypt. He tried not to imagine what lay decaying inside the gaping, dark maw yawning beside him. He fingered the St. Christopher medal at his neck.

Did St. Christopher protect against zombies?

Whatever the hell Eugene had to show him had better be good. Where in the piss was he, anyway? This was all his stupid idea.

Chink. Chink. Chink.

Suddenly, Rabbit heard a heavy thud. The long scrape of something being dragged over stone stripped his nerves like nails on a chalkboard. His head turned toward the strange sound. He noticed a wavering orange-yellow glow hovering over the tombs just a few narrow alleys over. Rabbit scowled.

Eugene. Did that dumb ass go and build a fire in the middle of the damn cemetery?

Wait till I get a hold of that shithead.

Rabbit straightened his bony shoulders and stood tall, prepared to knock some sense into his practical-joking friend. The cemetery was a protected historical landmark. If they got caught dicking it up…

Rabbit didn't bother to finish the thought. He just knew he preferred dodging his dad's fists to the stifling confines of juvie.

His worn Converse dislodged a loose brick. It clattered to the stony pathway. The sound ricocheted between the mausoleum walls. A sudden pall of silence draped the cemetery. He braced himself. Here it comes, Rabbit thought. Any moment, Eugene, all buck-toothed two hundred and twenty-five ebony pounds of him, would jump from around the corner to make Rabbit wet his pants. Wasn't going to happen, Rabbit thought.

Ha! I am Rabbit. I'm faster and smarter than you. A full sixty seconds passed.

Nothing.

A sobering thought occurred to Rabbit.

What if it wasn't Eugene?

He sucked in a breath and held it.

Just before his skin tinged purple, the solid thud of a drum echoed through the night. A second, deep boom followed the first. Then another. Soon the rhythm matched the wild pounding of Rabbit's heart.

A deep baritone chanting joined the throb of drums. Rabbit dared a glance around the corner.

A flush of warmth rolled over him, his breath catching in his throat, as a wave of heat from a roaring bonfire rippled through the air. It swirled in a crackling cone near an opened tomb.

A large, darkened figure stood forward of the yawning black entrance. Rabbit was too far away to discern any more detail of the mysterious shadow.

He saw the open coffin with vivid clarity, however.

There, lying still in the open casket, was his friend.

Only Eugene wasn't Eugene.

Eugene laughed like a braying donkey. Eugene told ridiculously dirty jokes. Eugene could put away a full-size muffuletta from Central Grocery and still have room for a dozen beignets.

Eugene wasn't a lifeless, ashy brown. Eugene didn't have blood trickling from a bizarre symbol raked into his wide forehead.

And Eugene wouldn't lie there, docile, while a tall, top-hatted figure towered over him, skull face grinning, poised to plunge a blade directly into his chest.

Rabbit opened his mouth to scream.

Chapter Two

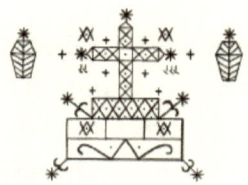

The scream ripped her from sleep. It wasn't until the Beretta PX4 was in her grip, a carbon black extension of her hand, that she realized there was no target. No threat.

The room? Empty.

The scream? Her own.

"Damn!" Hunter let the epithet fly. Another flipping nightmare. She collapsed backward onto the layer cake of pillows. They let out a gentle whoosh as her head sunk into the downy pile. Not that she *needed* seven pillows. Well, okay. Maybe they *did* make the king-sized bed seem less meaningless. No man had filled the space in quite some time.

Not since—well, there was no use dwelling on things you couldn't change.

Fact of the matter was, she just hadn't found one she liked of late. Pillow or man. Take your pick. In

Hunter's opinion, they were either too soft or too hard.

She grinned crookedly, courtesy of the chipped front tooth received from an over-zealous Mardi Gras fan. It simply amazed her what people would do for a cheap, plastic pair of beads. She grinned again.

Or a man.

Ah, the glamorous life of an 8th District New Orleans police detective.

Ugh! It was too hot to go back to sleep. Even at 5:AM, the standard sultry July temperature plastered her thin white undershirt to her svelte frame. Thunder rolled, an ominous growl, from somewhere in the distance.

Thank god. Maybe a good thunder shower would cool things off a bit. Hunter always said New Orleans only had two seasons—hot and wet. Both foiled her intentions for sleep at present. That and the startling images of her dreams.

She reached for the white-capped bottle on her nightstand. She squinted through the crust rimming her hazel eyes. The words "zolpidem tartrate" swam in and out of focus. With any luck, a few of the sleeping pills might coax her into a few hours of much-needed rest.

She gritted her teeth as she wrenched the bottle open.

Empty.

Hunter chucked it. It dominoed into a collection of its empty amber brothers. Much as she despised the idea, she was going to have to call Dr. Lacey...again. She fumbled for the television remote. Maybe some mindless infomercials would help distract her.

As the low hum of the set buzzed, the light of the

screen steeped the room in a hypnotic blue glow. Hunter settled back into her pillow Everest for some much-needed boob-tube sedation. She'd been pulling double shifts at the station, trying to close the recent onslaught of cases. Heat brought out the crazies.

Too bad half of them were on the city's payroll.

Ninety-seven. That's what they called her. It wasn't because that's what her slim frame weighed. Though at one hundred fifteen pounds soaking wet, it wouldn't be that far off the mark.

No. The reason she was just a number at the 8th was that, in the short time since she'd advanced from the rape unit to homicide, she'd made arrests in ninety-seven percent of her cases. Her male counterparts rushed to point out that arrests were not convictions. Hunter didn't really give a crap what they thought. If she could keep a creep off the street for even twenty-four hours, then that was twenty-four hours the public could breathe a little easier.

Tony Robbins suddenly extolled the career-advancing virtues of human brain consumption. The odd juxtaposition grated against Hunter's psyche like a face-puckering shot of Jägermeister.

"What the hell?" She focused on the screen. Somewhere amid her reminisces, the programming had segued into Romero's horror classic. She watched half-heartedly for a few minutes. She contemplated one of the shuffling, mindless drones.

Dated a guy like that once.

The zombie ate the face off some poor woman. A wry grin curled up the right edge of Hunter's full mouth.

Okay. More than once.

She covered her face with a pillow and collapsed back into her fluffy nest. She ground her thumb down on the remote's off button. What she wouldn't give for a little distraction!

The cell phone on her nightstand buzzed an urgent request for attention. A muffled "thank god" emanated from the mountain of down.

A standard-sized projectile sailed across the room as Hunter scrambled for the phone, nearly knocking over the Our Lady of Prompt Succor candle keeping watch on the dresser.

"Despré." Hunter remained silent as the caller relayed information. The welcome relief on Hunter's face morphed into stony determination. "I'll be there in thirty."

*****

The old man must have been upwards of sixty, the greasy gray hair lying flat and scant against his balding head. His overcoat had the mark of better days upon it, a finely tailored Hart, Schaffner & Marx. The straight-cut, single-vent check hinted at rich warm tones of brown, cream, and rust, but now, even in the dim haze of 6:00 AM, it just sort of smeared together under several years of grime and filth. As Hunter studied the mottled port-wine face, she wondered how things had gone so far south for this man.

"Y'all okay, Despré?" a deep, syrupy baritone startled Hunter from her reverie.

B.B. Benally's six-foot-five frame seemed to materialize from the eerie fog rolling in off the Mississippi River. In fact, Hunter pondered, the early mist had transformed all the morning residents—beat cops, harbor patrol, and a couple of puddle pirates from the Coast Guard—into ethereal specters. Insubstantial ghosts.

Even the great paddle wheeler *Natchez* seemed surreal as she floated silently in her moorings. The dreamy qualities brought all the startling images of last night's nightmare rushing back.

A face. Pale with death. The fierce, angry carving etched into the forehead. The incredible sensation of déjà vu washed over her.

She blinked her amber eyes with purpose, trying to dispel the violent image. She rattled her head. The lack of sleep was getting to her.

"Yeah. No. I'm good." She paused. "I'm good," she repeated, not sure if it was for Benally's benefit or her own.

"Okay. I hear you, partner. Sorry it's so damn early, but you know how it is."

Hunter grimaced and completed her co-worker's thought. "Crime never sleeps."

Benally nodded. "Call came in around five. Lucky break for us, too. If the old man over there hadn't been trying to fish breakfast out of the river, we might have missed this one. Current probably would have carried it straight out to the Gulf."

"So, where's the body?" Hunter's eyes combed through the fog, searching for the telltale medical examiner.

"Body? You see, that's the other thing." Benally scratched his close-cropped head. "It's not a body so much as it's a head."

Hunter's light cocoa skin turned ashen. She willed her lips to move.

"There was a carving. On the forehead." It wasn't a question.

Benally's eyebrows shot up in wary disbelief. "How in the hell did you know that?"

"I've seen it before."

Chapter Three

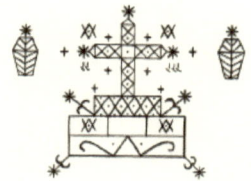

Hunter kept her gaze down, forcing herself to focus on the dirt smeared across her boot instead of the questions clearly brewing in B.B.'s mind.

She could feel his eyes on her, scrutinizing her in silence, waiting for some kind of explanation. But Hunter wasn't about to give him one—not a real one, anyway. She'd keep it simple.

B.B. shifted, crossing his arms as he watched her. "What do you mean you've 'seen it before'? You want to run that by me?"

She shrugged, her voice light but edged with something else, a hint of something unsettled. "You know how it is," she said, hoping her tone was flippant enough to shut him down. "Seen one creepy scene, seen 'em all. They just blur together."

B.B.'s expression didn't change. He wasn't buying it. "This isn't exactly run-of-the-mill. And from where I'm standing, you look a little more than… 'creeped out.'"

Hunter forced herself to look him in the eye, pushing back the faint tremor she felt in her hands. "Look, B.B.," she replied, her tone hardening just enough. "I'm saying I've been around enough messes like this one to see the patterns, okay?"

It wasn't a lie, not really. Not if she squinted at it sideways. But even as she threw up her usual wall of sarcasm, there was a cold prickle down her spine she couldn't quite ignore.

In her head, the image flashed again—a face, frozen and lifeless, a twisted terror etched in eyes that still seemed to stare back at her, even now. She knew that face, though she couldn't say how or why. Just like she'd known others, long before she'd ever met them, before they'd been claimed by tragedy.

The truth? She had no idea what her mind was trying to tell her anymore, and lately, the boundaries of her own head didn't seem as solid as they used to.

B.B. raised an eyebrow, his gaze probing, refusing to let her dodge it this time. He leaned in just a little, voice lowered. "Hunter, what aren't you telling me?"

The words clawed at her, and she could feel her usual defenses crack. A flicker of fear threatened to slip out, but she wasn't about to let it. She was Detective Hunter Despré, and she didn't break.

With a smirk she hoped looked confident, she fired back. "I'm telling you, I don't need to be a shrink or a psychic or whatever to pick up on the freak show at play here. It's called 'experience,' B.B.—ever heard of it?"

His gaze didn't waver, but she saw a flicker of

something, maybe worry, in his eyes. She didn't let him see her own hesitation, the hint of terror tightening in her gut.

With one last look at him, she forced herself to turn away, hoping he couldn't tell that her voice—cool and calm—was the only thing between her and the ghostly echo that had been clawing at her mind ever since she arrived at the scene.

Hunter turned away from B.B., shoving her hands into her coat pockets to hide the slight tremor that still hadn't left. She focused on the scene in front of her—the stark, gray light casting strange shadows across the twisted roots and damp grass. She let out a slow breath, keeping her gaze fixed straight ahead, even as the images she'd seen replayed in her mind.

The truth, if she could even call it that, was something she'd kept buried for years, hidden under layers of sarcasm and denial. A twisted part of her feared she might start believing it if she dared put it into words, to make it real. She'd lived with the half-dreams, the flashes of faces she didn't recognize but somehow knew. They were like puzzle pieces, their edges jagged and strange, that she tried to push away and ignore, even as they cut through her own thoughts.

But ignoring them didn't make them go away.

She let out a breath, thinking back to when she was a kid, her mind not yet crowded with the years of skepticism and self-doubt. Back then, she'd been… open.

She would wake up with strange scenes still fresh in her memory—images, people, places she'd never been. Sometimes she'd sketch them out, hoping that putting them on paper would make them make sense.

But they never did.

It was her mother who'd first noticed. She could still remember her mother's searching gaze, the way she'd hold Hunter's hand in her own, the fingers warm and firm. She had explained things to Hunter back then, describing their family's connection to their heritage, their ancestors, how sometimes those who'd come before left behind traces that some people—very few people—could feel.

She hadn't understood it at the time. Not really. It had felt like a bedtime story, a strange family secret woven into the patterns of their lives. Her mother had tried to prepare her, guiding her with wisdom and care. She'd called it a "gift," though sometimes, when her mother thought Hunter wasn't looking, her expression turned somber, as though she, too, could see the dark edges of this "gift."

And then... Serafine.

The memory sharpened, clear as a knife's edge, but Hunter's mind jerked back, stopping herself from revisiting those thoughts. She wasn't going there.

Not today.

She clenched her fists in her pockets, trying to calm herself. She could almost hear B.B. behind her, his presence like a stone lodged in her thoughts, pressing her with unasked questions. Her friend, her partner—he would understand. Well, he'd *try* to understand, at least. But Hunter couldn't risk that. Couldn't risk watching him look at her like she was slipping, or worse, that she was crazy. She'd worked too hard to keep this buried, to act like everything in her life was well-ordered and logical, like she was the same person as everyone else. Normal.

Sane.

"Hunter?" B.B.'s voice broke into her thoughts, cautious but persistent.

She threw him a quick glance, forcing her expression into something resembling a grin. "What's up? Still on about my 'experience' line?"

B.B. crossed his arms, giving her a look that was equal parts skepticism and concern. "Whatever you say, Despré. Just making sure you're all here."

"Oh, I'm here," she said, smirking, though inside, she wasn't so sure.

Hunter pulled her coat tighter, her smirk fading as she shifted her gaze back to the crime scene. She scanned the ground, the mud slick and cold, and took in the grim details with a practiced eye, all while keeping her own mind in check. The memories she wanted to avoid—no, *needed* to avoid—were still there, flickering at the edges of her vision.

She felt B.B. lingering beside her, his usual laid-back energy subdued, tempered by his own discomfort at the scene. She knew he had his questions, probably a million of them, but B.B. had a knack for reading the room, and he seemed to understand that pushing too hard would get him nowhere. He let her have her silence.

They stayed like that for a while, just the two of them watching as the CSU team worked, photographing every grim angle of the scene.

Hunter knew she couldn't stand there forever, and the waiting made her feel like the ground beneath her was shifting, as if it would swallow her whole if she let her guard down for a second.

She forced herself to stay present, keeping her mind anchored as she analyzed the details in front of her. But every so often, her gaze drifted back to the victim's face—or what was left of it.

It was in my dream, she thought, an unbidden flicker of memory pressing into her mind. She could still picture the face from her vision—its strange, twisted expression, the quiet resignation.

She hadn't understood it, hadn't known who it was or how it would all come to this. But that image had been clear—vivid enough to leave an imprint in her mind. And now, seeing it in reality, she was forced to admit that her nightmares were not just figments of her imagination. They were something else entirely, something she had spent years avoiding.

Hunter felt the familiar prickle of discomfort that came whenever she thought too long about the visions, that feeling like she was toeing a line between her world and something much darker. She'd been toeing it for years, stepping close enough to feel it but never close enough to acknowledge it fully.

Her mother had always said that some things defied explanation, that they were woven into life itself like an invisible thread. And even though Hunter had never completely accepted that notion, she couldn't deny it anymore, not with the girl's face staring back at her from the muddy ground.

Her jaw tightened as she took a step back, breathing in the damp air and trying to steady herself. She wouldn't let herself fall into the trap of overthinking, not when the clock was ticking, and they had work to do. There was too much at stake to let her mind wander down paths best left alone.

"Need a minute, partner?" B.B.'s voice jolted her out of her thoughts, anchoring her back in the present.

"Yeah," she replied, fighting to keep the fear out of her voice. "Maybe a minute… or two."

The cool, damp air settled heavy around her as she stepped away from the scene, letting the voices of the CSU team, the flash of cameras, and the murmur of police radios fade behind her.

She focused on her breath, the slow, rhythmic in-and-out, steadying herself, knowing that one lapse was all it took for her mind to wander back to darker places she couldn't afford to go.

The truth she wouldn't admit—not even to herself—was that these visions weren't just haunting her sleep. They were creeping into her waking hours now, tangling with her sense of reality in ways that left her feeling isolated, like she was seeing the world through glass.

It wasn't the first time she'd felt this, but it was getting worse, and part of her feared it wouldn't stop.

The vision of the girl's face had been disturbing enough, but there had been others too, faces flashing in her mind with growing urgency, an awareness that pulled her closer to the edge each time. Her instincts warned her to leave it alone, to let it go, but the faces wouldn't leave her alone. They never did.

Just stick to the job, Hunter. There's no use trying to dig into things you can't explain.

But even as she took her own advice, she felt the

unease gnawing at her, growing louder, more insistent. She knew she'd have to face it eventually—she couldn't run forever.

B.B. watched her quietly—his gaze steady—his usual questions softened by something like concern. He was waiting for her, giving her the space she needed, but his patience wouldn't last forever. And Hunter knew she didn't have the answers he was waiting for.

As she walked, her mind drifted, unsettled, strangely aware of the distance between her and the rest of the world growing wider.

And God... was it lonely.

Chapter Four

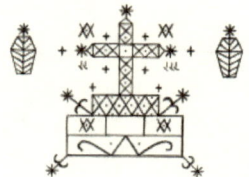

Mac Steele stared at her. She was beautiful in a childlike, impish way. The decapitated head stared lifelessly at him from the split garbage bag in which it rested.

Well, she had been beautiful once.

Death's toll had extracted beauty's blush from her high cheekbones. No pixie mischief danced in her lifeless eyes now.

The cloudiness of decay had already seeped into her cornea, a symptom that appeared within two hours—give or take—from death, turning the blue-green into a murky muddle. Mac made a mental note. It could help narrow the time of death window.

Chunks of bottled blonde crudely interrupted the girl's dark brown tresses, plastered with damp. He tried not to make any assumptions, but it was unlikely this girl was a lawyer or other nine-to-fiver. The alarming row of studs, a mix of sterling balls and sparkling stones, decorated a delicate ear. Mac sighed.

There would be no more music for her. No soulful stylings of Wynton Marsalis or Dr. John. The multiple piercings only supported his suspicions about her line of work. The question was—who cared?

Mac certainly didn't.

Nobody should, he thought. Lawyer, server, trucker, or stripper, this silent beauty needed someone to speak for her now. What the hell did it matter what she did to put food on the table? Hooker or homemaker, she deserved a voice. Mac bent close to listen.

"What's your story, sweetheart? Talk to me." He tilted his head, the strong straight jaw stubbled with shadow cocked. Listening, as if he fully expected her full, pallid lips to part and identify her killer.

A flash of the CSI's camera popped bright against the white mist. Mac shielded his eyes.

The young investigator shrugged. "Sorry."

"No worries." Mac waved it off. The kid was just doing his job. But as he examined the girl's horrific wounds, Mac decided there was *definitely* something to worry about.

Something positively evil.

He returned his attention to the young, dead girl before him. She couldn't have been much older than Hailey. Nineteen, maybe? Twenty, at most.

A smile tugged at the corners of his mouth at the thought of his fourteen-year-old sister. Scratch that. Fourteen and three-quarters. Hailey always made a point of reminding him of the fractional addendum.

"I'm practically old enough for my driver's license!" She persistently needled him over breakfast, over homework, over whether 11:30 was too soon to turn off the television and go to bed on a school night. The curly-haired, dark-eyed teen could really push the limits of Mac's patience.

"Learner's permit," Mac corrected. "And don't even let me catch you behind the wheel of a car. I've already got enough to worry about with you."

"Aw, come on, Mac! All my friends have their licenses already! It's not fair!"

No, it wasn't fair. It wasn't fair that some junkie had mugged his parents and left them to bleed out on a Faubourg Marigny street. It wasn't fair that he had had to drop everything and raise his kid sister. It wasn't fair that life served her up a menu of pharmaceuticals every day for breakfast when most kids her age were busy fighting over the last toaster pastry.

And it wasn't fair that some monster had snuffed out the light in this young girl's eyes.

His dark eyes shifted back to the dead girl. He surveyed the shredded tendons and ripped arteries dangling uselessly from the ragged base of what he was sure had once been a beautiful, slender neck.

Mac wasn't sure why, but he was reminded of a performance of *Giselle* he had taken Hailey to see back when she was in her dancer phase. For a while, everything had been tulle and pink. It had been like living in a frosting-flavored nightmare.

Pink-a-friggin-licous.

The prima ballerina had been beautiful, though. When Giselle danced the *grand scène dramatique*, "La Folie de Giselle," Hailey had sobbed her way through intermission. Mac would never admit it in public, but his eyes may have been a little moist themselves.

"Did you ever dance?" Mac almost whispered to the silenced victim.

"When I was a kid." The corpse spoke.

Mac scrambled backward, lost his balance, and fell squarely on his ass. He winced. The chunks of broken concrete and scattered oyster shells were unforgiving. Instinctively, he grabbed for his bruised backside.

"You good?" The disembodied voice queried.

A flush of embarrassment raced to Mac's high cheeks, deepening pink peeking through the early-morning stubble.

The feminine voice wasn't emanating from the deceased victim at all. A dark angel stood before him, a Creole beauty with haunted eyes and a very serious Baretta in her shoulder holster.

He gazed up at the slight woman with the NOPD shield clipped at her hip.

Great. A detective.

She stood over him, hands firmly stationed on her slim, cocked hips, looking remarkably assertive for such a small woman.

The apparent assertiveness was short-lived, however, as the detective took one look at the bodiless victim and lurched, gravity seeming to give way beneath her.

Mac had just found his own footing on the uncertain

surface when instinct drove him forward to snag her under the arms. His quick thinking saved the detective from a nasty introduction to the jagged berm.

"Whoa, there," Mac cautioned. "Maybe I'm the one who needs to be asking if you're okay."

She hung limp against Mac's muscled chest. Her button nose wrinkled as her body weight sagged against him.

"What is that? Lemon?" she sniffed and mumbled through ragged breaths.

Mac's brow wrinkled at the odd comment as he held her steady.

"At least you're not smelling burned toast," he murmured.

Summer citrus or not, they might as well have been on a garbage scow up the Illinois River in January for the spine-rattling shiver that suddenly vibrated through the woman's body.

Her grip tightened, some of Mac's chest hair catching under the shirt fabric she clutched in her fists. Mac winced. He followed her fixed, glassy stare toward the victim's forehead.

Mac had to admit. Even if the body had been intact, the symbol alone was wholly disconcerting. An angry red cross etched on top of a catafalque, a dais for the dead, glared from the victim's pale skin. Two coffins stood at post on either side, pinked now from being saturated in the murky Mississippi water.

"If I had to hazard a guess, I'd say the perp carved that first," Mac suggested, but he wasn't certain the detective was listening.

"Seriously, are you okay?" Mac reiterated. "Is this your first crime scene or something?"

His innocent comment jolted the detective like he'd hit her with the pungent ammonia and eucalyptus bite of smelling salts. She rocketed backward, electrified, out of his steadying embrace.

"Excuse me?" she spluttered. Her narrowed eyes flashed from amber to honeyed-green. Mac couldn't quite get a read on her—not that he'd ever had much skill in that arena. As far as he could tell, she was either ready to slug him or burst into tears. But which? She didn't look like she knew herself.

Almost instinctively, he drew his body into a crouching stance, hands raised to protect his face, but chose to drop them to his sides. Instead, he squinted, trying to decide if her ocular mood-ring display was for real or merely a trick of the uncertain morning light.

The detective did not warm to the uninvited study. "If I'm not interrupting, I was looking for the new M.E."

Mac suddenly realized how pointedly he was staring. He verbally backpedaled. "I wasn't, I mean, I was—I didn't mean. Oh, screw it. I'm Mac. Mac Steele, Medical Idiot."

Just great. Way to make friends, Mac. Strike one, you big dummy.

His unabashed sheepishness appeared to stay the detective's tongue. Her head tilted and her eyes narrowed as her gaze studied him. Mac cleared his throat.

"You don't look like most of the guys on the job around here," the petite detective finally replied.

"Thank you?" Mac replied, hesitation layered in his

voice.

The slim detective shook her head. "Nah. You remind me of this dog that followed me home once."

Mac scowled as she squatted near the victim and studied her. "Oh?"

"Yeah. He was a shaggy old mutt. You know?"

Mac drew a subconscious hand through his longish bangs.

"Had that kicked around look," the detective continued. "Begged my mom to let me keep him." She stood and dusted her hands on her backside. "But he had fleas."

Mac opened his mouth to protest, but she verbally bulldozed him.

"Anyway, I'm Despré. Detective Hunter Despré," she presented a hand. A peace offering, Mac supposed. He hesitated. She punctuated the air between them as she jabbed it forward again.

"Come on, then. I'm sure you've had your hands in worse," she urged.

"Yeah." He noticed her eyes had receded back to a warm golden amber. "Sure. Detective Despré, then."

She shook her head, the barest hint of a smile crooking the corner of her mouth. "Just Hunter."

Hunter's gaze roved over the lookie-loos that had started to collect around the fringes of the scene. Mac watched as she scanned the crowd, making deliberate eye contact with people.

He looked as well, a little surprised at the number of faces gathering at this early hour. Tatted teens, runaways more likely than not, eager to see someone whose life sucked even moderately worse than their own. Ogling tourists stumbling on their way for Café du Monde beignets to soak up last night's Bourbon Street debauchery, eyes red as their Minnesota skin pinked from days in the New Orleans sun.

He spotted the shimmering sequins of a few entertainers, drag artists and impersonators from someplace like Mag's 940, he supposed. He squinted.

Was that Dolly Parton?

Mac shook his head and refocused. When he looked back at the crowd, one face popped. It wasn't tattoos, or sunburn, or startling Bianca Del Rio makeup that made him look twice—it was the fierce, intense gaze that suggested more than just morbid curiosity.

The slim detective must have noticed it, too, because she took a step forward. But as soon as she moved, the face vanished, melting into the crowd.

"Damn it," the detective spat, but immediately regained her composure.

"You thinking the perp's in the crowd?" Mac queried.

"Maybe. Maybe not," Hunter replied. "Either way, folks around a scene like this read your body language. They can almost sense what you're thinking. You give off the attitude that this is just another piece of meat? You're just gonna make your job tougher. Someone in this crowd might know something. You've gotta show you care, or you're not gonna get spit from any of them."

Mac's head bobbed in appreciation.

"Easy enough," Hunter continued and dropped again to squat near the victim, bringing her closer to the indelicate reality of the dead girl's world. "Especially when you do."

Okay, Mac thought. Maybe he'd let the shaggy dog comment slide.

"Tell me a story, Doc," Hunter nearly whispered.

"She hasn't been in the water long. Probably less than twenty-four hours, even given the plastic trash bag. Otherwise, the critters would have munched on her like the buffet line at Golden Corral." Mac winced as Hunter's face screwed up in a distasteful grimace.

And...let's just go back to the mutt analogy and point me to the doghouse now.

Mac admonished himself silently. He shook his head.

"Yeah. In case you haven't noticed, I'm not so good with people. It's even worse if they have a pulse. Probably best I opted for pathology instead of obstetrics. The dead don't really complain too much when your hands are cold." Mac chuckled weakly.

Hunter's gaze remained flinty.

The facts, Steele. Just stick to the damned facts.

"Sharp force trauma. Her head was severed from the body at around the fourth, possibly fifth, cervical vertebrae. Most likely with an axe or hatchet. Maybe a cleaver. I'm not seeing the serrations typical when a toothed weapon is used. I'll know more after I get her into the lab, where I can get a better look at the kerf marks on the bone itself. And since I don't think she put herself in the bag, I can almost guarantee homicide."

"What kind of monster would do something like that?" Hunter asked.

Mac sighed heavily.

"A really nasty one—or desperate." The last word came almost as an afterthought. It hung oddly in the air as his gaze glazed over. He gave his head a shake as he noticed Hunter's narrowing stare.

Mac cleared his throat. "It gets worse. You see this and this?" He pointed to several individual blood vessels. "Whoever did this, they did it while she was still alive."

Hunter blanched. She swayed.

"Detective Despré?" Mac began. He wasn't quick enough to catch her this time as Detective Despré solidly hit the deck.

Chapter Five

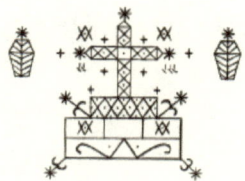

The candle's flame danced on the wick, throwing whispering shadows on the wall nearby. Hunter struggled to hear what the shadows were saying.

Blood.

Sacrifice.

The vague words swam in and out, much like Hunter's consciousness. She clutched through the darkness that threatened to pull her back down.

She tried to remember what had sent her spiraling into the dark recesses of her memory. What was the startling image that had come to her just before…before what? Damn it! What had happened? Her neurons fired on every synapse she could muster. All she managed to recall was lying in her bed and receiving a summons to come to the *Natchez* wharf.

Her bed. This wasn't her bed. This wasn't even a

bed. She shot upright and promptly slammed her head on the interior roof of a car.

"Shit!" Hunter gingerly rubbed the sore spot on her scalp and drew back a sticky hand. "Huh?"

She retracted her hand and looked at the bright red palm. Blood. Her blood.

Oh, that was just great! She had probably contaminated the crime scene. Of all the rookie moves!

Goddamn it!

Her memory came back in disjointed pieces, images she struggled to puzzle together. She vaguely recalled gravity reversing itself—the pavement rushing toward her like an IMAX 3D. Someone must have carried her to the car, a vintage four-door Volkswagen if she wasn't mistaken, and laid her on the backseat. They had taken pains to fold up a jacket and fashion a makeshift pillow. The anonymous act of kindness tugged briefly at her heart. Not a helluva lot of that going around these days, she thought.

Who had the Good Samaritan been? She allowed herself a moment to ruminate, or at least that's what she told herself. Honestly, she was just giving her throbbing head a moment to recover.

She grabbed the jacket. Her nose wrinkled as a furrow creased her brow. She held the jacket to her nose. A familiar scent tickled her memory.

Lemon.

The good doctor. Maybe not inherently a jackass, she considered, remembering Steele's awkward conversation.

She wiped the smear of blood from her palm onto

the leg of her jeans. The stain darkened, already oxidizing in the copper-tinged air.

Blood.

The ominous word drifted back to the forefront of her mind. Blood and sacrifice. She remembered the flicker of an unsteady candle flame as it danced in the warm breeze—the same warm breeze brushed her cheek.

Had it been a dream?

It was getting harder to tell. As she watched the warp and woof of the denim stain a dark scarlet, she realized reality and the visions in her head were weaving together into a disturbing tapestry.

"Yeah," she thought out loud. "A regular freaking death shroud."

She gingerly prodded the wound on her head. She winced. She looked around the small car. Empty coffee cups. Crumpled fast food wrappers. Not exactly a neatnik, the good doctor, but no candle.

She spied a faded photograph of a young girl who looked to be about ten years old. The photo had been fastened with care, a pewter guardian angel clip keeping it safely attached to the driver's side visor. Hunter tilted her head, studying it.

The young girl played in the snow, an expression of wild abandon lighting up her small, heart-shaped face. Hunter recognized that look. She'd worn a similar one. She recalled the year New Orleans experienced its first white stuff in thirty-five years.

The only other time the city went that nuts? When the Saints won the Superbowl. Neither happened that often.

The hint of a smile lifted the corner of her mouth,

catching her off guard, the unfamiliar expression making her keenly aware of just how long it had been since she had genuinely smiled. She closed her eyes and took a deep breath, letting air fill her lungs, and allowed the dimples to deepen, creasing the smooth bronze of her skin.

Her eyes opened, and her gaze returned to the photo. The girl was cute. Her eyes seemed a little puffy, but hell. Half the city suffered from seasonal allergies. Long, curly hair. Dark. Like the doctor.

A daughter, maybe?

Hunter didn't remember seeing a wedding ring, but what did that really mean these days, anyway? She knew plenty of people who had kids and no spouse. She made a note to herself to investigate. Shouldn't be that hard. She *was* a detective, after all.

The photograph was well worn, tattered, and frayed at the edges, color leached from the corners—a photo held and looked at often. Whoever the girl was, Hunter had an inkling the doctor cared for her greatly.

The basso profundo blat of the Natchez horn shredded her reverie. The abrupt sound made her jump, and her shoulder bumped into something small but solid. It tinkled against the smudged glass of the windshield. Her eyes drifted to the key dangling oddly from the rearview.

The key was old, a long shaft tapering from a rounded bow, and a notched bit at the end. She nudged it with her finger. It swayed on its dirty ribbon, bringing Hunter a fresh recollection of vertigo.

The cell phone buzzing on her hip made her jump. She smacked her head on the roof—again.

"Sunuva—" The epithet hung on unfinished air.

The driver's door opened, and Hunter tumbled into an awkward pile at Mac's feet. Once again, Hunter's reality turned upside down.

"I'm beginning to think you really like me the way you keep throwing yourself at me," Mac suggested.

Hunter scrambled to put herself to rights, but her body voiced its disagreement as she swayed precariously. Mac sat her back on the car seat, being careful to help her avoid hitting her head on the car frame.

Hunter protested. "I've gotta go."

"Yeah, hang on there, Dirty Harry. The only place *you're* going is the hospital. You smacked your head on that concrete pretty hard. Twice now. You could have a concussion."

Hunter attempted to protest. "No. No hospital. I have a case to solve."

"The victim's on the way to the morgue. Trust me. She'll be there after we get you checked out. Hey," he smiled. "Doctor's orders."

Hunter opened her pert little mouth to protest again, but since she was now seeing two of the good doctor, she decided it might, in fact, be in her best interest to play along. She slumped back against the seat.

"Fine. You win."

"Really?"

"Yeah. But no hospital. You're a doctor. Right?"

Mac shrugged. "That's the rumor."

"You." Hunter jabbed a close-clipped finger into Mac's chest. "You check me out. That's the deal."

"Don't think that I haven't," Mac muttered, but his eyes popped wide as Hunter leveled a questioning, if slightly confused, stare at him.

"Okey dokey, then." Without hesitation, Mac changed the subject. He closed the passenger door and folded his tall frame into the driver's seat. He turned the key in the ignition and the old VW rumbled to a shaky start.

"Baaaaaby, baaaaaby, baaaaaby, oh!" A former teenage heartthrob warbled at an ear-piercing decibel. Hunter's hands flew to her ears as Mac fumbled with the volume knob. Once the prepubescent crooning was silenced, Mac managed a weak grimace and shrugged his shoulders.

"Little sister," he mumbled.

Hunter nodded slowly, halfway because her head still throbbed and halfway in a show of visual sarcasm.

"Right," she drawled, stretching the word to its capacity.

The sudden disappointment that flooded Steele's face caught Hunter more than a little off-guard. If she didn't know any better, he looked like a batter who'd just struck out in the bottom of the ninth.

Chapter Six

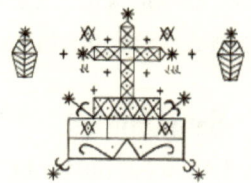

The flat-bottomed pirogue glided through the murky, gray-green waters of the Honey Island Swamp. Circular eddies swirled in the wake of the small boat as he punted it along with the long, twelve-foot pole. The swamp was a 250-square-foot tract of bottomland timber situated a little less than an hour outside of New Orleans proper. The swampy marshland earned its name from the honeybees said to populate one island in the swamp.

The bees weren't the only thing that could be found in the swamp, though. Louisiana's very own Big Foot, the Honey Island Swamp monster, was rumored to prowl through the gray green trees—if you believed the tourist hype.

And then, of course, there was Handsome.

The pilot's dark, wary eyes pried through the uncertain sunlight that filtered through the lacy swathes of pearly gray Spanish moss shrouding the ancient cypress trees. He searched the green, fungus-covered banks for the fifteen-foot alligator that laid claim to this part of the swamp. He had no quarrel with the leathery reptile and would prefer to avoid a tussle. It didn't help matters that the swamp guides egged the old boy on with whole skinned chickens—and marshmallows. Give the tourists a taste of the Louisiana backwater. Go ahead. All works out fine till one of them winds up on the menu.

A low-hanging clump of moss brushed the top of his head as the boat floated along. Funny thing, Spanish moss. Wasn't Spanish. Wasn't even a moss. Though it relied on trees like cypress and oak for support, the bromeliad actually pulled all the nutrients it needed from the air. The plentiful clumps of moss once served as a thriving Louisiana industry, stuffing everything from pillows to mattresses to seats on passenger trains and cars.

He knew it well from another of its more arcane uses. The moss was a staple in creating voodoo dolls. Any authentic *houngan* or *mambo* knew a doll stuffed with any material less than Spanish moss would lose much of the power it was intended to carry over its intended victim. Perhaps he would gather some to take back with him after his task was complete.

His black gaze drifted toward the lifeless form lumped near the bow of the boat. His tall, massive form provided ballast against the dead weight of the body. The dark-skinned boy, thick around the middle, had been unwieldy. He had been forced to dump him in the boat like an anonymous sack of potatoes, and nearly upended the pirogue. The boy hadn't complained, though.

Of course, it was difficult to complain when you were dead.

It seemed as if nature itself held its tongue as well. The swamp was eerily silent now. As if it had sensed some great evil was on its way and had pulled up roots to seek refuge in some safer locale. In fact, he half expected one of the cypress knees to lift from the brackish water, rooted foot and all, and start sloshing off toward the Gulf.

But all remained quiet, save for the rhythmic slosh of the punting pole. The left side of his thick-lipped mouth twisted upward in a crooked leer. He knew better.

The swamp quivered. It quivered with unseen life that lurked just beyond the knobby knees of the Old Man Cypress. As if to prove his point, the winding screech of millions of cicadas suddenly punctuated the silence like an alarm. The soft whoosh of a white egret gliding overhead seemed to whip a nearby barred owl into a fervent hooting frenzy. The insistent chirrup of frogs chorused angrily, proclaiming their disapproval of his presence in their swamp.

Let them quarrel, he thought. Though nature played its part, he did not serve the lesser creatures of the Divine. He served the *lwa*...and the *lwa* were hungry.

Chapter Seven

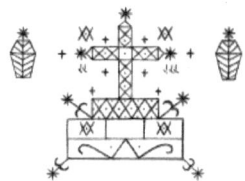

"Order up!" The tinny ding of the bell was almost lost amidst the din of the lunchtime crowd at Sabine's. A whirlwind in white dervished behind the counter. The long expanse of polished cypress was laden with Southern decadence. Pecan pies. Sweet potato pies. Tarte à la Bouille with its golden sweet-dough crust and custard filling. The whirlwind deftly snatched up a towering plate of fried chicken and mashed potatoes and quickly delivered it to an eager diner, without missing a beat.

"You're slacking, Eldridge!" the dervish teased the cook. "Took you two whole minutes to plate that bird. Try to keep up, will ya?"

The strapping African American waved a set of metal tongs at his challenger. "Don't you be pushing me now, Sabine. You givin' me half a mind to step out on you and leave you with this crowd."

Sabine Louviere flashed a brilliant smile against her flawless mocha skin. She leaned in and whispered conspiratorially toward the young lawyer seated next to her at a table. "Big old bear wouldn't do any such thing. He just wants everybody to think he's a mean old grizzly. He's just grouchy 'cause we're a bit shorthanded today."

"Keep on pushin', Sabine. Keep on." The big man grumbled as he hefted a sharply honed cleaver over a bare-naked chicken. "I'd have fired that boy a long time ago."

Sabine's laugh tinkled like a set of happy wind chimes. She knew Eldridge wasn't *really* mad at her. And she was sure Rabbit had a good reason for being late. He'd show—sooner or later.

"Y'all enjoy that food, now, hear?" She gave the lawyer a friendly pat on the shoulder and continued on through her restaurant, greeting each table with a friendly smile and ensuring the satisfaction of each and every customer.

Truth be told, there was hardly a way for anyone to be cross with Sabine Louviere. The thirty-something beauty with the cloud of soft, dark hair and sparkling obsidian eyes was always ready with a joke or a friendly word.

Widowed at a young age, many women might have allowed their grief to swallow them whole. Especially considering the horrible trauma of watching her husband go the way he did.

But not Sabine. She was made of sterner stuff. She had taken the modest sum left from her husband's life insurance policy and bought one of the many abandoned historic buildings that peppered the French Quarter and flipped it into a culinary sketch of the South.

Friends argued against such a risky business venture—most restaurants failed in their first year—but Sabine's mama didn't raise a fool. The restaurant was perfectly situated near the Supreme Court Building and within walking distance of tourist-burgeoning Bourbon Street and Decatur. Then there was the *coup de grâce*.

It was next door to the 8th District police station.

Sabine knew she had a built-in clientele. After weeks of personal elbow grease, a few creatively hung Boston ferns, and a bit of loan money, Sabine's opened its doors offering a humble, but delicious menu of mouth-watering Southern comfort food: red beans and rice with Andouille sausage; jambalaya with duck and Tasso; shrimp and crawfish étouffée; fried chicken served with thick, buttery mashed potatoes; and a characteristic collection of sweets like the richly flavored pralines crumbled over vanilla bean ice cream.

Hungry patrons salivated and flocked. Sabine's quickly became *the* place to dine. Her tables flourished with a who's who of New Orleans—doctors, lawyers, judges—and, of course, NOPD's finest.

One of those finest sat at the corner booth, chasing the last few crumbs of sweet potato pie on his plate with his fork. B.B. Benally finally gave in and pinched the last tidbit with two long fingers and popped it into his mouth. He gave a contented sigh and leaned back against the booth. A satisfied grin spread across his wide, flat face, accenting the high cheekbones of his Native American heritage.

"Well, now, if that ain't the prettiest sound I ever did hear." Sabine slid into the booth next to the detective.

"Mm-hmm," Benally agreed. "Sabine, honey, I

gotta tell ya. You've outdone yourself again. That was *the* best sweet potato pie I ever wrapped my gums around."

Sabine slapped him lightly on the arm. "That's what you said last week, B.B."

"That's right. And every week, I swear it gets even more scrumptious. If I didn't know any better, I'd swear you was working magic back there in that kitchen."

"No magic. Least, none that I'm admittin' to, anyway." The pair shared a laugh.

"Well, you must be doing something to do all that you do. Running this place, helping out at Ozanam Inn, and volunteering at Doc Mac's clinic? You're a saint. A scrumptious saint, but still a saint."

"Speaking of scrumptious, where *is* that partner of yours?" Sabine asked.

Benally's eyes immediately lost that half-asleep look. "Oh, you'd best not let her hear you say that. She's liable to cuff you and bring you up on obstruction of justice charges. She figures bein' a woman gets in the way of her doin' her job. Glass ceiling and all."

Sabine sniggered. "Aw, hell, honey. What use is it in being a woman if you don't use what heaven gave you?"

She purposely let the peasant blouse slide slightly off her shoulder, exposing an adorable dimple at the top of her shoulder blade.

Benally cocked an eyebrow. "You angling for a bigger tip, Sabine?"

"Have we met? You know I'm always angling for something," Sabine giggled. "Seriously, though, where is that gal? Tiny as she is, I ain't never known her to pass up Eldridge's cookin'."

"We rolled out on a call early this morning. She took a bit of a tumble. Doc wanted to check her out. Nothing too serious. Her damned head's too hard for it to have done too much damage."

Sabine chuckled throatily. "Now who better hope she don't hear?"

B.B. chuckled. "I tell you, though, I'm glad Doc's givin' her a look see. She started spoutin' some mumbo jumbo down at the dock. We pulled a real nasty one. Can't say it's that surprising in this heat, though. We tend to see the less Christian side of folk this time of year. But this? This one was worse than anything I've ever come across in my whole damn career. Here's the weird thing. Hunter said she's seen it before. Now, I've known that gal since she was in blues. Nothin', and I mean *nothin'* like this ever came through the parish before."

Sabine shrugged. "So?"

B.B. leaned back. "So, what the hell was she talking about?"

A moment of silence passed.

B.B. sighed, then drew his eyebrows together in an opposing scowl. He cast a curious glance around the room. "Say. Why are you waiting tables, anyway? Where's that juvenile delinquent you hired?"

"Rabbit's not a delinquent. Poor boy's just misunderstood."

"Yeah. Right. Like he misunderstood the sign in the French Market that says 'shoplifters will be prosecuted'. Girl, I've rousted him and his chowhound of a friend, Eugene Watson, from the stalls over there trying to use the old five-finger discount. More times than I can count."

Suddenly, a ruckus clattered through the typical chat and din and clink of flatware on plates. Eldridge's deep, growling baritone rumbled from the kitchen. Heads swiveled toward the clamor, curious. Sabine pursed her lips.

"Rabbit," she murmured.

She was certain Eldridge was giving the teen a talking to, but the only thing Sabine wanted the people in her restaurant talking about was the food, not arguments between her employees. She stood and excused herself from B.B.'s table in a flurry of white, willowy grace.

"Excuse me, B.B. Seems like there's something that needs tending in the kitchen. Let me send Corrine over with a fresh cup of coffee to top off that pie. On the house." Sabine waved at the other server across the room and pointed to B.B.'s table, then rushed toward the kitchen to diffuse Eldridge.

When Sabine burst through the swinging doors of the kitchen, her face transformed. Gone was the sweet, endearing restaurateur. In her place? A Gorgon, face twisted into a stony mask of hardened fury. She had already risked too much and worked too hard to let anyone damage her bottom line with penny ante squabbling. Her right hand snatched up the cleaver, and she hacked it clean through a pork loin waiting to be seasoned.

"What in *the* hell…"

Sabine's voice died on her breath when she got a good look at Rabbit fidgeting near the back door of the kitchen.

The lid over the teenager's right eye had purpled into a shocking palette of violets and plums. His clothes were filthy, coated in a fine pink layer of mixed chalk and red clay dust. The hem of his t-shirt hung loose and ripped behind him, like a dangling, tattered tail.

The blood-crusted split in his lower lip had caused so much swelling that Sabine could hardly understand the frantic words that were tumbling out of Rabbit's mouth.

"Dead...Eugene...murdered!"

Sabine glanced over her shoulder through the kitchen window and into the dining room. More than just a few heads were turning now. She looked at Eldridge for some explanation. The big man just shrugged his shoulders. Sabine gently but firmly grasped Rabbit by the shoulders. Shuddering sobs racked the thin boy's body.

"Rabbit? Rabbit, I need you to calm down so we can talk about this." She saw B.B. stand up near his table. Sabine quickly looked back to Rabbit. "But not here. Let's go out back."

Rabbit nodded his mane of greasy, lank hair and let Sabine guide him outside to the service alley. Sabine sat the boy on an upturned apple crate and examined his injuries.

"Did your daddy do this to you?" she asked as she tilted his head toward the light for a better look at the bruise swelling his eye closed.

"Yeah," he sniffled. "I tried...I ran home to try...about Eugene...he wouldn't listen."

Sabine clucked her tongue as she twisted Rabbit's head this way and that, ignoring his whimpers. "I tell you what, that Pete Scarpetta is a complete waste of human flesh. I know nutria's what got better souls in 'em."

Sabine finished her exam of Rabbit's damage. "You need to go to the clinic and get Doc Steele to check this out.

You'll be damned lucky if it doesn't get infected with all this dirt you're carrying around with you. Where have you and Eugene been rattin' around *this* time? And where *is* that boy? I got half a mind to box his ears, but good."

Rabbit leaped to his feet, cutting off Sabine's rant. "That's what I've been trying to tell everybody. Eugene's dead! I saw it! At the cemetery! St. Louis Number One! This huge guy! Least I think it was a guy. And he looked huge! He had a black hat and a skeleton face. He had this big ol' knife and Eugene was all dead! In a coffin. I shoulda helped him. Like he helped me with Pop. You know, he cracked him with a beer bottle the other day to save my ass. I shoulda done something. Anything! He was my best friend. But I didn't. I ran. And now Eugene's dead!"

Rabbit slumped back onto the crate, tear-streaked face in his hands. Sabine's brow wrinkled. "This ain't some kinda prank, now, is it? It's startin' to sound like something Eugene'd pull."

But Rabbit just shook his head.

No one could deny something had scared Rabbit— scared him to the point where he would dare face his abusive father in an attempt to seek help. Sabine pulled Rabbit to his feet.

"Listen to me. I want you to go straight to the free clinic. Get yourself looked at. I'm going to go to the cemetery and check things out."

Rabbit vehemently shook his head. "No, no, no! You can't do that! The Skeleton Man! He'll get you, too, Mrs. Sabine. He'll get you, too!"

"Calm down, calm down. Won't nobody try nothin'

58

in the daylight. Hell, Carla brings her tourists through there all the time.

Rabbit was still shaking his head. Sabine ignored him and pressed on.

"If I find anything, I'll talk to B.B. You two are already in enough trouble with the law. You take this story to them, and B.B.'s liable to lock you up just for wastin' his time," Sabine warned. Rabbit looked despondent. Sabine patted his shoulder.

"I'm sure Eugene is fine. It's probably just one of his silly old jokes. He'll turn up, mouthful of something or other, laughin' at his own damn self, thinkin' he's some kind of Eddie Murphy comic genius."

Rabbit nodded hesitantly. Sabine ushered him from the alley.

"Now, git! I'll take care of this. Promise."

She watched as the tall boy loped off into the early afternoon. She shivered, even though the sun shone high and bright in the sky. Something about Rabbit's story had unnerved her. It wasn't the idea of going to the cemetery. New Orleans was filled with its above ground cities of the dead.

But the city was filled with something else, too.
Voodoo.

The religion of *voudon*, as was its proper name, worshipped many deities, many of them side-by-side with Catholic saints. But the deity that ruled over the dead, the king of the cemetery, was Baron Samedi. The *ghede* of the dead was represented most often with a tall black hat…and the countenance of a grinning skull.

A skeleton man.

Chapter Eight

"Tony Orlando called. He wants his yellow ribbon back." The small bell on the clinic door tinkled merrily at Hunter's thinly veiled jibe.

Mac had continued to press, wanting to take Hunter to the E.R., but after a revival of adamant refusals, which may or may not have involved a cloaked reference to discharging her firearm, he convinced her to at least allow him to bring her to the local clinic.

Hunter hadn't been too far off the mark. The Oretha Castle Haley Free Clinic may very well have been a wormhole to the 1970s, furnished in Naugahyde and avocado green. Hunter could just make out Simon and Garfunkel's "Bridge Over Troubled Water" scratching intermittently through the ceiling speaker in the clinic's lobby. She wouldn't have been at all surprised to see Redd Foxx come loping through the door, clutching his chest and calling out, "I'm comin', Elizabeth! I'm comin'!"

"Yeah, yeah," Mac replied as they weaved their way through the congested waiting room. "Poke fun 'cause I'd rather spend what little support I get from the state on amoxicillin instead of art déco."

Hunter pulled up short. "Wait. You run this clinic?"

"With whatever free time I have," Mac answered, quickly reviewing and signing off on a chart a nurse handed him. "I'm lucky to have a lot of help. Folks from the neighborhood volunteer their time—filing, answering phones, that sort of thing. Oh, and do you know Sabine Louviere? Runs that restaurant over on North Rampart? She's in here quite a bit. Did you know she was a LPN? A blessing in disguise, I suppose, seeing what she had to do to take care of her husband when he got sick. Gave it up, though, as soon as he died. To start her restaurant. Guess she'd had her fill of taking care of sick folks. I think running a restaurant was her dream all along."

Hunter grimaced with a pang of jealousy. She couldn't say she really had dreams any more. Her dreams were mostly just flat out nightmares.

Mac failed to notice the angst in her expression and kept talking. "Fortunately, she kept her license current, which is a godsend for me, let me tell you. When she offered to help, even with how busy she is? I gotta tell ya, the woman's a saint."

"I hadn't realized," Hunter murmured. All the times she'd sat with B.B. and eaten at Sabine's, she'd never really talked to the restaurateur. Hunter preferred to dedicate the RAM of her brain to rooting out perpetrators and bringing them to justice.

Human interface? That was more her partner's milieu.

And it seemed to be in the good doctor's repertoire as well, despite his claims to the contrary. Hunter watched with a keen eye as Mac stopped to pat the knee of a frail septuagenarian sitting nearby.

"Hey, Mrs. Jones. Arthritis acting up again?" Mac asked. The older woman nodded as Mac gently squeezed her shoulder. "Well, don't worry. We'll get you fixed up right as rain."

The old woman's face broke into a grateful smile and replied in a voice cracked with age. "Don't be jinxing us now, Doc. With that mess brewin' out in the Gulf, the less talk about rain, the better."

"Yes, ma'am." Mac grinned, honest joy spreading across his handsome face.

Man, what she wouldn't give for a little of that bedside manner.

The sudden, random thought jerked her to attention. She shook her head, a move she instantly regretted as the room began to spin. She gripped the edge of the reception desk and squeezed her eyes shut till sparkles danced. When she finally opened them, Mac's grin had dissolved from his handsome face, replaced with a worried frown. Hunter fought to reset her composure. The best she could manage was a biting quip.

"A regular knight in shining armor, huh?" She thumbed a gesture toward Mrs. Jones.

Mac seemed to accept her acerbic comment as proof of the status quo.

"I came down with the Red Cross after Katrina to

help. Things happened." Mac signed another chart then turned to face Hunter, the sheepish clumsiness replaced with steely resolve. "I stuck around."

Hunter's investigative instincts sensed there was more to that story. She kept her tongue, however, deciding that discretion was the better part of valor.

Stuck around.

His word choice danced around in Hunter's head, followed by an unspoken desire.

Wish more guys did.

She shrugged off the useless thought and followed as Mac led her down a narrow hallway with several doors. An odd juxtaposition of images adorned the hall walls.

A bachelor's degree from Harvard. A medical degree from Johns Hopkins. Pictures of a rumpled and dirty, but grinning Steele posed with a group of dark-skinned refugees in a survival camp.

Prep school poster boy meets Peace Corps.

The incongruity was jarring.

Hunter pointed to the picture. "Haiti?"

Steele nodded. "After the earthquake. You know, people are so quick to label Haiti as a Third World backwater, but you'd be surprised what you can learn from the people."

"Like a little voodoo?" Hunter suggested. Steele whipped around, a challenging look on his face.

Hunter's trim nail tapped a feature in the picture. "*Gris gris* bag. Here. Around your neck. Couldn't help but notice." Just like she had noticed the *veve* carved into their victim's forehead. Hunter caught a brief shudder.

Mac didn't seem to notice. A few moments of

silence simmered. When he finally spoke, it was with respect.

"I was going to say 'faith', but yes, the Haitian people's faith is firmly rooted in *voudon*."

Hunter's gaze locked on his. She'd never heard anyone outside the faith speak with such reverence. Her head cocked in curiosity.

"You seem to know more than a bit about it yourself," Mac interrupted her thoughts.

Hunter shrugged. "It's New Orleans. I know about as much as the average tourist. Marie Laveau. Voodoo dolls. Charms and talismans for what ails you. Luck, love…"

Mac studied the look in Hunter's eyes. He shook his head. "Nuh, uh. Not buying it. It's more than that."

It *was* more than that. But Hunter wasn't at all comfortable sharing the depth of her knowledge about it, not to mention the lurid carving on the victim's forehead with a complete stranger. She hardly felt comfortable admitting it to herself. To do so would lift the veil on a past she'd spent most of her life running from.

A past that was catching up…much too fast.

Hunter felt a claustrophobic pressure in the enclosed hallway. Her breath struggled, coming in short, shallow gasps. Her airways constricted. Just like they had on the dock. The room swam. Suddenly, her body lurched. Mac reached forward and caught her in the crook of his arm.

"Damn. We've got to get a better look at that head injury. Like, now. Esther, bring the portable x-ray into room seven right away." Hunter shook her head. She tried resisting Mac's strong embrace. She made a feeble attempt to wave him away.

"No. It's nothing, really. I'm fine."

"Like hell you are." Mac's penetrating gaze bored into Hunter's eyes. She dropped her lids, frightened of what he might see there. She turned her gaze back to the framed photo on the wall. She saw her own haunted look staring back at her, both in the reflecting glass and in the eyes of the quake survivors. They, too, had seen something coming.

At least they found solace in their faith and their lwa. The thought drifted through Hunter's head.

She was simply terrified.

Mac ushered her into a cramped exam room. The tiny space was clean but sparse. A couple of informational medical posters were tacked to the walls, outlining the symptoms of the common cold and flu and stressing the importance of repeated hand washing. A faded plastic chair kept sentinel in the corner, its worn surface testimony to the countless mothers who'd sat there, waiting anxiously for the diagnosis of a sick child.

Mac propped Hunter up against the wall and grabbed a white lab coat from the hook behind the door. He pulled his arms into the sleeves. His biceps flexed and Hunter felt a sudden, surprising flush of warmth flood her.

What the hell?

She looked up at the posters and felt her forehead.

Maybe I'm coming down with a cold.

She dismissed the thought and continued to survey the room. An elevated exam table ran the short length of the left wall, its cushioned surface covered by a protective layer of hygienic tissue. It crinkled as Mac patted it with his hand. "Alley oop."

Hunter's shapely eyebrow shot up, any last dregs of awkward warmth immediately dissipating. "I'm sorry. Did you just say 'alley oop?'"

Mac offered an awkward grin and scratched the back of his head. "Um, yeah. Sorry about that. Habit. Most of the patients I see here are under twelve or over sixty."

"No worries." His candor brought another unpracticed smile to Hunter's face. "It was actually kind of…funny."

The stretching muscles in her face felt strange.

Maybe it's the flu. She wouldn't bring herself to admit anything else. Couldn't, she corrected. She felt an uncomfortable tightening in her chest. The simple fact of the matter was, there just wasn't room for anything but the job right now—in her life or her heart.

The pain squeezed. Hunter lowered her head, her chocolate-colored hair fanning across her embarrassed features. At least, she hoped so.

"Let's just get this over with," she barked and tried to maneuver past Mac. The room's abbreviated dimensions, however, made it impossible to push past without brushing up against him. At six-foot-one, he had her by an easy eight inches. They performed a clumsy tango until Hunter found herself, once again, pressed against the doctor's chest, hands splayed across the firm, broad muscles. Tiny jolts of electricity sparked through her fingers before she gave a forceful push and squeezed past.

She hoisted herself onto the raised table, exhaling lightly with the effort. The move put her at eye level with

Mac. As her amber eyes caught the dark, studied stare of the doctor, she suddenly tried to recall if she'd brushed her teeth that morning. Mac reached for her face, the tips of his warm fingers brushing just under her jawline. He leaned in close.

Instinctively, Hunter's own hand shot out and grabbed the doctor's arm in a vise-like grip.

Mac pulled backward, his eyes widening, then immediately softening. He spoke, his voice gentle and low. "I just need to take a look at you, Detective Despré. I need to check for signs of a concussion."

Hunter loosened her grip. "Yeah. Sorry. Of course. Do what you've gotta do."

"You sure?" he asked. "'Cause it's going to be a lot harder to work with a broken wrist."

"Sorry." Hunter nodded and dropped her hand. "I just want to get back to work."

She wasn't sure exactly who she was trying to convince.

Mac dragged an ophthalmoscope from the pocket of his coat and leaned forward again, albeit cautiously. Hunter managed a stupid, apologetic smirk as he shone the light into her right eye. Hunter squinted against the bright beam. Mac clucked his tongue.

"So, tell me, and be honest. Are you prone to dizzy spells?" Mac asked as he continued his examination. "Blackouts?"

Hunter considered which answer would get her back to the precinct faster. Honesty took a backseat. "Hey. It's New Orleans. Between Jazz Fest and Bourbon Street, who hasn't blacked out a time or two?"

It wasn't a total lie.

Maybe just a little gray around the edges.

Mac pursed his full lips dubiously before looking at her left eye. "Headaches?"

Does the six-foot-plus one in front of me count?

She kept the quip to herself and shook her head instead. "I'm on the city's payroll. Headaches are in the job description."

Mac straightened to his full height and slid the ophthalmoscope into the pocket of the lab coat. "You feel any nausea today?"

Whatever awkwardness Hunter had been feeling was replaced with seething anger. She planted her palm flat on the crinkling paper shield and vaulted herself from the table. "Yes. Yes, I have felt nausea today. I still do! I feel absolutely sick to my stomach that some monster ripped that poor girl's head off her shoulders and tossed it into the Mississippi like it was nothing more than garbage. So, if you don't mind, can we wrap this up so I can get back out there and find the asshole responsible?"

Mac blocked her exit, his brows knit with concern.

"I still need to take some x-rays," Mac started.

"Then take them."

"There's something about this girl—this case— that's affecting you. You know something. What is it?" Mac urged.

Hunter's eyes widened. How could he possibly know?

Benally.

She instantly regretted her off-the-cuff admission to her partner. About seeing the startling image of a mutilated girl before.

But the weight of the burden had become too much for her to bear alone. Suddenly, all the energy drained from her body and she collapsed fully into Steele's embrace. There was no strength to deny it anymore.

"It was a calling card."

"For what? For whom?" Steele prodded. The answer escaped her lips as little more than a whisper.

"Death."

Chapter Nine

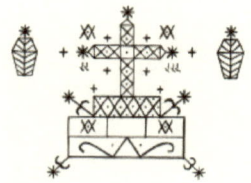

Leroy Oates enjoyed his job as a *diener*. He didn't even mind that the word derived from the German for *servant*. The work was quiet. The customers rarely complained, and it had allowed him to improve his Halo scores markedly.

Fact of the matter was, most of the women he met just weren't into guys who spent their workday hauling dead bodies from the morgue coolers onto autopsy tables. It was a job hazard that left his social calendar wide open.

The job also had a way of twisting your perception of humor. He recalled one particular blind date his buddy had railroaded him into accepting. On a humorous whim, he had purposely held his hand on his cold glass of iced tea before shaking the hand of the young woman who arrived for the dinner date.

"Hi. I'm Sheila," she offered with a shy, hesitant

smile.

"Hi. I'm Leroy. I work with dead people." She instantly recoiled at the dead cold temperature of his proffered extremity.

Apparently, the humor was lost in translation. He wound up enjoying a three-course meal for two solo. But on the plus side, the crab cakes were excellent.

Being a diener also served as a constant reminder of human mortality. He had seen all types pass through the cold, sterile examination room—tatted-up gang members, soccer moms, rich Wall Street types, older folks, and even small children. Not to be trite, but death really *was* the great equalizer.

So, it was no great surprise, then, that he was in no rush to meet a girl, start a family, and wait…wait for the inevitable end we all came to.

The best we could hope for, Leroy thought, was to meet a peaceful, if anonymous, end—one hopefully a little less violent than some victims that presented before him.

Take the young woman who'd been reduced to the thin file in his hands. Currently listed as a Jane Doe, he was transporting her body from the bank of stainless-steel coolers to the exam room.

Normally, Leroy would have rolled a sheeted gurney toward the mottled silver wall to help ferry the body from Point A to Point B. It seemed superfluous in this case, however. Poor girl was a little light in the body category.

Body or not, there was still procedure.

After he removed the young woman's head from the foggy chiller drawer, he hoisted it into the metal basket of the calibrated scale near the waist-high autopsy table.

Ten and two-tenths pounds. Leroy scratched a notation in the file. He calculated an estimated total body weight for the head with the sightless eyes. If the average human head comprised about eight percent of total body mass, then it was likely this woman weighed around one-hundred and twenty-seven pounds. He made another note.

Of course, there was no need to position the foam-like body block under the body to prepare for the requisite Y-incision. No body. He began the macabre modeling session for the "as is" photographs, to document the body as it is first seen in the autopsy room.

"Ready for your Glamour Shots, darlin'?" he asked. The flash popped multiple times in succession until Leroy was satisfied he had compiled a detailed portfolio. Setting aside the camera, he performed a cursory visual examination. His alert brown eyes roved over the skin's pasty white surface. Just above the ragged edge of skin at the base, he noticed a darkened patch of epidermis. He lifted a swatch of the limp bleached hair to inspect the mark. In the bright light of the surgical lamp, he could make out the tips of a butterfly's wings.

Leroy smiled. Tattoos were good. They could help in the identification process. Another note.

The butterfly wasn't the only definitive mark on Jane Doe's skin, however. Leroy examined the angry symbol carved on the slight hill of her pale forehead.

"You just weren't having a good day, were you, honey?" he commiserated out loud as he drew a sketch of the carving in the margins of the report.

Leroy reached for his lead-lined apron and used the X-ray to take detailed films of the abbreviated corpse.

When the prosector began the internal dissection and examination, it behooved medical personnel to be aware of the interior inclusions that might not be readily apparent on the skin surface—broken bits of weapon, hidden detritus, and other possible shrapnel.

The forensic odontologist would be able to determine further details about the victim, approximate age, telltale country markers, and even definitive identification when dental records, including fillings, crowns, etcetera, were matched in the system. He would forward them as soon as he had taken a full and accurate set.

As his nitrile-gloved hand removed the last bitewing from her mouth, a momentary glint caught in the shaft of light pointing from the surgical lamp.

Leroy squinted, making sure it wasn't a trick of the light. He reached over to the instrument tray, neatly aligned with its standard collection of autopsy tools—scissors, Hagedorn needle, long-handled scalpel, bone saw, enterotome, and skull chisel—and picked up a pair of tweezers.

He folded back the victim's upper lip and gingerly grabbed the flake of gold leaf trapped in the crevice between her right central and right lateral incisors. He held it up to the lens of the light.

"What the hell?" he muttered.

Chapter Ten

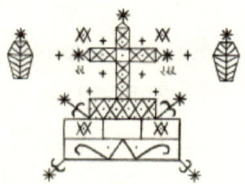

"What the hell, Captain?" Hunter echoed Leroy's epithet all the way across town to the Quarter, albeit for a wholly different reason.

The glass door to the captain's office was closed, but it may as well have stood wide open for as clearly as the entire squad room heard the mezzo bellow that emanated from within.

"I'm sorry, Despré, but I've got no choice but to put you on medical leave." The captain met Hunter's complaint with an even-tempered bass.

Hunter pile-drove each step into the scarred tile as she paced back and forth in front of the captain's desk. Mac had tucked himself into a corner, allowing Hunter a wide berth. Benally sat in one of the generic office chairs lodged under the closed Venetian blinds, silently watching the events transpiring before him.

It might have been the Navajo blood that accounted for his taciturn tongue. It also could have simply been the concept of losing one too many arguments to strong-willed, legally well-represented women.

After three divorces, it seemed he had learned *something*. Even if it was just to know when to shut the hell up. At any rate, he maintained a stoic reticence as the argument between his co-worker and superior officer bubbled heatedly.

Captain Rudolph "Rudy" Spiers was not a small man by any stretch of the imagination. Granted, the vast expanse of pectoral muscles and bulging biceps earned through twenty years in the Army had sagged a few flaccid inches south since his retirement from the service, but he was still in great shape for a man of fifty-five years.

Spiers' transition from the military to the police force just seemed like a natural segue for the brusque man. And his practiced leadership skills as a staff sergeant made for an easy rise within the ranks to his current position as captain.

He could have been the goddamned Commander-in-Chief. It wasn't shielding him from the fire and brimstone Hunter currently rained down on him from the other side of the desk.

"Why?" Hunter pressed firmly for a more valid explanation.

Captain Spiers leaned back in his chair, hands clasped behind his head. "It's been brought to my attention that you sustained a head injury at a crime scene this morning."

Hunter whipped around and shot a withering stare at

Benally. He threw his hands up in mock surrender.

"Oh, for Chrissake! I got a tiny bump on my nut. People take harder hits than that at Best Buy on Black Friday! Come on!"

Spiers waved his beefy palms in the air before him. "I hear ya, Despré. I hear ya. And if that's really all it was, I'm the first guy that'd be willing to keep you out there."

"I hear a 'but' coming." Her eyes narrowed, dissolving from gold into a stormy green.

"But," Spiers began, "I've also got a doctor's report that says you passed out. Not once, but twice."

Now, it was Mac's turn for a visual castration. Even Benally cringed.

Spiers tried a different tactical approach. He leaned in, fingers tented in an almost prayerful gesture. A softer edge dulled the severity in his tone.

"Look, Hunter." The captain used her first name, but it did nothing to quell the tension visually tightening in Hunter's shoulders. "I know this girl—this case—well, I'd have to be a damned fool to think it wasn't hitting close to home."

Hunter opened her mouth to launch into yet another objection, but Spiers held up an arresting hand. "And you'd be a bigger fool if you're gonna try to tell me you're okay with this one."

Mac looked toward Benally, confusion in his eyes. Benally just shook his head.

"Explanation for another time, brother," Benally whispered. They turned their attention back to the verbal sparring match volleying between Hunter and the captain.

The captain began scratching notes in a file on his

desk. "Now, Doc here says you've got a concussion. It's not bad, but—"

Hunter threw her hands up in the air. Again, Spiers stopped her before she got a word out.

"It's enough that I'm benching you."

"C'mon, Captain!" Hunter protested. "I'm fine."

Spiers sighed heavily and sank into his chair. His big hand rubbed small circles at his temple. As he exhaled, his wide shoulders slumped with exhaustion.

"Gentlemen? You mind giving us the room?" The gravitas in his voice made it clear it wasn't a question.

Benally gave Hunter a sympathetic look, then lowered his gaze.

"B.B.?" Hunter's voice cracked. She forced a smile and took a step toward the tall Navajo, grabbing his arm. "Come on. Back me up, partner."

Benally's head shook almost imperceptibly. The tall man almost appeared embarrassed as he gently pulled his arm free and started for the door. Hunter's hand fell to her side. She wandered toward the window, the bright, sunny sky mocking her mood.

Mac shifted his eyes between the departing Benally and Hunter, a deep line cutting between his dark brows. He took a tentative step toward the female detective, then cast a doubtful look back toward the captain. Stoic resolve was all that could be found there. Mac turned back to Hunter.

"I'm sorry," he managed.

The now-familiar scent of citrus curled beneath Hunter's nostrils. The fresh scent she had come to associate with the handsome doctor.

The memory of being pressed against his chest

played like a movie in her mind, a brief clip quickly obliterated by the vision of the dead girl's lifeless eyes— her glazed gaze and the horrifying symbol gouged into her pale flesh. Hunter wheeled to face Mac.

"You're sorry? Tell that to the dead girl," she seethed. She leaned in toward Mac. "You got me benched? You may as well have killed her yourself."

Hunter pulled back as she read two expressions as they flew in tandem across Mac's face—disappointment and anger. Mostly anger.

Hunter cocked her head. She watched the muscle in Mac's strong, chiseled jaw working. Heard the grit of enamel as his teeth crushed together.

Recognition clicked. She'd seen the same expression in the mirror too many times over the years. It wasn't anger.

It was rage.

Red, raw, stinging rage. The knuckles on Mac's right hand blanched as his fist clenched, blood leaching from skin stretching taut over the tightening joints. Hunter returned her gaze to Mac's face, the lightning in her eyes flashing in contrast against the darkening clouds in Mac's own.

Captain Spiers stood, interrupting the brewing storm. "Stand down, Despré. The man's just doing his job. Which is what I need to get back to doing. Doc, thanks for taking care of Detective Despré. We appreciate it."

Mac's countenance transformed at the sound of the captain's burly voice. His hands relaxed. The skin pinked once more as blood flowed back through capillaries. He broke eye contact with Hunter and turned toward the captain.

"Yes, sir. I have some…other things I need to take care of before the weather turns. If you believe the weather guy." He turned on his heel and blew through the same door Benally had exited just moments before.

Hunter stared after him. The awkward pause in Mac's speech had cut through Hunter's own simmering anger.

Something—she wasn't certain what exactly— nibbled at her curiosity.

No, more like chewed.

Like a dog working at a bone. The boom of her captain's voice filled the room before she could really start gnawing at it.

"What the hell, Despré!"

Hunter whirled to face her superior officer. "Oh. Come on, Captain. Are you really going to listen to that Boy Scout? I'm fine. Really."

Spiers smacked two flat hands down on his desk.

"You're not fine. Far from it. And quit acting like you're the only cop on the planet who can do the damned job!"

"Maybe," Hunter countered, "but you know I'm the one who's going to give it a hundred and ten percent."

"Which is exactly my point, Hunter. You don't do anything halfway," Spiers sighed. "Look. I need you to listen to me, and not just listen, but hear me. You've been burning the candle at both ends since you've been back and maybe," he paused. "Maybe you came back too soon. Are you still seeing Dr. Lacey?"

Hunter cast her eyes down toward the floor.

Spiers exhaled. "I'm thinking it's time to schedule another appointment. Hunter. Get yourself right. Frankly, I've got no choice. You are officially off this case. Go home. Clear your head. Get the hell out of Dodge. Live a little."

"Live a little? Is that what you're gonna tell the family of the girl we found out at the docks? Live a little?" Flecks of spittle settled on Hunter's lips. "You don't just walk away from something like that."

Spiers' deep baritone struck with the authority of a judge's gavel. "No. No, you don't. And that's exactly why I want you off this case. Benally can handle it."

Hunter braced her own palms against Spiers' desk and leaned in. "You don't understand, Captain. I *need* this."

Spiers sighed. "You need *something*. That's for damn certain. This case? This case ain't it."

"Shit," he began. He studied her face. "Look at you, Hunter. The bags under your eyes have carry-on luggage for cryin' out loud. Have you been sleeping?"

Hunter thought of the collection of empty plastic amber bottles littering her apartment dresser. She shrugged, then crossed her arms across her chest. "Here and there."

He gestured to the belt on her pants—the prong pushed through a makeshift hole—sloppily scored when the standard holes obviously hadn't been tight enough. "And when was the last time you had a decent meal?"

Hunter opened her mouth to speak, but Spiers held up a staying hand. "Lucky Dogs don't count. Hell. I'm not sure they even qualify as actual food."

Hunter's shoulders sagged.

A gentle tone tempered Spiers' next words. "Joe's

death…"

"Oh, come on! Are we really going to do this again?" Hunter exploded. "This has nothing to do with Joe's death. Besides, I.A. cleared me."

"Settle down. That's not where I'm going with this. Joe should have waited for you before he breached that squat. I get that. Not gonna lie, though. Why you picked up the murder weapon still puzzles me."

"I don't know. I wasn't thinking straight."

"That's exactly what Internal Affairs thought."

"You mean why they suspected me."

"Well, it would have helped if you actually remembered more details of the event."

"My partner was killed." Hunter's voice cracked with emotion. "You don't think that kind of thing can screw with your memory?"

"Dissociative amnesia. Yeah, I got Dr. Lacey's assessment. And I know she cleared you for duty."

Hunter took a breath to speak. Spiers interrupted with a cough before Hunter could protest further. The captain leaned back in his chair and linked his fingers over the expanse of his stomach. "The department has rules for a reason, Hunter. You were dating a fellow detective. When things don't work out…"

"…it doesn't mean one of them just up and offs the other. Despite what everybody thought." Hunter completed the statement. "Joe and I were grown-ups, Rudy." She dared address the captain by his given name, but she wanted to drive her point home.

"Sure," she continued. "The personal relationship may have gone south, but he was still my partner. Are you telling me you wouldn't have grabbed the knife if your partner was lying in a pool of his own blood on the floor? You telling me you *really* think I—"

Her voice trailed off as the old, familiar fear threatened to overwhelm her. She swallowed it down, refusing to let Spiers see how much it still affected her.

"Do you really think I hacked off my partner's head with a machete because…because what? It pissed me off that he left the toilet seat up and drank out of the milk carton?"

"People have killed for less," Spiers reminded.

She ticked off her penance on long fingers. "I saw the department shrink. I served my suspension—every last second of it—while Joe's killer roamed free."

"Still," Spiers began. "Still roams free."

"Yes." Hunter's voice dropped to a whisper. "Still."

"Come on, Hunter. Do the right thing." Spiers gestured toward his desk.

Hunter sighed heavily. Her shoulders slumped. This was a fight she knew she wasn't winning. She unholstered her gun, its weight apparent in the loud thud it made as she set it on the desktop. She tossed her badge beside it and headed toward the door. She reached for the knob but turned, a final thought poised on her full lips. Finally, the words tumbled out.

"And you want to know if I'm sleeping," she scoffed.

She stormed from the office, shattering the inset glass pane. A shower of glittering diamonds danced on the terrazzo tile. Spiers shook his head and buried his wide face in his palms.

The crunch of glass underfoot broke the quiet. Benally gingerly pulled his foot up as he clasped the doorjamb to the captain's office.

Spiers rubbed his temples with weary concern. "What do you need, B.B.?"

"Sorry to disturb, sir, but you might want to check out the noon news broadcast." Benally pointed to the slim flat screen mounted to Spiers' wall. The captain hit the remote with a fat finger. The meteorologist for FOX 8 television glowed into high-definition existence on the formerly black expanse.

"Who told that man that toupee looked natural?" Benally groused.

But it wasn't the meteorologist that the captain concentrated on. It was the all too familiar circular swirl of white inhabiting the lower quadrant of the green screen map behind the awkwardly coiffed meteorologist. Spiers pushed up the volume. The meteorologist's voice confirmed what the men already suspected.

"The storm system we've been watching in the Atlantic has strengthened and definitely become more organized. The tropical depression has now been named Marisol, a late arriving thirteenth named storm of this year. About 220 miles off the east coast of Miami, its strongest winds are about 42 miles per hour. If it keeps its current trajectory, we expect it to make landfall near Fort Lauderdale, Florida."

"Hey, Boss," Benally began. "Isn't this how...". Spiers didn't offer Benally a chance to finish his statement.

"Yeah, B.B. This is exactly how Katrina started. Shit! If this storm turns out to be a repeat performance of that monster, we've only got three days before it clears out the city and every shred of hope we have of catching the animal that did this." He ground his finger down on the crime scene photo of the anonymous girl and the lurid carving staring at him from the open file on his desk. "And I just sidelined my best detective."

B.B. shook his big head, no offense apparent on his broad features. Instead, he offered a single word in response to the captain's declaration.

"Yup."

Chapter Eleven

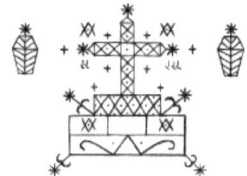

Sabine was distracted. The lunch rush had slowed. She should have been concentrating on turning over for the dinner crowd. *Kinky Boots* was playing at The Saenger, so they should be packed. But she stood, staring blankly at the wall as mounds of soapy bubbles rose in the basin and enveloped the stacks of white plates.

"You plan on washing any of them dishes?" Eldridge grumbled as he lifted a full black garbage bag from the trash can.

"What's that? Oh!" Sabine shook herself from her reverie and turned off the tap just before the bubbles cascaded over the stainless edge and onto the tiled floor. "Saints!"

Eldridge clunked the bag to the ground and tied off the top. "You shouldn't even be doin' dishes," he growled. "I thought that's why you paid that no account."

Sabine wiped her hands on her apron. Her brows came to a disgruntled peak. "Rabbit had no business being here today."

"You ask me, he ain't got no business bein' here *ever*." Eldridge offered a curt retort.

"Now, you take two steps back, Eldridge Brown. Don't go offering gospel on something you damn well know nothin' about."

Eldridge scoffed. "Gonna take more than the Good Book to help that boy find the path to righteousness. Boy couldn't find the moral high ground with a damned GPS."

He pushed through the screen door with the garbage. The loud bang of the dumpster and breaking glass echoed through the back alley.

"Yeah, well," Sabine muttered. "We all got our own personal demons."

"What's that?" Eldridge replied as he came back inside.

"Oh, nothing," Sabine answered. She untied the apron and pulled her head through the loop. "Look, Eldridge, I hate to ask, but can you handle dinner prep?"

"I suppose so, if you need me to."

"I do." Sabine grabbed her shoulder bag. "I got some errands I gotta run, and I'm afraid they can't wait."

She patted Eldridge's beefy ebony arm, smiling disarmingly. "You know I appreciate you, right?"

The big man let out a huff. "Yeah? Well, just so you know, I'll be 'appreciating' a raise soon."

Sabine's laugh tinkled as she dashed through the back door.

"And we out of garbage bags. Pick some up while

you runnin' them errands!" Eldridge called after her. He plunged his thick arms into the mounds of bubbles,

"Be callin' the damn place 'Eldridge's' soon." He started humming as the hidden dishes clinked beneath the soap.

*****

Sabine didn't enjoy turning the reins over to anybody, not even Eldridge, but Rabbit's hysterical explanation of the goings-on at St. Louis Number One had piqued her curiosity.

The sky had turned a steely gray. She was glad she'd grabbed her umbrella on her way out. She thought about Rabbit's vivid description of "the skeleton man."

Okay. So? Maybe she had grabbed the umbrella for other reasons as well.

As she made her way down the back alley toward North Rampart, she heard a long, low wolf whistle followed by a rough sandpapered voice grated over years of tar and nicotine.

"Well, well, well. If it ain't Ms. Sabine Louviere, the pride of the Crescent City. Ain't you just the belle of the ball?"

Sabine suddenly wished she'd worn her hip boots as well.

"Where you going all fancied up like that? You look scrumptious enough to be on your own damn menu, girl. You *must* be on your way to see Mr. Marcello. Mighty civic minded of you, now."

Peter Scarpetta leaned against the red brick wall, a

wooden Louisville Slugger propped beside him. He tapped a pack of Lucky Strikes against the palm of his hand, tamping down the tobacco. He knocked one loose from the pack and tilted it onto his bottom lip.

A flick of a yellow-stained thumb brought his scratched gold lighter to life. The dancing orange flame illuminated the telltale burst capillaries in his eyes. He wore a fresh bandage near the widow's peak of his oily, slicked-back hair. A red Rorschach pattern feathered from its center.

"Pete Scarpetta," Sabine declared. She stole a furtive glance back toward the restaurant door—Eldridge was a scream away—but thought better of it. Her business was just that—her business.

Scarpetta clicked his lighter closed with a distinct metal click and spread his arms wide.

"The one and only, sugar."

He pocketed the lighter and sauntered in Sabine's general direction. Her grip on the umbrella clenched a bit tighter, but fire danced in her eyes.

"Aw, what happen, Pete? Package store run out of Wild Turkey?" Sabine cracked, a surprising steel edging her voice. Scarpetta pulled up short.

"What's that supposed to mean?" he retorted, a sour cloud of leftover spirits assaulting Sabine's nostrils.

A beat passed before Sabine replied. She narrowed her obsidian eyes. "You're still standing upright."

The crack of his fist echoed between the brick walls. Fireworks burst in Sabine's head as Scarpetta's hand connected with the high cheekbone of her face. Still, she absorbed the blow without so much as a whimper. Instead, she turned slowly back to face Scarpetta, cold-blooded murder in her eyes.

"Well, now, that's better," she smiled menacingly. She wiped the trickle of blood oozing from the garish split on her cheek.

Scarpetta's chin disappeared into his neck as he pulled back in surprise. "Huh?"

"Least now you're picking on someone your own size." She sneered. "By the way, Pete." She hissed his name. "How'd you get that crack on that thick skull of yours?"

Scarpetta's cracked fingernails touched the criss-crossed bandage on his temple.

Sabine gripped her umbrella. "How'd you like a matching set?"

Her bravado didn't last long. Scarpetta slammed her lithe frame up against the brick. She felt the jagged bite of the edges. Her molars rattled in her jaw. But her pressing concern was the insistent point of the switchblade pushing into the lace of her blouse. A small flower of scarlet bloomed against the innocent white.

"You want to keep that sharp tongue in your head, now, hear?" Scarpetta hissed. "I can guarantee my blade is sharper."

He pressed the blade forward, just a touch. A fresh spread of red broadened on the original stain. "How I raise my boy ain't nobody's business but my own. Not Social Services, not that fat black kid, and certainly not some busybody greasy spoon manager who can't even get her own books straight. And speaking of business, you've got some with Mr. Marcello that needs tending."

Sabine wilted under his foul breath. "Tell Mr. Marcello I'll have his money. Business is good, but he ain't the only one I owe. There are food vendors, and I got employees to pay."

Scarpetta tilted his head from side to side, tongue clucking. "No, no, no. Now, you see, that's not how it works, doll face. You pay Mr. Marcello *first*. He wants his money, and he's sent me to collect."

A derisive snort escaped Sabine. "And he trusts you? A washed-up ball player more pickled than the okra you put in those weak Bloody Marys at that hole you bar tend at?"

The dig appeared to ruffle Scarpetta for a hot second before he leaned in again.

"We all got debts to pay," Scarpetta spat. He pointed his baseball bat at her face. "You pay yours, or the next time I crack you, I'm using *this* instead of my hand."

He tossed the bat into the air and made a surprising, deft catch with his left hand. He let it slide till the pommel of the handle nestled in the top of his fist and gave it an expert twirl before exiting the alley and leaving Sabine, cut and battered, in the darkening shade of the alley.

Chapter Twelve

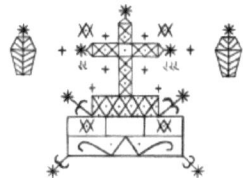

Hunter slouched into the chair across from Dr. Elizabeth Lacey, a soft leather cushion beneath her that squeaked with even the slightest shift of her weight.

She'd learned to keep still during these sessions, not wanting to give away anything with an unconscious twitch or move. If she stayed calm, composed, and answered only what was necessary, she could be out in under an hour.

Lacey adjusted her glasses, studying Hunter for a moment before speaking. "How are you feeling this week, Hunter? Are you getting any sleep?"

Hunter shrugged, her gaze sliding to the window. "Better than before."

"Mm." Lacey's pen tapped lightly against her notebook. "Enough to function well at work, I assume?"

"Enough to keep my focus where it needs to be," Hunter replied, her voice steady. Her tone was polite but clipped, signaling that she didn't plan on elaborating.

Lacey took a measured breath, her expression calm but determined. "Well, I'm glad to hear that, but the department tells me your sleep patterns are one of the concerns here. Difficulty sleeping, irregular hours. Anything specific that's keeping you up?"

Hunter's jaw tightened. "It's the job. You know how it is—shifts, late calls, paperwork. Doesn't leave much time to dream about unicorns."

Lacey raised an eyebrow, but a small smile softened her expression. "I think we both know it's more than that, Hunter."

Hunter didn't respond, instead shifting slightly in her seat, her eyes drifting again to the window, mentally pushing herself as far from the topic as possible. But Lacey waited, her calm demeanor an unspoken nudge, like she was gently probing for cracks in the wall Hunter had built.

After a moment, Lacey continued. "You know, a lot of people repress memories of traumatic events as a coping mechanism. It's not uncommon for someone in your line of work, especially with the pressures you've faced recently." She leaned forward, hands folded in her lap. "And if there are unresolved memories—"

"I don't have repressed memories," Hunter cut in, her voice sharper than she intended. She forced herself to take a breath, her jaw loosening as she offered a tight smile. "I just have a job that comes with baggage, Doc. Doesn't mean I'm carrying around some hidden trauma waiting to burst out."

Lacey didn't flinch, her expression remaining steady as she gave a thoughtful nod. "Okay. But if you're finding that certain memories, or... visions," she said the word carefully, "are making it difficult for you to function, I hope you'd consider discussing them. That's why we're here."

Hunter forced herself to meet Lacey's gaze, keeping her face neutral. She wasn't about to tell her about the visions, the faces that seemed to follow her even after she'd turned her back on them. "I'm fine. Really."

Lacey watched her for a beat longer, then leaned back, as if weighing her words. "All right. Let's talk about the medication you've been prescribed, then." She opened a file, flipping to the latest notes. "You're asking for a refill on the sleeping pills."

Hunter gave a nod, her expression carefully blank. "It helps me get the rest I need. Staying sharp, staying focused—those are non-negotiable for me."

Dr. Lacey looked at her over her glasses, her face unreadable. "Hunter, you're aware that these prescriptions come with potential side effects, yes?"

Hunter shrugged, brushing it off with a quick, casual smile. "Sure. I've taken them before. They're fine."

"Right, but I need you to be fully aware," Lacey replied, her tone firm. "These medications can cause side effects like hallucinations, loss of time, memory gaps. I'm sure you'd agree that these aren't things you can afford to ignore."

Hunter felt her pulse quicken at the mention of lost time, but she kept her expression smooth, her eyes carefully blank as she held Lacey's gaze. "I'm not experiencing any of those, Doc," she replied, her voice level. "Just good old-fashioned rest."

Dr. Lacey held her gaze for a moment, searching her face as if weighing the truth of her words. "Hunter, I'd like you to be honest with me. Have you experienced any strange episodes? Missing time, unusual dreams, things like that?"

Forcing a small, dismissive laugh, Hunter shook her head. "Not that I know of. Just sleep. Nothing else."

Lacey's lips pressed together, her expression thoughtful. "I trust your judgment, but I want you to know that if you do experience any of these side effects, you need to reach out. This isn't about pushing through or toughing it out. These things can affect your performance, and ultimately, your safety."

Hunter nodded, her expression cool. "Understood."

Lacey paused, as if deciding whether to push further. "Hunter, I know these sessions aren't your favorite part of the week," she said with a hint of humor. "But I am here to help you. And I believe that, with the right support, you can work through whatever you're dealing with."

"Appreciate it, Doc," Hunter replied, her voice softer but still carefully guarded. "But I'm good. Just need that refill."

Lacey didn't argue, instead making a note in her file before sliding the prescription paper across the table. "All right. But remember, if anything changes, or if you feel things aren't under control, I'm here. My door's open."

Hunter took the paper, offering a polite nod. "Thanks, Doc. See you next week."

Lacey watched her carefully as she left, her eyes thoughtful. But Hunter didn't look back. She'd gotten what she came for, and that was enough.

Chapter Thirteen

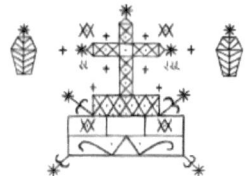

The door to the clinic slammed open, a gust of wind ripping it from Sabine's grip. Marisol hadn't even hit shore yet, and she was already being a Class A bitch.

Speaking of bitches…

Her hand went to her cheek, a canvas of purple and swollen flesh. Man might be a drunk, but Pete Scarpetta packed a hell of a wallop. She squinted through the pain as she wrested the door closed, her good eye darting around the sparsely furnished waiting area for Mac.

Her leg caught in the gauzy white fabric of her skirt pasted to her leg by the outside damp, leaving little to the imagination. "Dammit."

The humid air hung thick with an odd perfume—a curious combination of antiseptic and damp, the kind of scent that clings to the back of your throat and reminds you of decay.

Mac, his golden hair a disheveled crown atop his head, lumbered into the lobby, a fifty-pound sandbag slung in his arms. It was hard not to appreciate the flex of his muscles beneath the fabric of his shirt.

But that wasn't why she was here.

Mac looked up, startled surprise in his eyes, as Sabine approached. "Sabine!" A warm smile spread across his face, but it faltered, crumbled even, as he took in the damage to her face. "Jesus, Sabine. What in the hell happened?"

"Walked into a door?" The corner of her mouth twitched upward in a ghost of her usual grin. The dark joke did little to mask the gravity of her situation.

"Looks like that door could fight middleweight." Mac's blue eyes scanned her injury with the precision of a surgeon. He stepped closer, and the sterile light caught a scar on his side, a jagged line peeking just beneath his clothes.

"Something like that." Sabine kept her tone light, almost flippant, but her gaze remained sharp. The look in Mac's eyes changed—a subtle shift from carefree to pissed off. She'd seen the look often enough in the mirror—like a storm cloud passing over a sunlit field.

"This door have a name?"

Sabine pulled her gaze away.

Mac grabbed her softly beneath the chin and turned her face back to him. He leaned close and whispered. "Sabine?"

"Scarpetta," she sighed. "Pete Scarpetta."

"Goddammit!" Mac whirled away and kicked the innocent sandbag, a move he instantly regretted. "Ow!"

He reached for his injured toe, hopping like a leprechaun. Sabine stifled a giggle. Mac paused, a slow smile spreading across his handsome features.

"I know. Don't say it."

"What did that sandbag do to you, Doc?" Sabine said it anyway.

"Better that sandbag than Scarpetta's face. No, come on. It's not getting any prettier out there. Let's get that looked at." He nodded toward the back. His gaze drifted. "And maybe find you some dry clothes.

A slow smile spread across Sabine's face like it did anytime a man appreciated what she had to offer—thunder cracked outside—but now wasn't the time. "Lead the way, Doc."

Her steps squished wetly against the linoleum as she trailed Mac to the exam room. The fluorescent lights hummed above, casting an unforgiving glow on her bruised features. She perched on the edge of the examination table, paper crinkling beneath her.

"Okay, spill." Mac's tone was gentle yet insistent as he pulled on latex gloves with practiced ease. "What happened with Scarpetta?"

She inhaled sharply, her ribcage expanding with the weight of unsaid words. "It's Rabbit. Scarpetta's got his claws in that boy." Sabine's voice growled low, tinged with syrupy bitterness. "Thinks he can slap around the kid whenever he's feeling small—which is often."

Mac's jaw clenched at the image of Rabbit, small and wide-eyed, cornered by Scarpetta's menace. His blue eyes darkened, storm clouds gathering in their depths as he listened.

"Let me see that eye." Mac's voice dropped an octave, no trace of humor left. He positioned himself close, his presence enveloping, as if his broad shoulders could block out the world's ugliness.

"Only if you promise not to kiss it better," Sabine quipped, but her laugh echoed hollowly, a cracked bell in a deserted chapel. Her head tilted back, exposing the violet canvas of her skin to his scrutiny.

"Wouldn't dream of it." The corners of his mouth lifted in a half-smile. His fingers moved, deft and gentle, as they probed the perimeter of her swelling, his touch a whisper against her bruised flesh.

"Any dizziness? Blurred vision?" Mac's clinical questions cut through the tension as he flashed a penlight in her eyes.

"Vision's fine. Just feels like I've gone ten rounds with a sledgehammer." She flinched only slightly when his thumb brushed too close to the tenderest spot.

"Looks like you'll live." Mac stepped back, stripping off the gloves. "But that eye will be a beauty for a while."

"Great, 'cause I wasn't standing out enough already." Sabine swung her legs off the table, her movements controlled and graceful.

"Stay put while I grab some ice."

"Your bedside manner's crap, Doc," she called after him, a smirk playing on her lips despite the pain. "But your rescue complex is top-notch."

Mac returned with a cold compress and applied it to Sabine's eye. She jumped, the chill of it a stark contrast to the humid air that seeped through the cracks of the aging clinic. The storm outside continued to gather strength, angering the sky until it rumbled its disapproval.

"Rabbit's scared, Mac." Sabine's dark eyes reflected a storm of their own. "Scarpetta's left more than just bruises on that boy, and I ain't talkin' 'bout what you can see. The boy's running scared, and now with this storm, I worried even more."

The icy pad in his hands trembled slightly. "I swear, I'll find him, Sabine. And after the hurricane passes, we'll figure something out."

Sabine sat up straighter, wincing as the movement tugged at her tender skin. "I'm worried sick 'bout the kid, Doc. Let me handle the storm prep here. You need to focus on finding Rabbit and keepin' him safe from that rat bastard."

Mac hesitated. "Sabine, it's a big job—boarding windows, securing supplies. Hell! You've got your restaurant to think about, too. For one woman… that's an awful lot."

A hot flash of anger welled in Sabine, threatening to boil over. "You forgettin' who you talkin' to? When Tim got sick, it was me by his bedside—day in, day out. Nobody else. I was the one turnin' him over, changin' him, feedin' him till he was nothin' but skin and bones."

Her words hung heavy in the air, each syllable a weighty reminder of the nights she fought sleep, the days she battled despair, all the while playing nurse, cook, and guardian angel to a man slipping through her fingers.

Mac turned, his blue eyes softening, reading the tempest behind her sharp gaze. "Sabine, I'm sorry. Truly. I didn't mean to imply—"

"Save it." She took a deep breath. "Look, I know you feel some kind of guilty 'bout leavin' this mess to me." Her hands found her hips in a familiar stance that brooked no argument. "But I ain't some delicate flower that'll wilt at the first sign of hardship. Goddammit, I always find a way."

"I know, I know. I get it, and I'm sorry. You're more than capable. I just…" His voice trailed off.

The corner of Sabine's mouth quirked upward, her dark eyes glinting with a challenge. "Don't you worry none. If I get into a tight spot, I'll holler for Eldridge. That old bear may grumble, but he'll come runnin'. He always does."

"Alright." Mac's voice was tinged with reluctance, but edged with trust. "Just promise me you won't take any unnecessary risks."

"Cross my heart." She gestured flippantly. Her hands remained steady as she took the list Mac handed her.

"This is everything that's got to get done before Marisol slams into the city. Call if you need anything."

"Wouldn't dream of it."

"Okay then. I'm going to look for Rabbit." Mac grabbed a rain slicker from the coat rack and dragged one arm through it before he turned back to Sabine.

"Go!" She shooed him out the door. Mac nodded and stepped out into the wind and rain, leaving Sabine alone.

Outside, the wind picked up, carrying whispers of rain and debris along empty streets, a prelude to the tempest brewing on the horizon. Sabine moved through the clinic with purpose, her movements fluid, calculated, as she started securing windows, checking supplies—making sure everything was tied down or tucked away. She thumbed through a few loose files on the reception desk, jotting a few notes before slipping them on the shelf where they belonged.

She paused by a window, watching the palm trees bend, their fronds flapping wildly like the broken wings of some tropical bird. A smirk tugged at her lips.

Let the storm rage.

She'd walked through worse and come out with her head held high and her heels clicking defiance on the other side.

"Bring it on," she murmured to the howling winds. And the clinic, with its creaks and groans, seemed to brace itself alongside her.

Chapter Fourteen

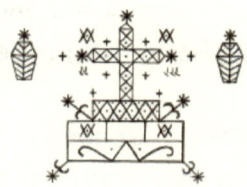

The bright blue sky over the tall, white steeple spire of the St. Louis Cathedral belied the pending weather threat pushing into the Gulf of Mexico. Last night's showers were only a humid memory. Hunter held a hand up to shield her eyes as she walked past the Cabildo and stared up at the bell tower.

Damn Benally, she thought as she stewed over the events in the captain's office. He hadn't offered a shred of help. Just let the captain toss her off this case. He was her partner, for Chrissake! Partners were supposed to have each other's backs.

The dramatic sense of irony was not lost on Hunter.

Hi, Pot. The name's Kettle. She mentally berated herself.

She'd seen the unease in Benally's eyes. Most of the time, he did a fair job of disguising it. But sometimes, when he thought she wasn't watching, Hunter could see it. It was a look she'd seen on the faces of most of the cops at the 8th at one time or another. New Orleans was just one of those towns. Everybody knew everybody—and that included their business. That went double for the police force. Nothing was sacred.

Or secret.

A rumored New Orleans Mafioso boss had said it best. "When two people have a secret, the only way it stays a secret is if one of 'em's dead."

Yeah, right, mused Hunter. *Everybody* knew Hunter's secret—from God right on down to the corner liquor store owner. And somebody *was* dead.

So much for Mafia adages.

Despré's "secret"? She was defective goods. Most of the men in the department had learned to steer clear of the diminutive detective. Atchafalaya Basin-sized chips on your shoulder didn't earn you too many rounds at Pat O's. Her less-than-friendly attitude wasn't the real reason people steered clear, however. Most of the cops on the force just considered her bad *juju*.

That's what happened when you lost a partner.

And it was worse when you were the number one suspect.

So, Hunter thought as she looked up at the towering steeple, she couldn't really blame Benally if he wasn't ready to jump in and play Captain America.

She shrugged noncommittally. Fine. If she wasn't going to get any help from him, she would not let that stop her.

She would just seek help from a higher authority.

With that, Hunter lowered her hand, allowing the bright midday sun to flood her face. She sucked in a deep breath, then squared her shoulders and marched up the wide white steps and through the heavy doors of the Cathedral.

*****

The St. Louis Cathedral was the oldest cathedral in North America. Founded in the early 1700s, the first church on the site was erected in 1718. After a succession of several churches built on the site, it was the third church that was elevated to the rank of cathedral.

Now, it dominated the northern end of Jackson Square in the heart of the Vieux Carré, rising between the two equally historic buildings, the Cabildo, the former seat of colonial government in New Orleans, and the Presbytère, currently a state museum, built on the former site of a Capuchin monk residence, or, as its name aptly distinguished, a *presbytere*.

Hunter listened to her boot heels echo on the marble floor after she crossed herself with holy water. Still, she knew she wasn't safe from her demons. Not even here, under the watchful gaze of the saints that kept guard over the flock. They kept their silent sentry from their stained glass and richly colored portraits in gilt frames and murals high above on the arched ceiling near the heavens.

But Hunter's devils were much closer. She felt their influence deep within her with every breath she drew. For her, there was no real sanctuary.

Even the cathedral itself wasn't protected from the evil that men, or nature, do. It had succumbed to fire on Good Friday in 1788, a dynamite bombing in 1909, and hurricane damage on two separate occasions.

Hunter's heart leaped into her throat as the opening measures of Schubert's "Ave Maria" trumpeted from the Holtkamp pipe organ perched in the loft near the rear of the cathedral. The organ had returned to its home relatively recently. It had not fared well during Hurricane Katrina and had to be sent back to the Holtkamp factory to be rebuilt. Hunter let out a derisive chuckle.

Too bad you couldn't send people back to the factory to be fixed.

No. Humans were far frailer than organs. There were just some things you couldn't come back from.

No matter how badly you wanted to.

As she genuflected in front of the impressive altar, however, her thoughts turned to Mac Steele and something the Medical Examiner had said. He had commented on the unwavering faith of the Haitian people in their religion, *voudon*. He was not wrong. At least not about that.

Voudouisants did indeed turn to their faith for many things. Protection. Strength. Guidance. Hunter was in short supply of all three at the moment.

She deposited a dollar in the tithe box and lit a novena candle. As she watched, the bright yellow flame flared to life and danced above the pure white votive. It was more an act of desperation than faith. Hunter had wandered so far off the path she was completely lost in darkness. She wondered if it was pure folly to imagine that this small flame could help illuminate the way back.

"Well, if this ain't a sight for sore eyes. Now I *know* a storm's a comin' if Ti Mambo Brigitte has found her way back into a house of faith."

A full, throaty chuckle echoed from behind Hunter.

Hunter whirled to see a mountain of a woman swathed in blood red fabric. The satin clung, tightly knotted in a kerchief on her high, proud ebony forehead, draped across her more than ample bosom, all the way around her wide belly and heavy, curved hips down to her sandaled toes dolloped in crimson polish.

Hunter rose to her feet and dipped her head in salutation. "Reverend Mother."

"Don't you 'Reverend Mother' me, girl. It's Reverend Mother Queen Rosalie and you ain't gettin' away without givin' me a hug. I know your mama taught you better than that! Now, you c'mere and show me some lovin'!"

The big woman swept Hunter into two enormous arms and smothered her in a tight embrace. When she finally let Hunter up for air, the large woman let out a belly laugh. "Mmm. Nuh-uh. Gimme some more of that! Now, that's better!"

A Cathedral docent shot Reverend Mother the evil eye. Reverend Mother merely pursed her lips and clucked.

"Oh, I know that scrawny little chicken ain't trying to shush Reverend Mother now. This is a house of love and praise, and I am gonna lift same up as loud as I damn well please." The big woman's voice echoed against the marble—loud enough for angels to hear.

A smile cracked at the edges of Hunter's stern mouth. The repeated use of unfamiliar muscles was making her cheeks ache. She reached for Reverend Mother's arm, which was now firmly stationed on the woman's ample hip.

"Come on, Reverend Mother. Let's not do anything we'll regret. More specifically, that I'll regret." Hunter tugged her toward the exit.

Hercules probably had an easier time wrangling the Nemean Lion. Hunter realized how fitting the big woman's self-appropriated theme song was: "I Shall Not Be Moved".

"Please," Hunter begged.

Perhaps it was the edge of desperation in Hunter's plea that melted Reverend Mother's resolve. It may have also been the snappy jazz brass trumpeting from the outside street. In any case, Reverend Mother whirled in an unexpected grace of red satin toward the door. Hunter followed through the side door and out into the welling crowd on St. Ann.

"Mmm, mmm, mmm. Now, ain't that the most beautiful B-flat you ever did hear? Damn, but those Marsalis boys can whomp up a tune!" Reverend Mother's eyes closed as she swayed with a slight bounce in time to the cheery second line.

Travelers often had an array of options when choosing how to soak in a city's culture. You could admire regional works of art hanging on the walls of austere museums or hip galleries. You could take in a show at a local theater or cabaret. You could treat yourself to a plateful of gastric bliss at local restaurants with their home-grown cooks and chefs.

But the absorption of culture in the Big Easy was more passive. Sure, one could pursue any of the aforementioned activities. Local artisans *did* ply their wares, brightly painted canvases on the rod-iron fences of Jackson Square. Celebrity chef and favorite son, Jon Besh, dished up nirvana flavored with nostalgia at The American Sector restaurant at the National D-Day Museum.

But in New Orleans, you could stand stock still on the banquette and still steep yourself in culture. The gumbo of accents flavored by Spanish and French and just a pinch of New York—a sort of Bronx with a softened edge. The lackadaisical pace of conversation with locals.

Culture burbled up in the streets, a twenty-four-hour party, and everyone was invited—come rain or shine. Day and night.

The second line parade dancing past Hunter and Reverend Mother was a prime example.

Rooted in historical tradition, second line parades burst forth in neighborhood streets with the sudden intensity of a summer shower. The brassy herald of a trumpet rolled between the historic buildings like thunder. The kaleidoscopic wardrobe of color punctuated the crowd like rainbow-dazzled lightning. Participants even sported umbrellas, parasols of satin and lace, not to avoid the rain of celebration and music, but almost to conduct it as owners jabbed them skyward to the beat of the brass and drums.

Second lines descended from fraternal organizations and neighborhood societies of the 1800s who catered specifically to the African American community. These clubs would frequently offer burial services, insurance, and even loans to their members. The parades arose as both a means to honor the recently departed and to advertise club services. The mourners and club members established the "first line" of what essentially became a musical, moving block party. Bystanders who fell in step, strutting and singing, behind the kerchief-waving revelry formed the infamous "second line". Death became a spirited celebration.

The spirit had definitely taken hold of Reverend Mother as her hips swayed and her ample bosoms bobbled. Almost possessed, it seemed for a moment she would be swept into the passing throng, a willing victim. But Hunter's tightening grip anchored her to reality. Reverend Mother's finely penciled brows folded into matronly concern.

"*Soc au lait, cher*. Something's playing the devil with you. What's goin' on in that pretty little head of yours?" Reverend Mother's voice creased with worry.

"It's nothing. Really." Hunter's voice wavered.

Reverend Mother's face morphed from concern to stoic resolve. "Don't you be sugarcoatin' the truth. You know how I feel about lyin'. It's the Devil's native language."

Hunter nodded. She swallowed hard. If she took this step, she'd be Alice tumbling down the rabbit hole. Her jaw set.

"It's happening again."

The color drained from Reverend Mother's face.

Chapter Fifteen

The water rushed over his body, its warmth enveloping him like a comforting embrace, a momentary escape from the harsh reality outside the bathroom door.

He stood, unmoving, under the cascading shower, his eyes closed, allowing the steady stream of droplets to beat against his skin. The steam clouded the air, transforming the small room into a sanctuary, where everything beyond the walls ceased to exist, if only for these precious few minutes.

The sound of the water splashing against the ceramic tiles echoed in the confined space—rhythmic, almost hypnotic. It was a relentless, steady drumbeat, a reminder of the world outside, yet at the same time, it was distant, as though time had slowed.

The water's heat, at first intense, now melded with his skin, easing tension in his muscles and sending a soothing warmth through him.

But there was no escape from the chill deep within his chest.

Each droplet felt like it was purging something from him, scrubbing away the grime, the dirt, the blood. As the water streamed over his torso, it traced the contours of an old, jagged scar that slashed across his skin—a permanent reminder of battles fought and lost, of a past that could never be forgotten, no matter how much he tried.

The scar was the embodiment of everything he had endured, a testament to survival, but also to the wounds that never truly healed.

His somber mood matched the gloom that settled in the back of his mind, where memories and regrets lay in wait. He hadn't meant to drift so far into his thoughts, but the weight of them pressed down on him, a burden he carried even in moments of solace like this.

He stood still, letting the water run over him, but inside, there was nothing still. His mind churned, restless, teeming with shadows of things best left buried.

The scar. That cursed mark. It was more than just a line of raised flesh.

It was a brand.

A constant reminder of failure, of pain, of survival that came at a cost too high. What had it all been for? He often asked himself that question, standing in this very spot, under this very stream of water, hoping for answers that never came. There were no answers, only silence and the steady beat of water hitting the tiles.

Inside, he battled demons that seemed determined to claw their way to the surface. The darkness in him was an old friend, something he'd grown accustomed to over the years.

It lurked in the quiet corners of his mind, waiting for moments like this to rise, taunting him with doubts and fears. He wasn't the man he had been—he wasn't even sure if he was a man anymore, or just a hollow shell carrying the weight of past sins.

There was always that feeling—like a dam about to burst—held together only by his will. But his will was faltering.

Each day, each sleepless night, he felt the cracks forming, growing deeper, more pronounced.

There was a part of him that feared what was coming. That familiar gnawing in his gut, the unease that settled like lead in his stomach.

He could sense it, just beyond the horizon—a storm, an event, something or someone that would upend what little control he had left. It was inevitable. He'd lived long enough to know that calm was nothing but an illusion, a brief respite before the chaos returned.

Even here, in the privacy of his own home, in the shower's warmth, he wasn't safe. His thoughts kept drifting back to that feeling—that something was on its way, something that would drag him down into the abyss he had fought so hard to avoid. Was it a person? A ghost from his past? Or maybe something darker, a consequence of his own making?

The doubts were always there, scratching at the edges of his mind. The feeling that he couldn't outrun the consequences forever. That the darkness inside him was winning. No matter how hard he fought, it always came back.

His hands twitched at his sides, the fingers curling involuntarily into fists. The motion was small at first, but it grew—tightening until his knuckles turned white under the strain.

He squeezed harder, as if the act itself would release some of the tension coiled within him, but it didn't. His body was wound tight, muscles flexed under the heat of the water, as though preparing for a blow that hadn't yet come.

In his mind, there was a war raging. Not one fought with weapons or words, but with silence, with memories, with the constant, gnawing sense of doom.

He wanted to believe that he could fight it, that he could emerge victorious. But the truth was, he wasn't sure how much longer he could hold out. How long until he snapped?

Finally, after what felt like an eternity, he forced his fists to unclench, his fingers loosening with a visible effort. The water was cooling, its once comforting warmth now turning tepid, a reminder that even this fleeting moment of solace was slipping away. He was being pulled back into the world, whether he liked it or not.

He took a breath, his chest rising and falling slowly as he reached for the knob to shut off the water. The steady drumbeat of droplets hitting the floor stopped, leaving only the soft sound of the drain gurgling as the last bits of water swirled down.

For a moment, he stood there. Naked. Wet.
Exposed.

He watched the steam dissipate, and the cool air crept into the room, raising goosebumps on his skin.

And then, as he stepped out from the shower, something caught his eye.

The drain.

A swirl of red diluted in the water, spiraling down into the darkness. He blinked, staring at it for a long moment, feeling the weight of it settle in his chest.

Blood.

Chapter Sixteen

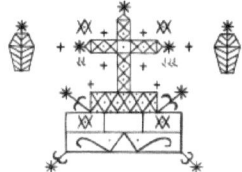

If she was being honest with herself, the little dust-up with Peter Scarpetta had shaken Sabine, but she remained determined. Rabbit's father was a real piece of work.

If the darkening stain on her blouse was any sign, Rabbit had every right to be afraid of the man. But something the boy had seen had driven him to confront his abusive father, regardless. Something that had scared him even more than the drunk beatings his father dished out like pecan pie. Sabine meant to find out what.

As she approached the entrance to the cemetery, a last gaggle of tourists, packed together, bobbled awkwardly through the wrought-iron gates, a run of pink salmon swimming upstream.

Sabine adjusted the oversized sunglasses on her face and stepped aside to let them pass. A costumed tour guide led the pack, spinning wild yarns about Marie Laveau and the voodoo curses she wreaked from her house on North Rampart.

Sabine smirked. Marie Laveau may have been a voodoo queen, true. But more powerful than that, she was a shrewd woman.

The beautician for the wealthy white and Creole women of New Orleans had practiced the art of listening far keener than any voodoo ritual. Through the quiet whispers of her vast network of spies, Marie became privy to all manner of intimate secrets and private fears—secrets and fears she used to her clever advantage, along with a smattering of her own personal dramatic flair and significant acquaintance with spells—till she became the most powerful woman in the city.

Whites of every class beseeched her for aid with their dealings and dalliances. Negroes perceived her as their leader. Indeed, she often offered her skills to them gratis. Meanwhile, upper-class politicians lined her pockets to secure elections, while high society types walked in off the banquette and laid down ten dollars for a trifling love powder.

To implore the help of Madame Marie became synonymous with *haute couture*. Even now, Sabine thought wryly, people of all walks of life from the farthest-flung corners of the world flocked to her grave, the one with the famed red "XXX", and asked for her aid in life, love, and the pursuit of happiness.

Sabine had always felt a certain kinship with the famous voodoo queen. She prided herself on being a shrewd woman as well. She knew how to take a situation and use it to her own advantage.

She also knew how to deal with anyone who got in her way.

She squared her shoulders and pushed past the throng of sunburned tourists.

Who came to New Orleans in the dead of summer, anyway?

It was hell on earth. Give her a tropical island, quenched by trade winds, and surrounded by jeweled sapphire waters. You could keep this simmering soup bowl with its murky Old Man River.

She warrened through the cemetery "streets," striding forward until she came upon the white-washed, three-stacker scratched over with triple crosses. She squinted through the irritating glare that seeped through the cloud cover, trying to detect any telling signs of Rabbit's harrowing exploits of the previous evening.

A fat streak of greasy carbon suggested *someone* had made a fire. Sabine squatted low to investigate. She ran her fingers through the black and rubbed them together. Too big to have come from an overturned novena candle or discarded crack pipe from some junkie.

Maybe Rabbit *had* seen something happen here. She took a closer glance around the tomb. A curious clump of debris caught her eye. She bent low.

"Lucky Strikes?" She picked one cylinder up in her fingers and slowly rolled it. It hadn't been lit. Just a random pile of the unused cigarettes.

But as she looked closer, it wasn't random at all. They were neatly stacked in a little pyramid formation. Like someone had taken great care to place them there.

"So, not just tourist trash," she mused out loud.

A wink of purple flowers peeked curiously from mounted vases on the crypt.

"What did you see, my little blossoms?" she asked. "Tell me. Did the Baron pay you a visit?"

She fingered a bloom and a single purple petal fluttered, lifeless, to the ground. She noticed another, darker stain of red near the toe of her sandal. The scarlet in the stain had oxidized, forming the dark russet characteristic of iron oxide.

Dried blood.

Sabine straightened and used the sole of her sandal to blot out the telling evidence. That's when she saw it. A distinct sized-fourteen footprint. A sudden sound captured Sabine's attention. She whirled.

The groundskeeper, a thin, frail man wearing a *dŏulí* against the threat of skin cancer, shuffled close. He paused at the cloud of gray dust billowing up around Sabine. Sabine quickly faced the tomb, crossed herself, and bent her head in simulated prayer. In truth, Sabine prayed to no higher power. God stopped listening long ago.

Every woman for herself, now.

Her full lips murmured in hollow appeal. The man shambled along, leaving Sabine to her silent devotions. Once he was out of sight, Sabine gathered the folds of her billowing skirt in clenched fists and bolted from the cemetery. Whatever Rabbit had seen, Sabine knew one thing for certain.

The dead don't bleed.

Chapter Seventeen

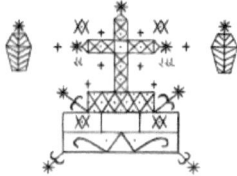

Piety. A reverent devotion. *Desire.* A fervent wanting. In life, the two concepts didn't intersect. It wasn't happening for Hunter. It didn't happen in the Lower Ninth Ward of New Orleans either.

Piety Street began at Chartres, near the "Rusty Rainbow," a ruddy metal sculpture arcing over a stretch of public green space. Visitors could cross over the rail tracks to the riverfront into the Piety Gardens and Crescent Park and jog, walk the dog, or enjoy an unobstructed view of the French Quarter round the river's bend. They could even glimpse the old WTC building towering over the Central Business District.

One block over, there was no rainbow and certainly no pot of gold at the end. Desire started near the same point and ran parallel all the way past St. Claude into the Upper Ninth Ward where entire neighborhoods lay in ruin, still, nearly two decades after the devastation of Katrina. Skeletal buildings, pock-marked with graffiti tags, sat caged behind fences, powerless to stop nature from reclaiming her own.

Hunter wasn't sure what lay between piety and desire on a philosophical level, but as she followed in the Reverend Mother's wake, she felt the tug of a past that held a firm root between the two—Rosalie Alley.

Reverend Mother Queen Rosalie took great pride in telling her flock and, truthfully, any soul who gave a willing ear, that the alley was named after hers truly.

Fact of the matter was the alley *was* named after a neighborhood personality and, when pressed, Reverend Mother challenged any person, living or dead, to have more personality than her.

The alley was a narrow passage in the Bywater neighborhood of New Orleans. Not a through street, but more of a grassy, graveled lane bordered by planked fences adorned with vibrant and lively depictions of dancing *ghede* and flaming hearts. A weathered, welded Baron sculpture kept watch over the alleyway entrance, perched high atop a power line pole. A rusted cigar gripped tight in tin teeth. A paint can top hat sat at a jaunty angle on his russet-colored head. A colorful character.

And if the Baron and Reverend Mother didn't provide enough local color, there was always the Bywater itself.

In the colonial era, the area was predominantly plantations, but at the turn of the nineteenth century, the area saw a shift. As the section became more residential, the Bywater bubbled, an eclectic melting pot of nationalities. You could find French living next to Spaniards. Creoles living side-by-side with folks of Native American descent. And it wasn't long before the area saw an influx of immigrants from Ireland, Germany, and Italy. Large numbers of French Caribbean immigrants also settled into the neighborhood. It wasn't surprising, then, to see *Voudon* take a foothold.

Reverend Mother and Hunter passed a large black and purple painting of a grinning skeleton. Hunter imagined the top-hatted barebones winked from an empty lens of his sunglasses.

The Baron was everywhere.

Reverend Mother tromped past pastel clapboards with ruby purpose until she came out onto the North Rampart side of the alley. She strutted up the steps of a bright blue shotgun and pulled open the painted red screen door. Hunter watched as the big woman angled her girth to slide inside. Hunter hesitated on the curb.

Reverend Mother popped a red-kerchiefed head back outside and waved her forward. "Well, come on, now. We got work to do!"

Hunter took a deep breath, squared her shoulders, and stepped inside.

She followed Reverend Mother out to the walled-in courtyard. She had forgotten how open it was. Open and warm.

Several wide ceiling fans swirled from weathered pergola beams in lazy rotation, making a minimal swath through the summer heat. Loving art dedicated to the *lwa* adorned the walls.

The prominent feature of the space, however, was

the tall *potomitan*, a giant blue pillar centered in the room. Hunter searched her memory for its significance.

Oh, yes. Gran Bwa's Mapou tree.

A connection between the physical and spirit worlds. Thick bodied snakes encircled the pole, painted with multi-colored scales. Hunter looked up at the broad blades of swirling fans. Her head swooned. The lids of her eyes grew heavy.

The banana leaves were broad, too, like great, flat fingers of a giant. They waved in the night, ushering in the stars. Mama had just tucked her in. Serafine, too, though her little sister struggled against bedtime like she did every night—every night till Mama gave her the doll she cried for. Hunter's doll.

A candle kept watch at the bedside, a silent sentinel to keep the bad dreams away. But still they came. They came, unbidden, on the evening breeze. They brushed over the white sheets. They whispered in her ear. Whispered secrets of an unbearable truth.

She saw Serafine. Saw her pigment-pale skin. Her snowy hair plaited tight. Saw her standing at the river's edge. Saw the Baron waiting for her on the other side. The candle's flame danced wildly on its wick.

It danced...then sputtered and died.

"You got that coffee?" Reverend Mother snapped her fingers at Hunter.

Hunter shook herself alive. She looked down at the white, green-logoed cup in her hand and handed it, dazed, to Reverend Mother.

"Chain store brew." Reverend Mother clucked her tongue. "When we got Café du Monde right there." She gave Hunter a scolding glower.

Still, she popped the top and took a deep breath. "Well, it's blacker and hotter than my backside. Least that's good. That's just how he likes it. He prefer unfiltered cigarettes, but coffee'll do in a pinch."

She placed the cup with reverence on the altar at the foot of the *potomitan*, right next to a grinning skull. She gave a satisfied hum, sat her hands on her wide hips, and gave an approving nod.

"That'll be just fine. I always say we all got the spirits movin' in us. From us old folk right on down to the newborn babe. That's what binds us. But you know, each of us? Each of us got a special spirit. One who takes a particular interest in us. That's the one," she began. She drilled a fat finger in the middle of Hunter's forehead. "That's the one what own our head. I always said the Baron was your *met tet*, cher. He got something special goin' on for you and you gotta learn how to accept it, or there gonna be the devil to pay."

"But what if I want something different? What if this path, this way, is not the way for me?"

Reverend Mother took Hunter's pixie chin into her big hand and drew her close enough to smell the patchouli. "Better the devil you know than the one you don't."

A rooster crowed somewhere in the neighborhood.

Reverend Mother released Hunter's face. "'Nuff about that nonsense. Now, let's go see what the Baron's trying to put into that pretty little head of yours."

Hunter still wasn't sure she wanted to know.

Chapter Eighteen

The blade bit through the flesh without prejudice. It didn't care what manner of meat lay on the scarred slab. Its job was to cut—and cut it did—with efficiency, if not grace.

Thunk.

It came down in a practiced arc and cleaved through the fibrous pink. A soft suck puckered the air as the beveled edge pulled free of the adulterated muscle. A trickle of blood, warmed by the southern heat, rolled along the honed edge of the cleaver, until it let loose and sailed in a crimson arc across the room. It landed, a bold red flower, on the yellow kitchen curtain.

"Don't you be making a mess in my kitchen, Dante. You hear?" Reverend Mother scolded as a resounding clunk as the blade bit through flesh and bone. Hunter shuddered.

"Never you mind Dante," Reverend Mother patted Hunter's hand. The big man raised the blade for another cleave through the side of pork. "Good man. Always brings me a little bouquet of these bright purple flowers from the garden out in front of his double."

She pointed to the simple arrangement in the Mason jar centered on the table. "I ain't got the heart to tell him what they called."

Reverend Mother leaned in and whispered in Hunter's ear. "Devil's trumpet."

The big woman sat back and her voice returned to normal. "But what's the harm, I say. They pretty enough, so I let him bring 'em." She nudged one blossom with a red lacquered nail. The light scent of citrus drifted to Hunter's nose.

Lemon?

Hunter cast a curious look at Dante.

Thunk. His sharp blade cleaved another section of pork rib.

"Poor boy may be simple, but he know sticks in a bundle are unbreakable." She leveled an accusing eyeball at Hunter across the table. "Don't matter who we are. We all got our part to play."

"Dante," she addressed the tall man. "Blessings on you again for taking time from the butcher shop to get them chops ready tomorrow's fry up."

Dante gently lay down his cleaver and wiped his bloody hands across the white expanse of his apron. He dipped his bald head reverently. "Wasn't no problem, Reverend Mother. I serve."

"Amen," Reverend Mother replied. She turned back

to Hunter. "We got ourselves a hurricane ceremony tomorrow. Erzulie Dantor don't usually say no when she get a good meal. And we'll be feeding her good, too. Lord knows we need it." Her brow furrowed. "Things ain't lookin' too good out in the Gulf this year."

That's right. Hunter nodded almost imperceptibly. She'd lost hold of the calendar since Joe was gone.

She'd lost hold of a lot of things.

It was almost the third Saturday in July. The day the faithful implored the Black Madonna for protection against the awesome destructive power of nature's fierce tropical storms.

Hunter wasn't sure if she could be counted among the faithful any longer.

"You'll be there, of course," said Reverend Mother. It wasn't a question.

Hunter sighed. "I'll try."

"What's this 'try' business?" Reverend Mother fussed as she deftly shucked her fifth ear of corn. "There ain't no such thing as 'try'. You either do or you don't."

Hunter suppressed a chuckle. Jedi wisdom spouting from the full red lips of a voodoo *mambo*. She shook her head.

"It's just I've got this thing going on right now, Reverend Mother. A case. And it's a whole lotta ugly with no good explanation."

Another solid thunk resounded from the chopping block. Hunter glanced at the tall, dark man slicing the marbled pork. He seemed focused on his task.

Still, Hunter watched as he set the cleaver aside and picked up a thin boning knife. Her eyes followed as he executed a fine cut that denuded the pork from the shank, but Hunter noticed the tension in his ebony muscles, the furtive glances from the dark eyes. Something eerily familiar padded around the edges of Hunter's brain. The rip of corn silk from a fresh cob interrupted before she could hone in on what it was.

"Sounds like somebody's causing a heck of a ruckus." Reverend Mother pulled another tuft of corn silk loose from a cob, oblivious to Dante's keen interest in their conversation.

"That's not the half of it. They're killing people, Reverend Mother." Her next thought caught like a sticker burr in her throat. She swallowed painfully. "They're killing them and marking them with the Baron's *veve*."

A deafening and sudden clatter exploded behind the two women. Dante stood, slack-jawed, as the entire platter of chops lay upended at his large feet. For a moment, he stayed rooted to the spot, then burst into a flurry of dark motion.

"I'm so sorry, Reverend Mother. I didn't mean nothin'. It just slipped. The whole thing. She just slipped outta my hands. I'll clean it up right quick."

"Oh, Dante, baby, don't you worry none. Ain't nothing but a trifle. We'll set it right."

"I got some more pork at the house. I'll be sure to bring it along for tomorrow." The large man bowed and nodded and bowed some more before he finished rescuing all the lost pork and carried the platter from the room.

The cleaver lay abandoned, forgotten on the tile floor. Hunter wished fervently that she could abandon the horrific visions of the mutilated head in the Mississippi as easily. But every time she closed her eyes, the dead girl's milky ones stared right back at her.

She moved to retrieve the blade. Reverend Mother kept a wary eye. Hunter picked up the imposing tool, slowly rotating it in her hands. She looked up after Dante.

"It's…it's like…". Hunter broke off in mid-sentence. She swallowed hard.

Reverend Mother broke the silence. "Like the last time?"

Hunter nodded wordlessly.

"Like every time. It's Joe. It's Serafine. It's everything. All over again." The sound of her sister's name spoken aloud sent a spine-shuddering shiver down her spine.

"None of that business was your fault, child, and you know it," Reverend Mother scolded.

"How can you say that?" Hunter snapped back, swinging the knife in a wide arc. "*Everyone* blamed me!" Her voice fell to a strangled whisper. "They do. Every time."

"And them's always a pack of fools." Reverend Mother deftly disarmed Hunter, setting the knife on the table. "Especially when it comes to what happened to your sister. You was nothing but a child then."

"And so was Serafine. Mama cried, Reverend Mother. She cried so hard. Couldn't even lay Serafine to rest proper. Not without…without…". Hunter's voice trailed off again. The memory was too painful. "She could hardly even look at me after. Hardly spoke to me. Right up till the day she died."

A heavy silence crushed Hunter. When she finally

raised her head, green eyes implored Reverend Mother. "It's like *I* was the ghost. Not Serafine."

Hunter slammed her hands on the counter. She cursed under her breath and shoved herself away, grinding her heels in a furied pace across the kitchen.

"I saw it, Reverend Mother," Hunter hissed through clenched teeth. "Saw the whole goddamned thing before it happened. Just like with Serafine! And just like Joe, damn it all!"

Reverend Mother jabbed a cylinder of yellow corn at Hunter. "I'll thank you not to blaspheme in my church, thank you very much!"

Reverend Mother stood, her size filling the kitchen less than her sheer power of will. She leveled a severe scowl at Hunter. "You might have been a child then, but you ain't no more. The Baron is workin' through you, girl. Workin' through the dead to try and help you save the livin'. Problem is, you ain't listening!"

"What do you mean, I'm not listening? All I ever did was listen. I tried telling people. I tried to tell them about Serafine. About Joe." Her breath caught. "You say I'm not listening. Well, what am I supposed to do when people won't listen to me? They all just think I'm crazy. And you know what? I'm starting to believe them."

Reverend Mother walloped Hunter upside the head with a cob of corn.

"Ow!"

The big woman stood, towering over Hunter. "You forgot *everything* you been taught about the faith? Girl, you *know* the Baron! He the *lwa* what got control over the dead. He using them to speak to you. Just like last time and the time before that. Can't you see, girl? Somebody? Well, somebody be working some bad hoodoo. They trying to send folk to the Baron before he say they ready. And one thing you know the Baron don't abide, it's being told what to do."

Hunter grimaced at the irony.

Reverend Mother's features softened. She reached for Hunter's hand. "The Baron is giving you everything you need to stop this evil, child. He's given you the sight so you can help these folks. But ever since Serafine, you've got blinders on to what he been trying to show you."

The voodoo priestess sat and folded her arms across her ample bosom. "If you gonna get through this, there's only one question left."

"What's that?"

Reverend Mother leaned in close.

"Do you believe?"

Chapter Nineteen

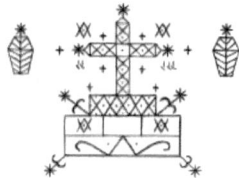

There were things you knew in life. Things that just *were*. There were things you were told, and you accepted them as *fact*.

Then there were things you took on *faith*…even if they defied rational explanation.

Mac believed. He fingered the small lump hidden under his shirt. He had to. Otherwise, it was all for nothing.

What he had a difficult time believing was there was some reasonable explanation for gold in the evidence sample his assistant showed him.

The first hints of Hurricane Marisol had begun peppering the city. The patter of light but insistent rain smacked against the transom window. New Orleans might not have basements, but city officials still liked to keep all evidence of gore and carnage from the curious eyes of the public and American Express-carrying tourists. So, bottom floor of the Earhart Expressway building and raised windows it was.

"You're certain it's gold?" Mac asked.

Leroy nodded. "One hundred percent positive. Did an *aqua regis* test. Speaking of aqua, you are soaked, my man."

"I think that's *agua*, pal." Mac dried his shaggy hair with a towel as water pooled around his feet. "But, yeah. I guess I do kinda look like a drowned rat, huh?"

Leroy snorted. "That's putting it mildly. Looks like you soaked up half of Lake Pontchartrain. Won't catch me outside in weather like this. Nuh uh. No way, no how." Leroy jabbed a thumb toward the rivulets of rain trailing down the short glass. "A person could catch their death out there."

Mac halted his vigorous towel drying. For a moment, he seemed lost in thought.

"Boss?" Leroy called. The diener's voice jolted Mac from his reverie. Mac stepped forward and squinted at the tiny sample. Something niggled at his memory. He tried to bring it to the surface but, like himself, lay drowned beneath a flood of other thoughts.

"Gold tooth, maybe?" Mac suggested, considering where Leroy had found the flake.

Leroy shook his head. "Nope. Not even so much as a filling in sight. I don't know what other choices this girl made in her life, but she had a *killer* dental hygiene routine."

Mac looked dubiously at the diener. Leroy looked duly sheepish. He threw his hands up in defense.

"Too soon?"

The faint mumble of a weather report scratched from the radio on the counter.

Mac's brow furrowed. "Hey, can you turn that up?" Leroy obliged, rotating the tuning dial until the broadcast came through loud and clear.

"The storm system we've been watching in the Atlantic has now been classified as a Category One hurricane."

A queasy feeling flopped Mac's guts.

Leroy passed a concerned look to his superior. "You worried?"

"Definitely not planning a beach trip. Let's just say the clock's ticking," Mac replied.

He returned the evidence to the tray on the exam table. The gold fragment was just a part of the larger mystery this anonymous girl presented.

Stranger still were the results of her tox screen. Mac analyzed the results as the doors to autopsy swung open. B.B. Benally strode in with his customary casual swagger and a stainless-steel thermos in tow.

"Tell me something good, Doc," the tall Native American graveled. "We got this little lady's name, rank, and serial number?"

Mac rose to meet the detective with a hearty handshake. "Wish we did, Detective Benally, but we seem to be coming up with more questions than answers."

"Damn it," Benally grunted. "I was hoping to get home and board up my windows, but what can you do? And please. It's B.B. Might be old-fashioned, but with this hurricane dancing out in the Gulf, if the mayor calls for an evac there's a distinct possibility we might be shackin' up together. Least we can do is be on a first-name basis. Can you tell me what you *do* know?"

Mac reached for a thin paper report on his desk.

"*That* I can do. But I don't know that it's going to make you any happier. We took a sample of the vitreous humor."

"And it was no laughing matter," Leroy chuckled, earning him scolding glances from both men.

"Ahem." Leroy tugged at the collar of his shirt, which just seemed to have gotten about two sizes too small. "I'm just going to go write up some reports and leave you gentlemen to it."

With that, the young man retreated through the double doors into the nether regions of the morgue, taking his gallows humor along with him.

Benally shook his head. "Y'all got some weird folks working down here."

Mac shrugged. "Leroy's weirder than most. But I gotta say, he does excellent work."

"If you say so, Doc. Still don't think he's gonna make the Christmas dinner invite list, though. So, what *do* you have for me?"

"Initial assessment at the scene was accurate. The neck was severed from the body between C4 and C5. Kerf marks show it was likely done with a cleaver. And somebody pretty strong, to boot. Even so, it took more than one blow to separate the head entirely."

"Jeezus. Poor baby. I hate to ask, but what else?"

"Like I said, we didn't have a lot to work with in this particular case, so we pulled fluid from the eye and ran tox on it instead of a blood sample. We screened for the basics, of course, but considering the type of assault, we also threw the net a little wider to include classes of substances that might incapacitate the victim or make her more pliable. Flunitrazepam, gamma hydroxybutyric acid, and ketamine."

"Benally folded his muscled arms across his broad chest. "Roofies, GHB, and Special K. The damned Holy Trinity of date rape drugs."

"Yeah," Mac replied. "I've got to believe she wouldn't just lie there and let something that horrific be done to her without putting up a fight. But from the little we have to work with, we can't see any evidence she put up any kind of struggle."

"And?"

"And not a single one popped."

"Well, shit."

"Hold on. Don't throw in the towel just yet. We did find *something* in her system."

B.B. held out his hands. "You gonna keep me hanging?"

"Scopolamine," Mac finally admitted.

"Scopolamine?" The big man pondered silently for a moment. Mac didn't interrupt. Eventually, Benally shook a long finger in the air. "Wasn't there a scare a while back about a version of scopolamine being used transdermally on business cards to subdue would-be victims?"

"Yeah, but that's more of an urban myth. More likely, our girl ingested it. Probably in a free drink or food."

"That's why I always pack a thermos, brother." Benally shook the metal cylinder in his hand. "I'll run it through ViCAP and see if any similar cases pop. Did we get *anything* that might help identify her?"

Mac flipped to the second page of the report. "We did note a portion of a tattoo. Not enough to track down a particular artist or studio. But it might help corroborate her identity if we get more information."

A pensive look crossed Mac's face. "Speaking of more information."

"Uh oh." A worried frown etched wrinkles on Benally's otherwise smooth face. "I feel an interrogation comin' on. Can I plead the fifth?"

Mac shrugged. "I'm not putting you on the stand. I was just…curious. About Detective Despré."

"Yeah," Benally warned. "We all know what curiosity did for the cat, brother."

"My interest is strictly clinical, I assure you," Mac replied, waving his hands defensively.

"And I don't need to have a string of letters behind my name to tell you that you are 'clinically' insane if you're even thinking of gettin' Detective Hunter Despré up on your exam table."

"I mean, technically, I already have," Mac replied.

"Come again?" Benally suddenly looked ruffled, and he squared up to the doctor.

"When I evaluated her for a concussion! Jeez. Thanks for the credit, huh?"

Benally backed away. "Yeah, of course. Sorry about that. Guess sometimes I think of that kid like my own daughter. If I had a daughter. 'Course, I can't seem to keep a woman long enough to start a family of my own. Not that I'm complaining. I like my Monday night poker games and walking around the house in boxers." Benally apparently noted the curious hitch in Mac's brow.

"Not at the same time, of course," he explained. "I tell you, though, if I had had a kid, I would like to think she'd be as scrappy as Hunter Despré. Kid's gotten a bad rep. Lot of guys in the department give her the cold shoulder. Not gonna lie, though. What happened to her old partner was bad news."

Mac leaned forward. "What *did* happen?"

Benally looked over his shoulder like he was about to betray some confidence.

"Now, mind you. I don't believe half the scuttlebutt swapped around the station watercooler, but I know Joe Moreno deserved a better end than the one he came to. And Hunter? She deserved a damned sight better than to be accused of his murder."

Mac sucked in an audible breath. "Murder?"

Benally's head bobbed in the affirmative. "She and Joe were following up a lead on a body drop in the Quarter. Some boarded up hole-in-the-wall. Local squat for addicts and homeless. According to Hunter, Joe went in without her. The way the story goes, when she got in there, he was already dead. By the time anyone else got there, Hunter was leaning over him, knife in her hand, nothing but her prints all over the handle."

"And that was enough for them to suspect her?" Mac queried.

Benally hitched his shoulders. "Rumor had it the two of them weren't just partners on the squad. They tried to keep it on the D.L., but a cop shop is worse than a girls' high school when it comes to airing everybody's business. It's like that old shampoo commercial—this one tells two friends, and so on, and so on. Thing of it was, it didn't end so great between 'em. Might have been the stress from all the secrecy and sneaking around. But—and again, we're talking rumors—it was because Joe had started seeing somebody else."

"Was he?" Mac prodded.

Benally shook his cropped head. "Nah. No way, if you ask me. That was all a bunch of bullshit. Hunter was the one who started pulling away. Girl's married to the damn job. Twenty years on the force and I ain't never seen someone that driven. Like she was trying to outrun the Devil himself."

He paused.

"Almost like she was…possessed."

The loaded word hung in the cold, damp air, stretching like a balloon waiting to pop against the silence. Benally finally pushed the pin.

"You ask me, there was just no way Joe was gonna compete with that."

"And that's all they had on her?"

"Enough to launch an Internal Affairs investigation. Spiers put her on suspension, of course, but I think it was more to give her time to wrap her head around Joe's death than he believed what I.A. was investigating. They tried, mind you, but they couldn't come up with enough to make anything stick. Case is still unsolved."

Mac stared down at the open file, lost in his thoughts. He was beginning to think he understood more about the beautiful detective than he realized. There were things that drove him, too. Thunder rumbled.

Mac's eyes drifted back to Jane Doe's file. He

scanned the paperwork, running a finger down the column of information. Suddenly, he paused.

"Huh," Mac mumbled.

"Huh, what?" Benally countered.

Mac looked up. "She's O-negative."

Benally shook his head. "Yeah. Well, I try to be a positive Pollyanna. Enlighten me, Doc. What's that give us?"

"Not a lot. But this other factor?" He tapped the report several times in rapid succession.

"*This* is a breadcrumb."

"What do you mean, 'a breadcrumb'? What are we, like, Hansel and Gretel? I ain't much of a reader, Doc. More of a *Game of Thrones* guy myself. Hot chicks and swords."

"You know that series is based on a book, right? Books plural, actually," Mac countered.

Benally waved him off. "Whatever. Just give me the Cliff Notes version, Doc. Sometimes this medical mumbo jumbo is a little above my paygrade."

"Yeah. No. Sorry," Mac apologized as he shook himself from his reverie. "Our victim wasn't only O-negative. She was Lutheran-b negative."

"So, you're saying we've got a hate crime on our hands? Somebody killed her 'cause she ain't Catholic?"

Mac's eyebrow shot up. "You know, if I didn't know any better, I'd say Leroy's sense of humor was becoming contagious. No. It's an antigen system used in blood typing. Lutheran-b negative occurs in less than .2% of the population. Combine that with the O-negative factor and it's crazy rare."

Benally whistled long and low. He rocked on the heels of his crocodile boots. "Now *that's* something."

"Yeah." Mac agreed. "Yeah, um, it is. I need to go take care of something. Can we pick this up later? Maybe tomorrow?"

"Yeah. Sure, Doc," Benally replied. "Just don't take too long. We're on the clock!"

He tapped the face of his wristwatch as Mac grabbed his keys and pushed through the swinging double doors of the morgue. Benally shrugged, then cracked open his thermos and poured himself a steaming cup of black go juice. Leroy re-entered carrying an empty beaker.

"Oh, hey. Is that chicory? Don't mind if I do!" he chortled and held out the empty beaker for Benally to fill. Benally blinked twice, then filled the jar. Leroy clinked the beaker against Benally's own cup.

"Cheers!"

Chapter Twenty

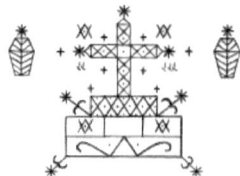

The shotgun double on Burgundy was pink. Not carnation. Not blush. A tiny gingerbread cottage decked out in flat-out Pepto-Bismol pink. Two ceiling fans lazed over the porch. Normally, they cut through the thick summer heat. Now, lingering drops of rain just spun from their edges.

The first weak outer band of the storm system had passed over the city, leaving pockets of standing water in low areas. The frequent potholes dotting the streets morphed into miniature lakes that could swallow unsuspecting compact cars. The evening sun dipped low on the horizon and soon would wink out. Still, the summer heat clung to the remains of the day. A light breeze blew through the air, carrying the steamy, acrid scent of hot cement. Dante's broad nose wrinkled.

Potted Areca palms waved a rustling welcome from

the landing. A cypress swing swayed on one end, its gentle rhythmic rock inviting a long stay with a tall, iced tea, or maybe even something a little stronger. Even the bright purple flowers in the garden beckoned, a sweet, citrusy scent wafting from their upturned trumpet blooms.

Dante couldn't wait to get as far from the house as possible. But there was something that needed doing, first.

The sudden, sharp rap of hammering startled him. He looked to the house next door where the neighbor anchored sheets of plywood to his front windows. Long, sharp nails jutted between the man's lips, preventing the traditional "how's ya mom an' dem." Instead, he raised his hammer in greeting. Dante returned the wave with a hesitant nod. His neighbor went back to hammering.

Dante shook his head. If Erzulie Dantor wasn't pleased with their offering tomorrow, there weren't no hammer strong enough to protect against her fury, he thought.

He tried not to worry. After all, Reverend Mother had been calling on the *lwa* for many years. But the *lwa* of love and passion was also wild and aggressive. Hot tempered and fiercely strong, she could both protect and punish.

Set koud kouto, set koud pwenyad. Prete'm dedin a pou m'al vomi sang mwen. Sang ape koule.

His thick lips silently murmured the words of Erzulie's song, seeking strength from their meaning.

Seven stabs of the knife, seven stabs of the sword. Hand me that basin. I am going to vomit blood. The blood runs down.

"Give yo' son strength, Mama Dantor," his deep

voice whispered. As if in answer, a wave of water splashed through the air, pushing Dante forward. A small smile twitched at the corner of his wide mouth. He paid no mind to the passing car whose wheels had thrown up the water from the street. He knew it had been Erzulie, and that she was with him.

"I serve," he intoned.

He stepped toward the three-foot rod-iron fence bordering the property. The gate creaked a warning as he stepped through. The whites of his eyes disappeared into the ebony of his face as he scrunched them closed against the sound. When he dared open them again, he seemed alone in the tiny yard, with only the purple flowers for company.

He ventured another step.

"What are you skulkin' around for?" The voice came from behind the closed screen door. Dante held a beefy hand to his eyes and squinted against the glare. "Gets a gal to wondering when a man goes sneaking around his own house."

The screen door squeaked open and Sabine Louviere padded barefoot onto the porch.

Dante removed his hat and bowed his head. He crushed the brim of the porkpie in his fingers. "Sorry, Ms. Sabine. Wasn't sneakin'. I know you work hard and wouldn't be wrong of you to be tired. Didn't want to wake you if you was catching a snooze," Dante mumbled in his deep voice.

Sabine leaned against a column. "That's so sweet of you. Wasn't sleeping. In fact, I gotta get back to the restaurant before Eldridge puts me on the menu, but I appreciate the thought."

Dante ducked his head. "No worries, Ms. Sabine."

He made a move toward the second door of the double. His foot never made it to the first step. Sabine planted herself at the top of the stairs. Dante's eyes darted between his front door and the bronze beauty between them, but his anxious glances turned to curiosity as the furrow between his brows suddenly deepened.

"What happened to your face, Miss Sabine?" He gestured to the swollen welt on her cheek.

"What?" Sabine queried, a puzzled frown twisting her ruby lips. An embarrassed hand flew to her face. She turned slightly away. "It's nothing."

Dante took a bold step up. The abrupt movement put him at eye level with the petite restaurant owner, even though he remained two steps below her.

At first, Sabine pulled back, a response hinting at her instinctive choice between fight or flight. Her follow-through, however, was wholly incongruous. She straightened her shoulders, pushed out her small but shapely breasts, and cleared her throat.

"Fact of the matter is, Dante, I was waiting for you to get home," she challenged.

Dante retreated one step down, giving Sabine the advantage once more. "Why's that, Ms. Sabine? You need me to finish puttin' up the boards? For the storm? So the windows don't get broke?"

"I would certainly appreciate that, Dante. I got some of 'em, but I don't have time for the rest. Like I said, I've got to get back to the restaurant pretty soon."

"Yes, ma'am. I know we made a deal when you

rented me the space, and I'll do my part, but I got something I gotta do first. For Reverend Mother. We got the ceremony tomorrow, you know."

Sabine crossed her long arms over her rounded bosom. Dante looked away.

"Good old Reverend Mother," Sabine commented. "How is she these days? Still preaching to the faithful?"

Dante's expression morphed to one of stony resolve. He stood straighter and looked Sabine in the eye. He reclaimed the taller step. "The Reverend Mother don't preach. She serve. Like all the faithful. She serve the *lwa*."

A throaty chuckle burbled from Sabine's throat. She rubbed a hand over Dante's balding head. "Oh, simmer down. I didn't mean any disrespect."

The look on Dante's face belied his doubt, but he remained silent.

Sabine ruffled her fingers through the palm fronds. "The Reverend Mother can serve whomever or whatever she wants. It's a free country. Though I've got to say, I've been around the teacup rim a time or two and I ain't never seen no magic that works better than money in the bank."

"Voodoo ain't magic," Dante mumbled.

A moment of silence passed. Dante dug into the plywood of the step with the toe of his boot.

"Was there something else, Ms. Sabine?" Dante pressed.

Sabine stood straight. "Yes, as a matter of fact. Just one last thing. I've just been meaning to ask you something. About some of the work you've been doing 'round here."

"Like what, Ms. Sabine? I do something wrong?"

Sabine's curls bounced back and forth. "No, no, no. It's just there were some big plastic garbage bags out back a couple of days ago." She hitched a blood red thumbnail toward the side alley. You recall seein' them?"

Dante nodded.

"You know what happened to them?" Sabine asked.

"Took them to the dump."

Sabine pursed her lips, like she was mulling over Dante's reply. Finally, she gave a curt nod. "Of course. Thank you, Dante. Look, I was going to have a quick glass of tea before I head back. You want some? I think I might even have a full bottle of rum in there somewhere."

"I don't want no rum, Miss Sabine."

"Not for you, silly. For Erzulie Dantor. Didn't you say y'all have a ceremony coming up? I thought it might make a nice offering. That's how it's done, right?"

Dante's shoulders relaxed. "Yes'm. That'd be alright. Erzulie, she do like her rum, though Florida water'll do in a pinch."

Sabine's light laugh tinkled like the wind chimes dangling from the eaves. She waved him up. "Well, come on then."

Dante stepped onto the porch and accepted a tall glass of tea from Sabine. The ice cubes bobbled in an awkward little dance in the russet drink.

Sabine flashed a winning grin at Dante.

And Dante? Dante smiled right back.

Chapter Twenty-One

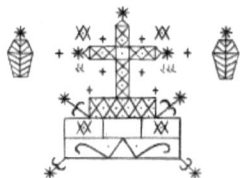

The air in the Bywater was thick and heavy, clinging to the skin like an invisible weight, as though the entire city was holding its breath. For all intents and purposes, it was.

So was Hunter.

Her boots squished and crunched against the graveled pathway of Rosalie Alley, the last light of day struggling through the heavy clouds above. The scent of more rain lingered—rain and something deeper, more primal—the tang of spices and wet earth mingling in a heady brew that tugged at her gut. She wasn't sure what had drawn her back here. She felt naked without the familiar weight of her gun and badge. Vulnerable.

She had wandered the streets for hours. Her feet brought her here, to this place, with its crumbling brick and faded murals of saints and sinners. A wry grin twitched at the corner of her mouth.

One out of two ain't bad.

Mostly, it was a typical July night in New Orleans—sweltering—with the heat coming off the Mississippi River in waves that shimmered through the streets. But at the corner of Piety and Desire, over eighty people had gathered, their faces illuminated by flickering candlelight, the faint glow casting long shadows across the cobblestone streets.

Damn it! The hurricane ceremony.

Mambo Reverend Mother Queen Rosalie stood at the center of it all, her tall frame draped in flowing white and red garments that fluttered ever so slightly in the breeze. Her head was adorned with a red scarf, tied tightly around her crown, and her eyes gleamed with a deep, quiet authority. Tonight, she would lead them in a sacred ritual— a ceremony that stretched back to the earliest days of the city, when the line between the physical world and the spirit world was but a breath away.

Hunter spun on her heel and headed in the opposite direction.

"Hunter!" Reverend Mother's sonorous tones stopped Hunter in her tracks.

She whirled with an enthusiastic smile plastered on her face. "Reverend Mother!"

"Child, why you be shoutin'?" Reverend Mother boomed, her arms akimbo as if she were holding up the sky itself. "Ain't nobody deaf here but the dead, and they ain't talkin'." She leaned in. "Or are they?"

"Where's Dante?" Hunter deftly changed the subject, peering past the priestess, half-expecting the giant of a man to appear with his slow gait and formidable presence.

"Late," Reverend Mother Queen Rosalie snapped, her eyes flashing like lightning about to strike. "You know he was to bring pork chops for the ceremony. Now we got nothin' but empty hands and hungry spirits."

"Damn. Weather's turning fast, too."

"Tell me somethin' I don't know. But if y'all think a little sky-water can wash away our spirits?" Reverend Mother hollers, her eyes blazing beneath the tightly knotted kerchief. "Hoo, you got another thing comin'! We got work to do. Dante may be lost to the wind, but we gonna feed the *lwa* tonight, no matter what."

Hunter's boots splashed through shallow puddles, the water seeping uninvited into her socks. She winced, but kept moving. Reverend Mother's blood-red garments fluttered and snapped like a defiant flag against the brewing tempest.

"What's the plan?"

"Plan?" Reverend Mother snorted, turning a steely gaze upon Hunter. "Child, when the world gives you lemons, you make lemonade. When it fails to give you pork chops, you get Popeyes!"

Laughter rippled through the crowd. Reverend Mother gestured grandly toward a young man scurrying toward them, his arms burdened with bags emblazoned with the fast-food chain's logo.

"Tonight, the ancestors dine on spicy wings," she proclaimed, and the flicker of candlelight caught the crimson polish of her toes as she pivoted back toward the altar.

"Anything I can do?" Hunter asks, her tone sharpening with anticipation.

"Keep your eyes peeled for Dante. Ceremony waits for no one, not even a wayward butcher." Reverend Mother turned on her heel and strode back toward the flickering candlelight of the gathering space.

Hunter turned her gaze to the alley's mouth, watching as the fat drops of rain began their descent.

Hunter shared Reverend Mother's concern for the butcher's absence, but for wholly different reasons. She hadn't liked the way Dante behaved at Reverend Mother's house earlier.

Nervous and twitchy? Good with a knife?

Hunter's fevered brain conjured violent images of the big man overpowering a young girl like their Jane Doe. Maybe her instincts had led her back here for that very reason. Her eyes scanned the crowd.

Around her, the throng buzzed with a mixture of excitement and trepidation. The night sky, dark and roiling with angry clouds, foreshadowed the monster stirring out at sea.

I only care about the monster that's already here.

Her gaze stopped on a familiar but unexpected face. "Mac?" Her pulse skipped.

He moved toward her with a confident, easy grace that made it hard to look away. His loose white linen shirt hung open just enough to reveal the toned, bronzed muscles beneath, the fabric shifting with every step like a whisper of wind against his skin. The matching linen pants brushed lightly against his legs, hinting at the strength they contained, while his leather sandals padded softly on the ground.

Blonde, unruly hair framed his chiseled face, catching an occasional glimmer from a passing candle, but it was his eyes—intense and electric blue—that held her captive, as if they could see straight through her. There was a wildness in them, something untamed that sent a thrill down her spine. His lips curved into a slow, devastating smile that spoke of promises and secrets, a smile that made her breath catch in her throat.

Hunter shook her head. What in the hell was going on? She looked up to the tin-top Baron on the pole, cigar clenched tightly in his metal grin. Hunter scowled. "What are *you* grinning at?" She huffed and turned back toward Mac.

Why was he here?

In one hand, he carried a fresh bottle of rum, its glass gleaming under the fading light. Rum was used in the ceremony, Hunter thought, but no—that couldn't be it.

Ceremony or no—as Mac neared, it was clear his attention was on her. There was a magnetic pull between them, an unspoken connection in the air, charged with anticipation. Every step he took seemed deliberate, sensual, as if the world had slowed down just for them, and when he finally stopped in front of her, his presence radiated heat, drawing her in closer, even as his eyes danced with mischief and something far more dangerous.

"Hey, stranger," he greeted.

"What in the hell are you doing here?"

Mac gestured. "I'm here for the hurricane ceremony. In case you missed it, we could use all the help we can get."

"Yeah, yeah, but why are *you* here? I never pegged you as a true believer."

"Right back atcha."

Mac's ballsy challenge brought an uncharacteristic grin to Hunter's face. "Fair." She gestured to his unbuttoned shirt. "Casual Friday?"

Mac looked down and bashfully started buttoning his shirt. "Damn! Yeah, I, uh, was in a rush. Had some things I needed to...take care of." He hesitated, suddenly avoiding eye contact.

Hunter tilted her head—but before she could press, Reverend Mother raised her arms to the sky, her voice ringing out over the crowd, clear and strong.

"Years ago," she began, "when the priests of St. Louis Cathedral stood at the banks of the Mississippi, they would carry Our Lady of Prompt Succor—blessed and sanctified—into the streets, where her gaze would meet the hurricane's eye." Her words painted vivid pictures in the minds of those gathered. "She would stand tall, unwavering, and turn the storm away, sparing the city from destruction. Her power has kept us safe for generations, her mercy a shield against the winds."

The crowd murmured softly in agreement, some nodding, others clutching their white candles closer to their chests. Before them, the altar dedicated to Our Lady of Prompt Succor was resplendent, adorned with flowers— lilies and white roses—and the soft glow of dozens of candles flickered in reverence.

"But there is another," the Mambo continued, her voice lowering, taking on a more ominous tone. "Erzulie Dantor." She let the name hang in the air for a moment, as if the very mention of it might summon the spirit herself. "Dantor is not like Our Lady. She delights in the storm, in the chaos and the mayhem it brings. And yet, if we make the right offerings, if we honor her properly, she can be persuaded to divert the storm's fury, to spare those who acknowledge her strength."

The altar dedicated to Dantor stood in stark contrast to the one for Our Lady. It was vibrant, chaotic—a riot of red and black. Dolls dressed in elaborate red garments sat among offerings of rum, cigars, and sweets. Bright red candles flickered alongside images of the fierce warrior mother, her scarred face gazing out over the crowd with a knowing, almost mischievous expression.

Mambo Reverend Mother Queen Rosalie's voice grew stern, commanding the full attention of those gathered. "Neither intercessor should be taken lightly. If you call on Dantor, you must be prepared to honor her with the proper offerings. And once she comes, you must leave her gifts in thanks—for her protection does not come without a price."

A hush fell over the crowd as the *mambo's* devotees prepared for the ritual. The drummers took their places, their hands hovering over the skins of the drums, ready to summon the spirits with their rhythm. The offerings had been laid out—white for Our Lady, red for Dantor. The people had donned the appropriate colors, some in flowing white dresses, others in red sashes and scarves.

"Tonight, we call upon the intercessors to protect us, to keep us safe from what may come," Mambo Reverend Mother Queen Rosalie declared. "But first, we must open the way."

With a signal from the *mambo*, the drummers began. The sound was slow at first, a steady, pulsing rhythm that seemed to echo the heartbeat of the city itself.

"Is, uh, this your first ceremony?" Hunter asked Mac as they lingered on the edge of the gathered crowd.

Mac shook his head. "Here, yes."

"But you follow the faith. You know about… everything that can happen?" She dared a look into Mac's eyes. For just a moment, she dared think about something beyond the horrors human beings were capable of.

Mambo Reverend Mother Queen Rosalie stepped forward, raising her arms and calling out in the old Kreyol tongue.

"Papa Legba, open the gates between the worlds! *Ayibobo*!"

The crowd responded in unison, their voices rising together in a powerful chorus. "*Ayibobo*!"

The air seemed to shift, as though something unseen had stirred. The *mambo* moved gracefully, her steps deliberate as she approached the center of the gathering.

"This," Hunter pointed, "this is the mock battle."

"Hm," Mac agreed. "The symbolic struggle between the forces of the spirit world and the physical world."

"Okay." Hunter nodded appreciatively. "Maybe you know a little something."

As the drummers increased their tempo, the *mambo* engaged in a ritualized dance, her movements sharp and powerful, as though she were fending off invisible attackers.

Hunter and Mac watched enrapt as the *mambo*

twisted and turned, her arms slicing through the air. Her body seemed to vibrate with energy, and for a moment, it was as if she were truly battling forces from another realm. The drummers played faster, their hands moving in a blur, the beat rising to a fever pitch. And then, with one final, triumphant movement, Mambo Reverend Mother Queen Rosalie struck a pose of victory.

"She's the bridge now—the bridge between worlds. The spirits will be called through her," Hunter whispered almost reverently. She had forgotten the powerful pull of the faith—and the passion it stirred.

The drums slowed, and the crowd, still humming with anticipation, swayed in time with the music. Mambo Reverend Mother Queen Rosalie knelt before the altars, offering rum and cigars to Danto, and candles to Our Lady. The offerings were made with great care, each gesture deliberate, each word spoken with reverence.

Mac started toward the altar with his bottle of rum. Hunter lingered behind. She had nothing to give.

Mac stopped, turning toward her with an outstretched hand. "You coming?"

Hunter offered a grateful smile and slipped her hand in his. Together, they placed the bottle of rum on the altar. As the offering was made, the crowd chanted. "*Ayibobo! Ayibobo!*"

The sound grew louder, and the energy in the air became almost palpable. People swayed and danced, their bodies moving in rhythm with the drums. Some raised their arms to the sky, calling out to the spirits in voices thick with emotion.

Mambo Reverend Mother Queen Rosalie bent down

to the ground, where she drew the *veve*, the sacred symbol that would summon the spirits. Her fingers pinched out the cornmeal with practiced precision, her movements fluid and sure. The *veve* took shape beneath her hands—intricate, powerful, a mirror of the spirit world made manifest in the physical realm.

As the last line was drawn, the crowd's energy seemed to reach its peak. The drummers pounded their drums with increasing intensity, and the chants of "*Ayibobo!*" echoed through the streets. The air was thick with the scent of incense and rum, the sound of the drums vibrating in Hunter's bones.

Then, the first of the possessions began.

A woman near the front of the crowd let out a sharp cry, her body convulsing as she collapsed to the ground. Two men rushed to her side, but she pushed them away, her body jerking and twisting as though she were a puppet on invisible strings. Her eyes rolled back into her head, and she laughed—a deep, throaty sound that sent a shiver through the crowd. She had been taken by the spirits, claimed by the power of the *lwa*.

One by one, others fell. Some danced wildly, their bodies moving in ways that seemed impossible, possessed by the spirits called down by the *mambo's* ritual. Others collapsed into the arms of friends, their eyes wide and glassy as the spirits flowed through them. The drummers played faster, the beat growing more frenzied with each passing moment.

Mambo Reverend Mother Queen Rosalie stood at the center of the chaos, her eyes closed, her arms raised to the sky. She swayed with the music, her lips moving in silent prayer. She was the eye of the storm, the calm amid the madness. Around her, the energy surged, and the boundary between the physical world and the spirit world thinned to the point of breaking.

The energy crescendoed. The frenetic pulse gripped Hunter. She surrendered to the ceremony, her body a conduit for the divine energies they had summoned. The world outside their enclave of raw spirituality fades, leaving only the here and now, the dance, the chant, the shared heartbeat of human and deity intertwined.

Hunter's breath came in quick gasps, half-drowned by the beating of the drums. Her honey-gold eyes stretched wide, caught in the spectacle unfolding around her. A wry smile ghosts across her lips.

If you can't beat the madness, then, hell—why not join the dance?

The faithful continued, locked in a moment out of time, where gods walk and the living met them halfway. In New Orleans, where the dead never truly rest and the living refuse to be cowed by storms, Hunter felt the thrum of the city's unbreakable spirit. It was gritty. It was raw.

It was home.

Hunter's pulse danced to the ritual drumbeats, the primal rhythm seeping into her veins. Shadows flickered in the candlelight, casting ghostly shapes that weaved among the frenzied bodies. Mac's blue eyes found hers across the room, and something unspoken yet unmistakably intense passed between them.

In a surge of movement, she was at his side, and his hands were on her, rough and urgent. Their breath mingled with the spicy scent of incense and rain-soaked earth as they moved together, drawn by a force far more compelling than the hurricane bearing down on the city.

"Take me," she moaned throatily, her need raw, as inexorable as the *lwa* whose presence infused the air with electric charge. She pushed him into Reverend Mother's house.

Mac's lips crashed against hers, and they staggered, half-falling, half-guided by their shared desperation. The heat of his skin burned through the thin fabric separating them.

There was no finesse in the way they fumbled with buttons and zippers, every action fueled by the wild energy that the ceremony had conjured. They were not gentle, but then, nothing about the night was.

Slick with sweat, they collided—a collision of flesh, breath, and spirit. It was a frenzied mimicry of the dance outside, where reverence gave way to passion, and caution lost to the wind. Hunter's world narrowed to the feel of Mac, the press of his body, the strength of his arms around her. Every touch felt magnified, every sensation amplified by the pounding of the drums.

"Oh, god!" She gasped against his mouth, words swallowed by another hungry kiss. Her sarcasm, her skepticism—everything was stripped away until there was only this. Only them. Only now.

They moved together, frantic and uncoordinated, pushed to the brink by the pulse of the ceremony. The line between sacred and profane blurred until it was impossible to tell whether they were driven by divine madness or mortal lust. It didn't matter. In that moment, they were both offerings and recipients, lost to the chaos they embraced.

As the climax shuddered through them, the room spun, the floor tilts, and the very foundations of the alley seemed to shake. Outside, the ceremony reached a fever pitch, voices raised in supplication and ecstasy.

Then, just as suddenly, it was over.

Silence crashed down, broken only by the persistent drumming of rain against the old brick walls. Hunter and Mac lie entangled amid discarded clothing, their chests heaving, gazes locked. The aftermath of what they've done—the rawness of it—settled over them like the damp chill of the encroaching storm. Hunter shivered.

"Here." Mac covered her with a swath of fabric. "Take this blanket."

Hunter looked at the blanket. "This isn't a blanket. This is Reverend Mother's nightgown. We'd better get out there." Hunter scrambled for her clothes and headed for the door.

"Wait! Hunter!" Mac called. He tumbled from the bed trying to catch her but got tangled in Reverend Mother's unmentionables and hit the floor.

As Hunter stepped outside, skin still flushed, a flock of pigeons was released into the night sky, their wings beating the air as they rose above the crowd. They circled overhead, their calls echoing in the dark, as if summoning the spirits to descend from the heavens. The crowd cheered, their voices joining the cacophony that filled the streets.

The night had taken on a life of its own, the power of the spirits mingling with the heat of the city, the scent of sweat and rum thick in the air. The ceremony was winding down.

Reverend Mother stepped forward once more. Her

voice, steady and strong, cut through the din of drums and chants. "We have made our offerings," she declared. "The intercessors have heard our call."

The frenzy of possession gave way to a deep, collective breath. Slowly, the drummers eased the tempo, their hands moving with less urgency. The spirits, satisfied with the offerings, retreated, leaving their vessels behind to recover from the overwhelming experience.

Maybe now New Orleans could rest easy. Hunter's phone buzzed on her hip. It was a text from Benally.

ANOTHER BODY DROP.

Rest easy?

Fat stinking chance.

Chapter Twenty-Two

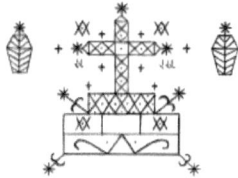

Back. Things were back where they belonged. That's how Hunter felt as she strode through the doors of the 8th.

Too bad Marisol disagreed.

As Hunter walked into the bullpen, leaving a wet, dripping trail, she found the entire precinct, eyes glued to the widescreen. A hurricane update held everyone rapt.

"Residents of the Florida Keys awoke this morning to discover their boats were not docked where they had left them the previous evening. Overnight, Marisol slashed across Florida, leaving fallen trees and flooding in its wake. Several deaths have now been classified as 'storm-related'. The National Hurricane Center downgraded the system to a tropical storm with top winds only reaching 65 miles per hour. This morning, however, the storm center has emerged from the Florida peninsula. Warm waters in the Gulf have contributed to an almost immediate re-intensification of the storm and it is now, once again, a Category One hurricane with top wind speeds reaching 80 miles per hour. The Gulf Coasts of Alabama and Mississippi are already feeling the effects of the outer squalls."

"So, where are we at, partner?" she whispered into Benally's ear as she snuck up behind him. The normally stoic Benally nearly jumped out of his own skin.

"Jesus H. Christ in a banana boat, Despré! What in the hell are you doin' here?" He gave her a puzzled frown. "And why do you look like you just won Wet T-Shirt Night at Treasure Island?"

Hunter looked down at her translucent white shirt. "Damn. Aw, screw it. If you're offended, take it up with H.R. and Mother Nature."

"I didn't send you that text so you'd come skipping back in here, you know. I just figured you'd want to know."

"You were right. Who was it? We have an I.D. this time?"

"Yeah." Benally's face grew somber. He nodded. "This one we know. Eugene Watson. Local kid. Some yahoo was pulling up crab traps out near Honey Island and pulled up Eugene as a bonus."

Hunter took the file from her partner's hand and started flipping through it. "What are we doing about it?"

Benally snatched it back. "*We* aren't doing anything."

Hunter scowled. "Oh, don't get your boxers in a bunch. The captain isn't even here. You know he's up at the State Capitol meeting with the Mayor and the Governor to see how they're going to handle an evacuation if it's needed. Remember the Superdome fiasco during Katrina?"

Benally grimaced. "What a mess *that* was. But seriously, if he finds out you're here, against orders…"

"All the more reason for us to solve this case quickly. *Before* he gets back. What do we have so far?"

Benally wagged his head in a long, slow shake. "I know I'm gonna regret this."

"Don't make me go all Nike on your ass."

Benally held up a warning finger. "Do *not*! I already got enough smart ass from the M.E.'s office."

Hunter cleared her throat. "Steele?"

"No. His helper monkey. The weaselly little guy with the glasses."

Hunter's brows knitted together. "Is that the guy that photocopied his backside on the office copier at the Christmas party?"

Benally nodded. "Gave whole new meaning to the phrase '*spread* some Christmas cheer.'"

"So, did they find anything?"

Before Benally could bring Hunter up to speed, a sudden flurry of activity at the reception desk drew their attention.

"Don't tell me he's not here. Detective Benally's like a homing pigeon with two settings. My restaurant or this station. The man don't deviate."

Hunter threw an accusing look at her partner.

Benally shrugged. "She's not wrong. Work to live. Live to eat."

Sabine Louviere looked in their direction from behind her Sophia Loren shades. She waved the duty sergeant away like a pesky fly. "Never you mind. I see him.

Glad to see my tax dollars at work. Eat your damned doughnut."

She scoffed as rainbow-colored sprinkles rained down the sergeant's blue shirt, then flounced away from the desk and headed in their general direction.

Hunter leaned toward Benally. "Something's sure got her worked up."

Benally cocked his head. "Don't nothing get Sabine riled up except business. Wonder if this has something to do with Rabbit."

"Rabbit?" Hunter questioned. "Pete Scarpetta's boy?"

"Yup. He showed up late for work at Sabine's yesterday. When he did finally show his face, there was some big ruckus and Sabine hauled his ass outside. Don't know whatever became of it."

"I think we're about to find out," Hunter suggested as Sabine huffed up to Benally's desk.

"B.B. Benally," she panted. She kept her shades on.

"Good morning, Ms. Sabine. What seems to be the problem? Lemme guess. That delinquent been sticking his hands in the till?"

"What?" Sabine shook her head, confused. "No. It's nothing like that. He didn't show up for work today. Some of us are still open for business, you know."

B.B. grumbled. "I'm guessing he's probably skulkin' about somewhere, sleeping off a tall boy nap. Apple don't fall far from that tree."

"Nuh-uh." Sabine scowled. "That's exactly why Rabbit won't touch the stuff. You know his good-for-nothin' father beat the hell out of him yesterday?"

All joviality drained from Benally's face. "Wait. What?"

Sabine nodded. "Beat that boy to within an inch of his life. I tried to get the whole story, but then he started blabbering all kinda nonsense about the cemetery, some big skeleton man 'round a fire, and Eugene being dead."

Hunter held up an arresting hand. "Wait. He said Eugene was dead? At the cemetery?" She shot a look at Benally.

Sabine bobbed her head. "I told him to go straight to Doc Steele's clinic and get looked at while I went and checked out the cemetery. Eugene might be a nuisance and a half, but there ain't no one else to look after him. So, I went to see what was what."

"You did what?" Benally growled.

"Oh, stop it. I can take care of myself."

Benally looked dubious.

"Point is," Sabine continued, "I didn't find Eugene, but I did find some Lucky Strikes. That's Pete Scarpetta's brand. I oughta know. I've taken 'em off Rabbit enough times, and I know he's stealin' 'em from his daddy. Boy don't pay for nothin' he can get for free."

"No argument here," Benally agreed. "But, Sabine," he grasped her hand gently. "Eugene's dead. He was found out near Honey Island...not a cemetery."

Sabine's eyes flew wide. She brought her hand to her chest and looked nervously at the detectives. "Rabbit told me Eugene cracked Pete a good one the other day. Took an empty Abita bottle to his head to stop him from wailing on his boy. What if Pete felt like returning the favor, only he took it too far? Wouldn't put it past the man."

Benally shook his head wearily. "Maybe so, Sabine, but, darlin', you ain't no cop."

Sabine folded her arms. "Maybe not, but what I am is a concerned member of this community. And if you know one thing about this town, you know everybody's your neighbor—whether they from down the street or 'cross the country."

Hunter flashed B.B. a *she's got you there* look and shrugged.

B.B. let loose a long, exasperated hiss before Sabine prattled on. "To throw salt on the matter, Rabbit didn't show today. I tried calling his phone. Kept running straight to voice mail. B.B., what if what happened to Eugene happened to Rabbit?"

"I'm sure he's fine, Sabine," Hunter assured.

Sabine tucked in her bottom lip. "I ain't so sure."

She pulled the glasses from her face. A violent palette of blacks and purples welled over her swollen cheek.

"Jeezus!" B.B. exclaimed.

"Well, that's not looking any better, is it?" Mac's voice sounded behind the detectives. Hunter turned just as the medical examiner pushed past them. Mac took Sabine's heart-shaped face in his hands and leaned in for a closer look.

"Who did that?" B.B. asked, but Hunter hardly heard him. Her focus was on how gently he was holding Sabine's face.

Hunter felt an unfamiliar tug at her heart. She felt a warmth flare between her legs as memories of the night before set her pulse racing. Mac didn't even acknowledge her. She tried to shake it off.

"Pete Scarpetta," Sabine answered B.B.'s query. "I asked him about his boy. Got this for my trouble."

"You want to press charges?" Benally asked, moving around the desk and taking Sabine's elbow. "Hell, even if you don't, I'll happily beat his ass for you. Consider it a public service."

A small smile dimpled Sabine's cheek to match the one at her shapely shoulder. Hunter leaped forward, placing her own petite frame between the two men.

Hunter looked at her partner. "Weren't you listening to the lady, B.B.? Sounds like Eugene already did." She let the weight of the implication settle before she continued. "Now, it seems like we've got one dead teen and one missing. Is that what I'm hearing, Sabine?"

At the words "dead teen," Sabine froze. Her eyes darted from Hunter's face and then to B.B.'s before settling on Mac. "Eugene?" she whispered. Mac nodded.

Something shifted in her expression. Hunter couldn't quite put her finger on it, but it unnerved her.

Sabine's delicate chin tilted up toward Mac's chiseled jawline. Sabine splayed her manicured hands across Mac's chest. "I don't know, Doc. I just got a bad feelin' about this. You've seen Rabbit at the clinic enough times. You know what Pete can do. If he's capable of this," she pointed to her cheek, "what else could he do?"

Hunter placed the unsettled feeling burbling in her gut. *Jealousy.*

She gritted her teeth as Sabine twirled a polished nail in a swirling pattern across Mac's shirt. He looked vaguely uncomfortable as he gently grabbed her wrist and lowered her hand to her side.

Hunter smiled to herself, although a bit unexpectedly. Sabine might be a good cook, but it appeared the good doctor wasn't ordering what she had on the menu. Hunter took a modicum of joy from the tiny victory.

Sabine quickly regrouped. "Anyway, I saw the story on the news. About the girl they found. Was it really just her head? In a garbage bag?"

The press had run with the story about the anonymous, decapitated head fished out of the river. The police had kept the detail of the *veve* to themselves, though. Hunter felt a momentary pang of guilt when she called to mind her conversation with Reverend Mother. Reverend Mother wasn't exactly known for her reticence.

The one thing Hunter *could* bank on, however, was Reverend Mother would never say or do anything to disparage the faith. She would likely take the *veve* detail Hunter let slip to her grave.

Before the guilt twisted Hunter's guts into a knot, Sabine leaned forward. Her voice was a strangled whisper. "I think Pete mighta done that, too."

"Peter Scarpetta is lower than the scum on the bottom of my shoe, Sabine, but certified asshole is a few steps off from cold-blooded murder," B.B. suggested.

"There's something else. Now, I ain't a believer, mind you. But Dante Molombe, the man who rents the double next to me? You know he's into all that voodoo mumbo jumbo, right?"

Hunter's heart jumped as Sabine's train of thought took a sudden left turn. How much of her conversation with

Reverend Mother had Dante overheard? Had the big man told Sabine about the *veve*?

Sabine's next words didn't indicate any knowledge of the voodoo connection, however—just an unfounded prejudice. "I hear him all the time chantin' all them nonsense words in the middle of the night. I heard they make sacrifices. You know he comes home all the time, covered in blood."

"He's a butcher." Hunter bit her words, a red haze clouding her vision. A red anger burbled up inside her. Sabine pressed on.

"Be that as it may, I've got concerns. The other day, I saw him carrying something away from the double. I didn't really think much of it until I remembered Rabbit's story about the big, tall figure with a skeleton face. Dante's big. Lord knows how often I've tripped over his big ass work boots on my porch. Now, I know they into some pretty wild things out in Rosalie Alley."

Mac shot Hunter a look. She ignored it.

Sabine pressed on. "What if this girl got herself on the wrong side of some kinda cult? What if Eugene did, too? What if Scarpetta is part of the whole thing?"

Hunter leaped to her feet. "Voodoo isn't a cult!"

Benally was right beside her, whispering in her ear.

"Remember, partner. You ain't even supposed to be here. Keep it cool. We'll straighten this thing out."

Hunter fumed inside but accepted her partner's reasoning with a ceding headshake. Benally turned back to Sabine.

"What did you see this Dante fella carrying, Sabine?"

169

Sabine took a beat before she answered.

"A black plastic garbage bag."

*****

"She's outta her damned fool mind!" Hunter exploded through the door, past the row of urinals, and collapsed against the wall, one foot propped. She leaned her head back next to the paper towel dispenser.

A uniformed cop who had been dousing a dissolving pink urinal cake, sputtered to a startled arrest.

"Hey, Hodge. How's Paige and the kids?" Hunter gave a dismissive wave.

Hodge nodded. His hands were otherwise occupied. He zipped up his business and beat a hasty retreat past Benally, who had walked in behind Hunter, Pete Scarpetta's file in his hand.

Hunter grimaced. "Ugh! What is it with guys? Don't any of you wash your hands? That's so disgusting."

"So, you *do* realize this is the men's room?"

Hunter's face tweaked in a visual "duh".

"Women talk too much," Hunter stated. "Which is exactly my point with Sabine. She dishes out gossip like it was a slice of her sweet potato pie."

"Not gonna lie. I love her sweet potato pie," Benally crooned.

"Come on, B.B.! You can't tell me you really believe some big, scary skeleton man is struttin' around New Orleans, killing people as part of some ridiculous voodoo ritual? Which, by the way, there is no such thing. In case you were wondering."

Benally shrugged. "Son of Sam talked to a dog. Ed Gein wore his mother's skin."

Hunter called foul. "Actually, he wore a skin suit that *looked* like his mother."

Benally ignored her. "And Trump got elected president. Who the hell knows *what* drives people to do the crazy they do. All I know is we got one dead girl, possibly two missing kids, and more questions than answers. I say we start finding some."

"Right." Hunter's tone tasted more of surprise than anything else. She stood straight.

"Right," she repeated. "So, what's our game plan?"

"Let's start close to home. Pete Scarpetta's place isn't too far from here. Go do a wellness check. Rattle his cage a little. See how *he* likes getting shook up for a change."

The restroom door swung open. Officer Renaldo Vasquez gave Hunter a sideways glance, stepped backward, looked at the door sign, then back at Hunter. Benally grabbed Hunter by the shirtsleeve and tugged.

"Vasquez." Benally passed the Latino officer with a chin wag.

"Hey, Vasquez." Hunter jabbed a finger toward the stalls. "If you ate from the food truck today, be careful. No paper in the third stall."

Vasquez blinked in utter confusion as the two detectives made their way down the hall.

Chapter Twenty-Three

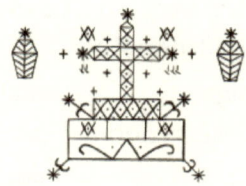

They didn't make it very far.

"Oh, crap!" Benally hissed. He did an abrupt about face, slamming Scarpetta's file into Hunter's chest and corralled her back down the hallway.

Hunter batted his arms away. "What the hell, B.B.?"

"The captain! He's back!"

"Shit!" Hunter spat. She took Scarpetta's file and turned.

Her about face was even more abrupt than Benally's. She ran smack into Mac as he hiked up the hallway.

"Oof!" The exclamation of expelled air was simultaneously uttered by both Hunter and Mac. A cascade of papers showered in a white waterfall of medical reports and criminal files, creating a total mess in the narrow hall. Hunter scrambled to put things to rights.

"Damn it, I'm sorry."

Mac had that deer in headlights look. It took him a moment to find his voice. "Detective Despré."

Okay, we're going with formality. Never mind that we were both overcome by the lwa last night and did things to each other that would not get a PG-13.

Hunter cleared her throat. "No, really, *Doctor*. It's my fault. I wasn't watching where I was going."

Benally leaned in toward Hunter. "We'll all be *going* to the unemployment line if the captain finds you here."

"I know. I know," Hunter hissed back.

Mac followed the verbal volley and bobbed his head. "Ohhh!" He let it out in a protracted drawl. "You're still not supposed to be here, are you?"

"Brilliant deduction, Doc. Guess that degree on your wall isn't just a Cracker Jack prize, huh?" Hunter's pulse hammered in her chest as she waited for the proverbial shoe to drop. The Boy Scout Medical Examiner was certain to rat her out. She'd be lucky to get parade detail when Spiers found out she was here.

"Are you kidding? I saved all my box tops for that."

Hunter's mouth dropped open in a surprised "O". Well, that certainly wasn't what she'd expected. It apparently wasn't what Benally had expected either, but he was quicker to react.

"You got a car, Doc?"

"Yeah."

Hunter protested. "That is not a car. That is a roller skate."

"Do not judge The Bug."

Benally sighed. "I don't even want to know. Just get her the hell out of here before the captain sees her."

He turned to Hunter. "Go check out Scarpetta. See what shakes loose. I'll take care of the captain. I'll meet up with you later."

They could hear Spiers shouting orders. The sound of his voice was getting closer by the second.

"Go! Now!" Benally ordered. Mac grabbed his sheaf of papers, then grabbed Hunter by the hand and tore headlong down the hall and out the back door into the crazy summer heat.

*****

The traffic on Decatur had ground to a standstill. Hurricane fever had gripped the city. The storm raging in the Gulf was still far away, but its effects were already being felt. Mentally, if not physically.

The Quarter thronged with wary locals who had suffered the fifteen-hour traffic jams during Katrina and were not looking forward to a repeat performance.

There were the skittish tourists, many of whom had never experienced the devastation of one of the Gulf's infamous storms and didn't care to. Taxis and rideshares lined the streets, packed with sunburned sightseers and their luggage, eager to get back to their boring, Midwest lives.

Then there was another demographic that flooded the historic Jackson Square area. The revelers.

A tradition lived among those who lived in the path of "Hurricane Alley", that strip of the warm water that stretched from the western coast of northern Africa all the way to the Gulf Coast of the United States. Hurricane parties.

Not a recent creation, hurricane parties could be traced back to at least the 1950s and 60s when the twin terrors of Betsy and Camille laid waste to the Mississippi shores. These unique social gatherings had gained particular prominence in the Southeast, where there were always those who either could not or would not evacuate during a hurricane warning.

These staunch homesteaders typically gathered in a central location, pooling critical supplies needed to survive an impending storm—water, flashlights, batteries, food...alcohol.

Yes, alcohol was often a critical component of such gatherings, as often was a thematic soundtrack like The Doors "Riders of the Storm" or, as in the case of the Faubourg Marigny area of New Orleans, the Weather Girls' "It's Raining Men."

The alcohol element of these parties created a compounded headache for the already inundated authorities, for too often, the unpredictable and dangerous natures of these violent storms called for quick thinking and reaction times. Sazeracs and a Sloe Gin Fizz were not conducive to same.

That's probably what gave rise to the classic urban legend of the infamous Richelieu Apartments party and the twenty-eight deaths that happened because of it, Hunter thought.

Too bad it never even happened.

Still, she thought, as she looked out of the smudged

175

Volkswagen window, Mother Nature could be a real bitch when taunted.

Better safe than sorry.

She almost wished she could get out of Dodge with them, but she knew she had a job to do.

One which she was not getting to anytime soon.

"Can't you make this Hot Wheel go any faster?" She groaned audibly.

Mac gestured out the window as a band of Tulane fraternity boys in roll-tide green stumbled in from of the stopped car. "You want me to run over them?"

Hunter waffled her hand. "Eh, maybe. I'm an LSU fan."

Mac chuckled. His thumb drummed the steering wheel.

Hunter adjusted her seatbelt, the silence in the car stretching as Mac navigated through the rain-slicked streets. She kept her gaze out the window, watching the passing buildings blurred by raindrops and her own reluctance to start this conversation.

Mac finally broke the silence, clearing his throat. "So… about last night."

Hunter glanced at him, her face neutral, even as her stomach knotted. "Yeah. That was… something," she replied, keeping her voice light and vague, hoping he'd get the hint.

But Mac pressed on, his grip on the steering wheel tightening. "Something good?" he ventured, a hint of warmth in his voice. "I was thinking… maybe it doesn't have to be just 'last night.'"

Hunter let out a low, almost incredulous laugh, her

hand running through her hair as she gave him a sidelong glance. "Mac, come on. You know how that went down. It was all the energy, the ceremony, the whole weather going wild outside. Just a perfect storm, if you ask me."

He raised an eyebrow, clearly not convinced. "You really think it was just the ceremony? Or are you telling yourself that because it's easier?"

Hunter huffed, folding her arms as she shifted in her seat, a teasing smile on her face to keep things light. "I'm just saying—things got intense. There was... a lot of tension. And we both know that has to go somewhere."

Mac shook his head, though he chuckled softly. "Tension, huh?" He cast her a quick look, his expression half-amused, half-incredulous. "So, that's all it was for you? Just blowing off steam?"

She rolled her eyes, giving him a smirk that she hoped came off more confident than it felt. "Look, I've got a lot going on. *We* have a lot going on. Not exactly the time for... I don't know, getting sentimental, is it?"

Mac glanced at her, his expression shifting, as if he were trying to gauge how much she actually believed her own words. "I'm not asking for sentimental. Just... maybe acknowledging it was more than just being possessed by the moment."

Hunter whipped her head around at his choice of words.

Possessed.

"What do you mean? A woman can't act on her impulses?" she spat.

He looked at her—almost clinically.

Hunter squirmed under the scrutiny. She shifted in

her seat again, suddenly uncomfortable. She let out a breath, keeping her tone light but avoiding his eyes. "Mac, I don't overthink things that don't need overthinking. Maybe it was just… a moment."

He looked back to the road, his jaw tightening slightly, the silence filling up with something heavier than either of them wanted to admit. "Right. Just a moment."

For a second, Hunter considered saying something more, something real, but then the moment passed. She shifted her gaze to the sun visor, where a picture of a young girl was clipped, her smile bright against the faded photo.

Hunter pointed up to the worn photograph clipped to Mac's visor. "Sister?"

Mac tossed her a surprised glance.

"You mentioned you had a sister when we were being serenaded by Bieber," Hunter offered by way of explanation.

"Uh, yeah," Mac responded. "Fourteen going on forty. Barely even in her teens and she's ready to take on the world."

"She looks a lot like you."

Mac looked up at the picture, wistful. "She does there, yeah."

"She live with your folks?"

Mac squirmed in his seat as the car inched forward. "Um, no. My parents are dead. Killed in a mugging. Not too far from here, actually."

Hunter's hands flew to her mouth as she took a sharp intake of breath. "Oh, my god! I'm so sorry."

"Why? It's not like you did it," he assured. "Just a junkie looking for a fix. Anyway, it's just Hailey and me now. It's not always easy. I swear she's going to be a lawyer someday. Always crafting new and convincing arguments on why I should let her get her driver's license." Hunter chuckled.

Mac tapped the photo. "But I keep this picture here to remind me of why I have to do the things I do."

"Guess we all have reasons for that, don't we?" Hunter surmised.

"So, what's the story with this guy we're going to check out?" Mac nodded toward the thick file in Hunter's lap. She looked down, opened it and began recounting the miserable tale of Rabbit's father.

"Pete Scarpetta. Aged forty. In and out of jail on a battery of charges—including but not limited to—drug possession, drunk and disorderly, check kiting, solicitation…jeez. Pick a letter of the alphabet. This guy's been charged."

MacKenzie growled. "Yeah. I know the guy. Waste of human flesh. What's our interest in him?"

"No. What's *my* interest in him. You are my Uber. Nothing more."

"Hey. I resemble that remark."

Hunter sniggered. "Anyway, we got a tip that he may be a person of interest in this case. He's the father of a boy who's been reported missing."

Mac turned. "Rabbit? He's not another victim, is he?"

Hunter shuddered. "God, I hope not. But that's why I'm going to talk to this scumbag. See what he knows and see if he knows where his son is."

She slapped the file closed.

Mac's thumb tapped a gradually accelerating pace on the top of his steering wheel.

Hunter noticed some dried blood crusted on Mac's knuckles. She shifted in her seat.

"What happened to your hands?" she asked.

"What?" Mac asked, startled. "This? I was trying to dissect the kitchen pipes under the sink. Hailey washes her long hair in the sink sometimes, which is ok, except now it's like Garfield puked in my pipes. Busted my knuckles up pretty good."

He forced a laugh. "That's what I get for trying to save a buck. I guess I should stick to dissecting people."

Hunter groaned.

"And we're back to strike one," he muttered.

*****

The peeling front door opened tentatively.

"What in the hell do you want?"

Peter Scarpetta's face looked like ground hamburger. He gingerly held a frozen steak over his swollen right eye and squinted at them with the left. He took one look at Mac and pulled back for a moment. Then he rolled his shoulders and stepped forward.

"Do I gotta repeat myself?" he barked.

Hunter shook loose the shock. "Mr. Scarpetta, Detective Hunter Despré. NOPD."

She moved to flash her badge and realized she was here strictly in an unofficial capacity. The captain still had her badge. Mac didn't miss a trick, though. He swiftly pulled out his credentials and shoved them into Scarpetta's face.

"MacKenzie Steele. Medical Examiner's office."

Bowl them over with bravado.

Hunter flashed him a grateful look.

"If you don't mind, we're looking for your son," she continued. "His employer, a Ms. Sabine Louviere, has reported him missing. We'd like to check and see that he's okay."

"Yeah? Well, as a matter of fact, I do mind. As you can see, I'm feeling a little under the weather and what's worse, I've ruined what was supposed to be a decent dinner for a change." He gestured with the slab of meat. "So, you can tell that busybody bitch to mind her own damned business and leave me and my son alone."

Scarpetta attempted to close the door, but Mac wedged a size eleven foot across the threshold.

"I believe the Detective asked to see your son." Mac towered over the shorter man. "Or do you need a side of frozen peas to go with your steak?"

Scarpetta stepped back and released his grip on the door, allowing the two officials entry.

The stench assaulted their nostrils almost immediately.

Something had died there.

But Scarpetta wasn't an idiot. A drunk? Yes. An abuser? Yes. A drain on the taxpayers' dollars? Definitely. But not an idiot. He just wasn't stupid enough to let them into his house if there was something that could link him to a murder, Hunter thought.

Right?

"I ain't gotta put up with this, you know. This is

police harassment. I should sue your asses. Leave this dump for good." Spittle flecked on Scarpetta's bottom lip.

"A dump might actually be more sanitary," Hunter quipped.

Her keen eyes searched for any telltale evidence in plain sight. Blood. A weapon. The pungent odor of decay was stifling. A sort of rancid, dirty diaper pail smell. Though Fourth Amendment annotations encompassed "plain smell" in evidentiary law, she still wasn't certain just what they were smelling.

She waved Mac over, holding a cupped palm over her nose.

Hunter used the cautious tip of a pen to lift a plate of science experiment that could have been pizza once upon a time.

"Want to tell us what happened to your face, Mr. Scarpetta?" Hunter asked as she continued to look around the squalid space.

Scarpetta's eyes twitched for a half a second toward Mac. But then that self-righteous expression slipped back into his face. "My employer and I had a dispute and my Union rep wasn't available," Scarpetta sneered.

What the hell was that about?

"Word on the street says you're collecting for Fine Frankie," Hunter pressed.

"Maybe yes and maybe no. Maybe he was doin' me a favor, so I was doing him a favor." Scarpetta talked in circles.

"What's that supposed to mean?" Hunter asked.

"Look! I owe him money, okay? I owe him a lot of money. Tulane didn't cover the spread!"

Hunter held an open palm toward Mac. "See? LSU fan."

Mac drifted from her side and waded through piles of sour dirty clothes and down through the hall. Her eyes darted between him and Scarpetta. Finally, she followed.

The first door had an official DOTD "DO NOT ENTER" sign bolted to it. A time-honored hallmark of a teenaged boy's bedroom. Mac pushed open the slightly ajar door. The room was remarkably neat in stark contrast to the rest of the house. Sure, there were heavy metal posters and a requisite Playboy pinup on the walls.

"Well, hello, Miss April," Mac murmured.

Still, Hunter saw over his shoulder that the bed was made, and a pile of textbooks was neatly stacked on the simple desk. There was no sign of criminal activity other than a little soft-core porn.

Hunter stepped aside and Mac backed out of the room and continued down the hall. She heard him jiggle the second doorknob.

"Hey," he called to Hunter. "This door's locked."

"What's behind the door, Scarpetta?" Hunter's gaze narrowed.

He folded his hands across the stained wife-beater. "I ain't gotta tell you. And without a warrant, I ain't gotta show you neither."

Hunter gritted her teeth so hard she knew Mac could hear the enamel grinding. Scarpetta flaunted a nicotine grin. She stomped down the hall and rattled the pitted door handle. She could just bust it down, she thought.

But it was a fine line whether exigent circumstances

would allow them to open that door. Add that to Hunter's authority not being 100% kosher, the line blurred to the point of invisibility. They needed something concrete. She just hoped it wasn't too late for Rabbit.

Hunter watched Mac walk into the kitchen. Shards of brown glass littered the cracked linoleum. Broken cousins of the assorted liquor bottles overflowing the waste can.

A steady drone buzzed near the sink. Green bottle flies danced an asynchronous waltz over the stainless-steel basin. Mac took another step closer.

"Lucilia sericata," Mac mumbled.

Hunter drew closer to him. "What's that mean?"

"Usually nothing good."

Scarpetta started rocking in his slides.

Mac craned his head over the lip of the sink. Hunter followed suit. The flies were thicker. They peered through the writhing, metallic green bodies and saw it. A heavy, broad-bladed cleaver rested suspiciously at the bottom of the basin, covered in blood.

Scarpetta bolted.

Chapter Twenty-Four

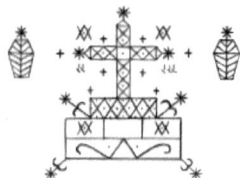

"The latest from the National Hurricane Center shows that Marisol, being fed by the Gulf's extremely temperate waters, has developed rapidly into a storm of some serious concern. Top winds have been clocked already at over 117 miles per hour, classifying her as a Category Three hurricane. With the eye of the storm only 325 miles southeast of the mouth of the Mississippi River, the governors of the Gulf states of Mississippi and Louisiana have declared states of emergency."

325 miles?

It seemed as if Marisol had landed square in the middle of the 8th District police station, Hunter thought as she read the captions on the television behind her captain.

A flurry of activity brewed at the reception desk as French Quarter residents piled in, asking worried questions about the storm, and alternative shelter, and what were the police's plans to handle potential looting if mandatory evacuation was put into effect. The desk sergeant was handling things as best he could, but it was stridently clear—the panic had started to set in.

What was happening out at reception, however, was no comparison to the tempest that roiled in Captain Rudy Spiers' office.

"What in the name of Jesus, Mary and Joseph were you thinking? Going to interview a suspect, in a high-profile murder investigation no less, without your badge, without your gun, without a warrant, and without your goddamned partner?" Spiers purpled and his eyes bulged.

"In my defense, I had Steele backing me up," Hunter offered. Mac shook his hands and head vehemently from the corner. Spiers whirled on the heel of a polished loafer. Mac could almost feel the crosshairs boring into his forehead.

"And who let *you* off your leash, Steele? As I recall, the M.E.'s office isn't even *in* this building. So, who gave you the authority to go out in the field and play cop, huh?"

Mac's eyes instinctively flicked to Benally. He tried to avert his gaze at the last second, not wanting to throw Benally under the bus, but it was too late. The detective practically had "Bluebird" stamped on his high, wide forehead.

Spiers redirected his wrath. "And where were you, Jessica Fletcher, while Nancy Drew and the Hardy Boy were off solving the mystery, Benally?"

Hunter leaned over to Benally and whispered. "I think he just called you old."

Benally rewarded her with a well-laced smack at the

back of the head. "With all due respect, Boss—they *did* find something,"

"Yeah, a room full of stolen televisions and stereos," Spiers sneered.

"And a murder weapon," Hunter piped.

"Of a rat. Scarpetta lopped the head off a rat. As filthy as that place was, it's no wonder CSU didn't find more bodies. House was a pigsty. Scarpetta will be charged with grand theft and possession of stolen property. They can try building an animal cruelty case as well, but good luck making that stick."

"We still don't know where Scarpetta's son is. We have a witness that claims Scarpetta abused the boy."

"And Child Services has been notified. Until he shows up, however, I'm afraid there's not much else we can do."

Mac kept stealing furtive glances at his phone and at the continuous weather report. Spiers planted two broad palms flat on the surface of his desk. His triceps flexed, visible even beneath the pinstripe of his dress shirt. He had long since removed his tie, his rocketing blood pressure making it more of a noose than a professional accessory.

"Are we keeping you from something, Doctor Steele?"

"Actually, Captain, yes. I'm needed at the hospital rather urgently."

Spiers looked puzzled. "The hospital? I thought all your patients were beyond medical treatment."

"Clever, Captain. Yes. Very clever. But I am needed, so if you're going to fire me, can we hurry it along so I can be on my way?"

"Fire you? I can't *fire* you. I can't fire a goddamned one of you!" He gestured at the television. "Have you seen this monster that's coming? The Governor is worried. Hell, I'm worried. It's 'all hands on deck'. Hell," he gestured out toward the lobby. "The crazy's already starting. I'd be shooting myself in the foot if I released some of my best people at a time like this. I don't have to be happy with it and, believe me, I'm not, but there it is."

He reached into his drawer and slapped Hunter's gun and badge on top of his desk. "Now, go find this monster," he jammed a fat forefinger into the autopsy photo of the dead girl, "before that one hits."

He jerked his thumb at the television screen.

Hunter grabbed her belongings and followed Mac from the captain's office before he changed his mind.

"Steele. Hey, Steele! Wait up!"

Mac turned. "What is it, Despré? I really have to get to the hospital."

"I know. Can I catch a ride? I want to see maybe if Rabbit showed up there."

Mac paused a moment, considering. "Yeah, sure. But let's get moving. I don't expect traffic has gotten any better with all the crazy out there."

Hunter took a sweeping look at the precinct and its chaos.

"Better than the crazy in here."

*****

"You're killing me."

Hunter groaned as they pulled into the parking

garage of Tulane Medical Center. It had taken them the better part of an hour to get to the hospital, which was only ten minutes away. Hunter could have controlled the rising agitation over that little snafu. But the purple and gold thrumming through her veins growled at yet another wave of the green.

"Hey, you wanted to come," Mac countered as he put the car in park.

They rode the patient elevators to the seventh floor. The ding of the elevator announced their arrival in the Abdominal Transplant Clinic. Staff buzzed like diligent worker bees through the hallways and near the nurses' station. A deep crease formed between Mac's eyebrows.

"What's wrong?" Hunter asked.

"It's not usually this busy up here," he commented. He stopped to speak to the duty nurse.

"Excuse me?"

The nurse, a pretty blonde whose dark eye circles belied the recent amount of sleep she'd lost, looked up. A stray hair worked loose from the clip that held it back. She blew it from her face.

"Yes? Can I help you?" The harried tone in her voice suggested she had more important things to do.

Mac gestured to the surrounding chaos. "What's going on?"

"We're canceling some of our surgeries and moving patients. There's a storm coming, or didn't you hear?"

"What?!" Mac cried. "No, no, no. They can't move her."

He tore down the hall. Hunter rushed after him.

Mac stopped in front of one of the patient doors just

as a dark-skinned physician was exiting. His stethoscope hung around his neck, dangling over the identification tag that read "Singh, Raj, M.D.". He looked down, scribbling notes into a chart.

"Raj," Mac grabbed his arm. "What's going on? Is Hailey all right?"

"Mac!" Dr. Singh gasped, startled. "You got my message. Yes. Hailey's fine. For now."

"I heard you're moving the patients."

Dr. Singh pursed his lips and tapped his pen on the edge of the metal clipboard. "We're moving some. For safety in view of the encroaching weather."

He dropped his eyes. "But not Hailey."

"Wait. What? Why? What's wrong? What's going on?" Mac tried to push past Dr. Singh and into his sister's room. The doctor restrained him.

"We had to do an emergency pericardiocentesis."

Mac's eyes popped wide. "You stuck a needle in my little sister's chest?"

Hunter looked confused. "I left my medical degree at home, guys. What's that?"

Dr. Singh looked between Mac and Hunter, unsure of their relation. Mac nodded.

"You can talk in front of her," he clipped.

"Hailey was complaining of shortness of breath. Her O_2 levels were extremely low, and she presented with pain upon lying back. We did an echocardiogram and saw her pericardium was distended. The fluid that had built up in her pericardial sac was putting pressure on her heart. Her blood pressure dropped dangerously low."

Mac rubbed his forehead. "Cardiac tamponade."

Dr. Singh shook his head. "This sometimes happens with patients in end stage renal disease, Mac. You knew this going in."

"I also knew her only hope was a transplant."

"And I did you a solid by moving her here and keeping her prepped if UNOS came back with a suitable donor, but you know what a longshot it is. Even with the extra points. Look, we did the procedure. She's got a catheter in place if the fluid returns. She's on oxygen and fluids and a low dose of norepinephrine to bring her blood pressure back up. We'll keep an eye on her, but between the hemodialysis and now this, she's not a candidate for transport."

Dr. Singh placed a reassuring hand on Mac's shoulder and squeezed. "Have a little faith, brother. Believe. That's all we can do at this point."

The doctor walked away, leaving Mac and Hunter standing at the doorway of Hailey's room.

Believe.

It was the second time in less than forty-eight hours someone had mentioned the word. Maybe it *was* time to pay attention.

But that would mean listening to the voices and visions in her head. And that?

Well, that was just insanity.

Chapter Twenty-Five

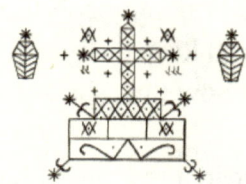

Insanity. That's *exactly* what this was, Fred Dreyfus thought as his back twinged with another heft of a sandbag.

Einstein said it. Doing the same thing, over and over, and expecting a different result? Freakin' insanity.

Why did people want to argue with genius?

Yet, Fred thought, here we are again. Stacking bags of sand on sand, trying to stop the inevitable surge of salt water that was going to wash over US-90 when yet another tropical storm hit.

When were the people of the Gulf Coast gonna realize to just pack it all in and move to South Dakota? No hurricanes there. No volcanoes. No tornadoes. No earthquakes. Yeah—he scratched his chin—South Dakota seemed like the place to be.

"Oof!" A lungful of wind expelled from his lips as Carl Flossy slammed another bag into Fred's paunchy midsection.

"These sandbags aren't gonna unload themselves, Dreyfus. Haul your lazy ass down past that outfall and reinforce the bag wall there."

Fred scowled as he took the latest bag from his supervisor and waddled toward the large cement culvert.

The culverts were an eyesore if you asked him. Giant round cylinders jacking up the pristine stretches of white sand beach along the coast.

They had been installed over the years to help drain local roads and coastal developments. With the casino boom from Long Beach all the way into Mobile, development had skyrocketed.

So, more pipes. More eyesores.

They served a purpose but created an undesirable secondary result—localized erosion. That didn't bode well in the face of a storm, especially not like the one this was shaping up to be. So, he supposed he'd better do what "Bossy Flossy" said or Fred better start doing his gambling over at Coushatta.

His feet kept sinking in the water-logged sand.

Schlock. Schlock.

"Damn it," Fred cursed under his breath.

The first outer squalls of Marisol were hitting. The storm surge was already saturating the sand. He grumbled as he was continually forced to pull his work boots free from the miring sediment.

The moist suck that sounded with every pull was nearly as loud as the crash of the angry waves pommeling the shore. The resulting spray stung his face with a million tiny needles.

"Ugh! Come on, man!" he lamented as he turned his face from the smarting spray.

The turn gave him a new perspective on the opposite side of the large culvert pipe.

He almost didn't see it at first. The unforgiving waves rolled in *ad infinitum*, preventing a clear, straightforward view. He tossed the sandbag to the wet sand with a loud *thwack*. He leaned over the culvert and squinted against the churning foam. Maybe he'd imagined it.

No, there it was. A bobbing flash of hot pink.

At first, Fred thought it was just a discarded beach toy, a floatie lost by one of the many sun-seeking tourists that had cleared the beaches days ago.

The waves flipped the pink object over and Fred fell back, flat and wet, against the sand. He scrambled to his feet, failing to find purchase fast enough to run screaming back to his supervisor.

"Carl! Carl! Carl!"

Flossy squinted through the rain and scowled at the sight of the tubby little man running toward him, arms flailing, before he fell flat as a pancake in the wet sand.

"Aw, what the hell is he bitching about this time? He'll get his break when the rest of us get a break, damn it," Flossy carped.

A coffee break wasn't the type of break Fred had in mind. He watched the news. He had seen the story about the bodiless head that washed up in New Orleans.

No. What he had just seen? The only type of break it meant was in a case for the cops.

The waves slammed the headless female torso

against the unforgiving cement of the culvert, over and over.

Insanity.

Chapter Twenty-Six

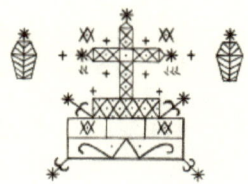

The room was dark. Someone had drawn the curtains closed. Night had fallen over the wet city, but distant bolts of lightning were still periodically lighting up the sky.

A wedge of fluorescence stretched across the floor as Hailey's door slowly opened. The only noise in the room was the blip of the pulse monitor.

"So, what's wrong with her?" Hunter's voice came out as hardly a whisper as she stood behind Mac in the doorway of his sister's room.

"Nothing. She's great. She's the most fantastic kid on the planet, as far as I'm concerned. But her kidneys? Her kidneys are trashed." Mac ran a scabbed, tired hand through his hair. "Focal segmental glomerulosclerosis. FSGS. It screws with the glomeruli, the kidneys' filters. Causes scarring which leads to damage. And, if you can't stop it, kidney failure."

"Do they know what caused it?" Hunter asked with hesitation in her voice.

Mac sighed. "With secondary FSGS, they can sometimes track it back to an underlying cause—kidney reflux, autoimmune disorders, or birth defects. With primary FSGS, though, it just sort of happens."

Hunter looked at the small girl in the bed. "Can they do anything?"

"There are some treatment options. Cyclosporine, Steroids. Diuretics to help with the swelling. But sometimes you just can't quite get ahead of it. The kidneys fail."

"Then what?"

"Hemodialysis will work. For a while. But she needs a transplant. Like, yesterday."

"Have you found a suitable donor?" Hunter asked.

Mac shook his head. "If we had, she would have had the surgery already. She's on the list, but…"

"I always thought family members made good options for donors," Hunter suggested.

"Sometimes." Mac grinned wryly. "But I'm running a little short on supply."

He lifted the edge of his shirt and exposed a long, thick scar on his side.

"Jeezus!" Hunter exclaimed, then clapped her hand over her mouth when Mac held up a finger to his full lips. "That's what that is?"

"Jeezus," she repeated in a softer, whispered tone.

"Yeah. Pretty ugly, isn't it?" Mac asked in a matter-of-fact voice.

"What the hell, Steele?" Hunter shook her head incredulously.

Mac lowered his shirt. "Remember that mugging I told you about?"

"When you lost your parents?"

"Well, I also lost a kidney. Tried to stop the mugger and got a switchblade in my side for the effort. Still got one good one, though." He sighed. "Unfortunately, that doesn't help Hailey much. So, we wait. Although, I don't know how much longer she *can* wait."

He leaned against the doorjamb and let loose a long exhale. "I'd kill for that kid, you know?"

Hunter watched the determined set in Mac's chiseled jaw and didn't doubt it for a second.

"Mac?" a weak child's voice called.

Mac sprang into motion. He rushed to his little sister's bedside and flipped the switch for the overhead bed light. "Hey, Moonpie."

"I told you." Her voice cracked. "You only get to call me that if you bring one."

Mac smiled. He fished in his pocket and brought out a cellophane-wrapped marshmallow pastry. "Last one in the store. Lemon. Just how you like."

Hailey's swollen face puckered. It had taken on that full-moon roundness that happened from consistent steroid administration. Hunter tried to hide her shock. Hailey looked nothing like the happy, carefree little girl she had seen in the picture in Mac's car.

"I *hate* lemon, Mac! Chocolate is my favorite, and you know it!" Hailey protested. Mac reached into the other pocket.

"Oh? You mean like *this* one?" He waggled the chocolate treat over her.

"Nerd," Hailey teased.

"Nerd?" Mac feigned offense. "You're the nerd. Putting up better Fortnite scores than your big brother? You're making me look bad, kid."

Hailey shrugged. "What else do I have to do lying in this bed all day?"

"Gee, I dunno. Read a book?"

"Blech!" She peeked over her brother's shoulder. "Who's your friend?"

Mac turned. "Who? That? That is Detective Hunter Despré. She and I, well, we're working a case together."

"She's a lot cuter than Leroy. You should keep her around," Hailey suggested.

"Hailey!" Mac scolded as he flushed beet red.

"What?" Hailey gave a weak shrug. "He's a good kisser, Detective, if you believe the sounds through the air vents at home, but guard your doughnuts. My brother is a sugar junkie."

"Hailey June Steele!" Mac resorted to using her full, given, Christian name.

Hunter felt a tug at her heartstrings. She gave a small laugh. She and Serafine used to joke around like that.

But Serafine couldn't laugh anymore. The girl they had found in the river couldn't laugh anymore. And if this little girl didn't get a transplant soon, she wouldn't be laughing anymore, either. The pain tugged.

Hunter excused herself. "It was nice to meet you, Hailey, but I have to go. Detective work and stuff."

"Sure thing, Detective."

"And it's just Hunter. Please."

Hailey nodded. "See you around, Hunter?"

Hunter forced a smile. "Hope so, kiddo. Hope so."

Hunter left the two siblings tittering like a couple of schoolgirls as she went to the nurses' station to see if anyone fitting Rabbit's description had been brought in. She met Dr. Singh at the desk.

"Dr. Singh, right?" Hunter queried.

The doctor looked up from his notes. "Yes? Oh, hello again. You're a member of the Steele family, right?"

Hunter was momentarily taken aback at the doctor's suggestion, but decided not to correct him. "Yes. Yes, I am. What are Hailey's chances? Honestly?"

"Honestly?" The doctor dropped his clipboard to his side. "There are no clear parameters in transplant cases. Someone in end-stage renal disease like Hailey can live close to four years with dialysis and proper care and as much as ten. But there are no definites. Especially in a case like Hailey's."

"What do you mean 'in a case like Hailey's'?"

The doctor tilted his head askance. "Well, as a family member, you're aware of her rare blood type, correct?"

Oops, Hunter thought.

I won't tell HIPPA if you won't, Doc.

"Of course, of course," Hunter covered. "I guess I'm just unclear on how that affects her transplant situation."

Doctor Singh still looked wary, but he continued explaining. "With Hailey's rare blood type, even if we found a willing donor, the chances they would be compatible with her are astronomical. She could have the surgery, but her body would likely reject the donated organ and we would be back to square one. Then, of course, there's the time factor. If a suitable match is found somewhere other than locally, medical personnel only have twenty hours to extract the donated organ, transport it here, and then perform the surgery. Sometimes you can stretch the window to thirty, but that's only if the kidney's been handled and stored properly. It's an enormous risk."

Hunter cast a glance back at Hailey's room. "But one worth taking, right?"

Doctor Singh nodded hesitantly. "When people are faced with mortality, they *are* often willing to take bigger risks. Color outside the lines, if you will." He paused. "An expired organ might not be the only option."

"Oh?" Hunter cocked her head. "Such as?"

"Well, you may or may not know, it's illegal to buy or sell an organ in the United States. The National Organ Transplant Act expressly prohibits financial compensation of any kind in exchange for human organs. But every fourteen minutes, someone new is added to the transplant list. Some are waiting for a heart. Some for a liver. Some, like Hailey, have to wait for years for a viable organ. Every day, twelve people die waiting on that list. If you're desperate enough, you might skirt around the edges of the law to get the organ you need to live. It's a situation of supply and demand, and it's created a 'red market.'"

"Red market," Hunter repeated.

"Yes. Where, for the right price, you can buy or sell anything you need—including a less scrupulous physician to perform the transplant. It's just a matter of what you are willing to do."

Hunter tried to absorb everything Doctor Singh had said. Suddenly, her phone buzzed on her hip. She looked at the caller identification. It was Benally. She hit the button and brought the phone to her ear.

"Despré," she said.

"Hey. You still with Doc Steele?" her partner asked.

Hunter peeked through Hailey's door to see Hailey giggling at her big brother's antics.

"Yeah. Why? What's up?"

"We caught a big break. Some poor DOTD worker in Long Beach."

"Mississippi?" Hunter sounded puzzled.

"Yeah. He found our missing body."

Hunter sucked in a huge intake of breath.

"They're transporting it here, since it's our case. There's some flooding along Highway 90, so it will be a bit. Captain wants you two here first thing in the morning. And bring your rain boots. Looks like this hurricane's gonna be knocking on our door before long."

"Got it," Hunter replied. "Anything else I need to know?"

"Yeah. To borrow a word from my new buddy Leroy, it's hinky as all hell."

"Hinky how?"

"She's missing all her internal organs. Heart, liver... and kidneys."

Hunter's wide-eyed gaze suddenly met Mac's from across the room and everything began to spin...again.

Chapter Twenty-Seven

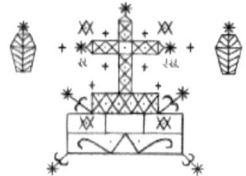

She was in the dark again, the only light bobbing uncertainly on a coated wick. The wind whispered secrets through the night, hiding in the shadows beneath the broad banana leaves.

"Wake up, cher. Wake up." It called to her. In the dead of night, the wind sounded a little like Papa.

Hunter's bare feet touched the cool ground. She looked at her sister's bedside, but the small mattress lay empty.

"Follow. Follow," the dream murmured. Hunter did follow—followed the whispers to the courtyard.

Then the dream became a nightmare.

She could not remember how she had gotten there— there in the courtyard where her sister lay. She could not remember how Serafine's tiny body wound up crumpled in her lap.

She remembered hating her sister. She remembered hating her for stealing the special doll Maman had made for both the girls.

Hunter had wanted to play with it first, but Maman favored Serafine. Always had. Serafine was her "special" child. A gift from the gods.

Hunter remembered wishing she did not have a sister. Wishing Serafine really was "zeru zeru", like she had heard Papa say.

A ghost.

The ghost whispered.

It whispered of blood. Pools and pools of crimson, draining from her sister's horrific injuries. Staining the flagstones. Staining her nightgown. Staining her sister's skin a wicked, evil red, the only color it would ever know.

She remembered the screams. They rolled, echo over echo in the courtyard, until she realized they were her own. She remembered picking up the cleaver, still slick in her sister's blood.

She remembered Maman rushing into the courtyard, screaming with horror at the sight. Hunter, holding her dead sister, murder weapon in her hand.

Then she awoke.

*****

Hunter wasn't certain how long she had been lying there. She heard the hustle and bustle of an emergency room behind the privacy curtain. Her head pounded in an irregular, insistent rhythm. She tried to reach her hand to cover her eyes against the bright fluorescent light, but the I.V. line in her hand tugged stubbornly.

"What the?" She looked at it curiously for a moment, then pulled it out. She winced against the pinch.

She focused harder on her surroundings. She looked up at the random, porous pattern on the ceiling tiles. Pareidolia made her perceive familiar patterns where none existed. One particular grouping of odd-shaped holes took on the shape of her sister's face.

Maybe she had needed that I.V. She shook herself alert.

The nightmares were getting stronger now. No, she corrected.

Visions.

Worry pinched the fine features of her face. She could only hope they were visions.

The alternative caused acid to churn in her belly.

What if they were memories?

"No!" she called out, her own voice in the empty space making her jump. She shook her head rather violently and instantly regretted the maneuver. She remembered what Reverend Mother had told her about the Baron. About what he was trying to do.

"He speakin' through the dead," the voodoo *mambo* had challenged.

Okay, fine. If that was the case, what was Serafine trying to tell her? What did the images of her murdered sister have to do with the present case?

Before she could answer her own questions, the privacy curtain slid back. Mac Steele stood on the other side.

"Good. You're here. We gotta go," she began. Hunter tried to stand up, but the room spun like a Tilt-O-

Whirl. Mac forced her back onto the gurney.

"No way, Scarecrow. You fall down more times than anyone I know. I'm not releasing you until you answer some questions," Mac warned.

"You know I have a gun, right?" Hunter rubbed her temples.

"No. What you *have* is an ass hanging out the back of a hospital gown."

"Wait! What?" Hunter sputtered. She patted herself down, suddenly realizing the doctor was telling her nothing but the naked truth.

"Who the hell undressed me?" she stammered, frantically looking for her clothes.

"I did. Nothing to worry about. I am a complete professional."

"Professional asshat, that's what you are! Give me my clothes!" she seethed.

"Not until you give me some answers. When was the last time you ate?"

Hunter raised a finger and opened her mouth to answer, but realized, suddenly, she had no answer to offer. She honestly couldn't remember the last time she had eaten. This case had been the one thing occupying her thoughts for the last forty-eight hours.

Her shoulders slumped, defeated.

"Aha! I thought as much. When we took your blood, your sugars were crazy low. We gave some glucose in the drip, but nothing beats a po-boy for what ails ya."

He handed her a grease-stained white paper bag. "Guard that with your life, though. Everyone's closing up shop. There's already some standing water in a few streets.

Pumps can't keep up. That might actually be the last fried shrimp po-boy for days."

Hunter looked perplexed. "Um, thanks?"

"Don't be too impressed. It's leftovers." His sheepish smile brought a sudden flush to Hunter's cheeks. "I ate the other half. And it had been sitting in my car, so the mayo might be a little iffy. But beggars can't be choosers, right?"

Hunter shrugged. "Probably safer than a Lucky Dog, right? Food is food."

"Right. But it's gotta be fast food," Mac continued. "Benally called again while you were passed out. We need to get to the station, like, yesterday. Then I have to get back here to be with Hailey. They are predicting this thing is going to hit New Orleans full blast in less than thirty-six hours. I've got to make sure she has what she needs."

As she struggled to pull on her clothes, Hunter recalled her conversation with Dr. Singh.

The odds of Hailey getting what she really needed were slim to none.

Chapter Twenty-Eight

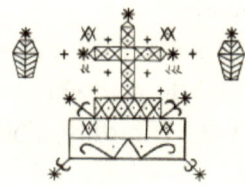

"Harmony Glazer?" Captain Spiers's voice bellowed. "Our Jane Doe's name was Harmony Glazer?"

Benally nodded. "Dancer at a local club."

The precinct buzzed with the usual late-night energy—phones ringing, detectives moving in and out, the clatter of keyboards filling the air. And then there was the amped buzz of the storm frenzy—people calling in to question where they could go if the mayor called for a mandatory evacuation, if there were any grocery stores, to report some minor looting.

Forget the storm landing. The crazy was already here.

Hunter sat across from Spiers, who leaned back in his chair, flipping through the file on Scarpetta.

"Frank Marciano's place?" Hunter asked between the throbbing tympani beats in her head. She rubbed her temples. At least they had diminished since she devoured the po-boy on the way over.

And, yes, the mayo had tasted a little iffy.

"Yup," Benally answered from his post at the right of the captain's desk. He paused, squinted at Hunter, then pointed to her chest. "You, uh, gotta a little something-something on your shirt there, partner."

Hunter looked down at the scattered French bread crumbs on her shirt.

"Damn it," she muttered. "Not my fault. Doc here forced me to eat."

She jabbed an irritated thumb toward the window where Mac stood staring at the rain hammering the glass. He shrugged.

Benally's mouth crooked at the corner as he bobbed his head. Mac managed a brief smile before Hunter whipped around. Benally quickly distracted her, pushing Harmony's file into her hands.

"About damned time," Spiers grumbled. "For a minute, I thought we were gonna have to tie you down to keep the storm winds from blowing you away."

Hunter flashed a sarcastic grin. Suddenly, she mused out loud. "Marciano's. That's where Pete Scarpetta works?"

"When he's not out breakin' people's arms, yeah," Benally answered. "Tends bar. We've fielded a couple calls out there when he gets a little too friendly with some of the girls."

"So, he knew our victim, then." Hunter voiced it as more of a statement than a question.

Spiers' wide nose wrinkled. "It's possible. If only

we could ask him. Oh, wait, that's right. Somebody scared him off."

Spiers scowled. Hunter stood her ground.

"Yeah, yeah," she countered. "Don't worry. Scarpetta's like a bad penny. He'll turn up."

"You'd better hope," Spiers replied. "If it turns out he knew her, I'd say that makes Scarpetta a person of interest in not just one, but two cases. His boy, Rabbit, and this poor girl."

"Harmony," Mac offered quietly from near the window. "Her name's Harmony."

Hunter caught the sudden, haunted look in the handsome doctor's eyes. She lingered there for a moment, studying him. He had uttered the name with a degree of familiarity—not like he'd only just heard it moments ago. She left it for now. She had other concerns.

"So, Rabbit still hasn't turned up?" she asked of no one in particular.

"No," Benally answered.

"Didn't Sabine mention something about Eugene attacking Scarpetta the other day?" Hunter questioned.

"Shit, yeah," Benally replied.

"Make that *three* cases," Spiers muttered.

A cold knot of dread twisted in her gut. A dead girl and a dead teen, both horribly mutilated, and one missing. Were they connected? She hoped not. She dreaded thinking that Rabbit had met the same gruesome fate as Harmony Glazer.

But Pete Scarpetta?

Her face puckered, and she shook her head. Sure, he had a reputation for pushing folks around. Hell, even amoebas were higher on the food chain, but Hunter was hard-pressed to believe him capable of this level of violence.

And then, of course, there was the *veve*.

"How did we identify her?" Hunter asked as she flipped through the file Benally pushed into her hands. "The girl, I mean. Prints?"

"Wasn't an option," Benally offered. "Whoever punched this little lady's ticket sure as hell didn't want to make it easy on us. Head in the Mississippi. Torso in the Gulf. For all I know, her hands might be halfway to Cuba by now."

"Jeezus," Hunter hissed.

"That's not the worst of it. Like I said, most of her internal organs had been removed. Lungs, heart, liver— even her kidneys."

Hunter's eyes immediately flicked toward Mac. A pained expression flickered across his face.

Spiers nodded. "And she might have stayed a Jane Doe, too, but another dancer at the club I.D.'d her. Denise Fontaine. Remember that bit of tattoo we found originally? It was part of a butterfly. Very distinctive design."

"How so?" Hunter asked.

"Glazer had a kid."

Hunter felt sick. The bitter taste of bile hit the back of her throat as Spiers continued.

"Little girl's name is worked into the scrollwork of the wings. We ran it on the news. Fontaine recognized it immediately. We confirmed the I.D. with dental records."

"Where is Fontaine now?" Hunter asked, anxiety fueling a sudden bounce in her stance. "Does she have the

211

kid?"

"She's in the lobby. And, yes, she's got Glazer's daughter with her. She'd been babysitting. Family Services has been contacted, but with the storm, they're swamped trying to take care of the kids already in the system. It might be a while."

The sound of a hinge squeaking caught their attention. Mac had one foot out the door.

"Going somewhere, Steele?" Spiers called.

"Yeah," Mac replied. Tension worked in the hard muscles of his chiseled jaw. "I just need to take care of something."

Hunter started forward before she checked herself. "It's not Hailey, is it? She's okay, right?"

An unexpected smile softened Mac's features. "She's okay. For now, anyway." His stomach rumbled, and the smile turned to one of embarrassment. "Bad shrimp po-boy."

Hunter's eyebrows arched high as her hand went to her own stomach. Mac mouthed the words, "I'm sorry."

"You, wait," Spiers pointed at Mac and then waggled a long finger at Benally. "B.B., I want you to question this Fontaine woman and do it quick. She's more nervous than a long-tailed cat in a room full of rocking chairs. I'm afraid she'll bolt at any minute. And you two," he pointed to Hunter and Mac. "I want you two to pay a visit to Rapture. Kick over some rocks until you find the one Scarpetta's hiding under."

Hunter shifted in her seat, turning slightly to glance at him. Mac's gaze was fixed on the far wall, his arms crossed over his chest. There was something off about him—his usual presence, steady and assured, had given way to something more closed off, distant. It wasn't the first time she'd noticed it, but tonight it felt more pronounced. She stood and walked over to him.

"Mac?" she prompted, a soft nudge to bring him back into the conversation.

He blinked, his focus snapping back to her, but the hesitation in his eyes lingered for just a beat too long. "Yeah," he said, his voice quiet. "I'll go."

Spiers raised an eyebrow but said nothing, nodding his approval. "Go. Tonight." Lightning flashed outside the window. "Time's running out."

Hunter stood, ready to move, but her mind was already ticking over the details. She knew Marciano's reputation—the danger that came with stepping into his world. Rapture was no ordinary club. It was a place where deals were out together... and other things were... broken.

Mac moved toward the door, his steps a little too deliberate. Hunter's eyes tracked him, catching the subtle shift in his posture, the way his shoulders tensed. Something in her gut twisted. She followed him out into the hallway, the fluorescent lights above casting a harsh glow over everything.

"Hey," she called out softly, reaching out to brush her hand against his. It was meant to be a reassurance, a connection—but the moment her fingers touched his, Mac flinched.

He pulled his hand back quickly, almost as if the contact burned him. Hunter froze for a second, her brow furrowing. Mac gave her a tight, fleeting smile, his gaze slipping away.

"Sorry," he muttered, his tone distant. "Just…a lot on my mind."

Hunter swallowed, the subtle distance between them growing heavier. She forced a nod, though her eyes searched his face for something familiar, something to hold on to. "Yeah. Me too."

They walked in silence down the hall, the noise of the precinct fading as they neared the exit. Hunter couldn't shake the unease that had settled in her chest, the way Mac had pulled away from her so easily. It was subtle, but it was there—a line drawn between them, and she didn't know how or when it had appeared.

*****

The low rumble of the Volkswagen's engine filled the silence between them. Hunter sat stiff in the passenger seat, the tension coiling tight in her muscles.

Water sluiced in the gutters, tiny rivers heading for the storm drains en route to join the murkier, swirling waters of the Mighty Mississippi. Hunter watched her gaze unfocused.

Rain pelted the windows, but it did nothing to wash away the heaviness that lingered between her and Mac. Neon lights from the passing streets flashed over his face, casting quick shadows that seemed to highlight every sharp angle of his features.

He had said little since Spiers had given the orders. His fingers gripped the steering wheel, knuckles pale in the dim light. The road ahead stretched out like a dark promise, leading them straight into the heart of the French Quarter—

and to Rapture, the strip club that wasn't just notorious for its dancers but for the secrets it kept.

Secrets owned by Frank "Fine Frankie" Marciano.

Mac's voice cut through the steady hum of the engine. "Spiers thinks this is where we'll find our next lead on Scarpetta?"

Hunter glanced sideways, her eyes narrowing. "You sure you're up for this?"

Mac didn't answer immediately, just kept his eyes on the road, fingers tapping the wheel in that restless way that had her on edge. "I've handled worse," he finally muttered, but the way his voice tightened didn't match the words.

Hunter leaned back, her eyes scanning his profile. Something had shifted since the hurricane ceremony. The skittishness wasn't just nerves anymore—it was something darker. And the more she watched him, the less she understood. His reluctance, the strange avoidance since they'd been together, and now... it all felt wrong.

"What is this really about, Mac?" she asked, her voice cutting through the tension. "You've been off since... well, since the ceremony, and I can't shake the feeling there's something you're not telling me."

"What?" Mac's grip on the wheel tightened, but he didn't look at her. "You don't think Scarpetta's connected to everything we've seen so far?"

"I think," Hunter began, choosing her words carefully, "that if you know more than you're saying, now would be a good time to let me in on it."

Mac glanced at her, the flash of neon from another club highlighting his blue eyes, intense and unreadable.

"You think I'm keeping something from you?"

Hunter's stomach tightened at the challenge in his voice. Her mind flashed back to the conversation with Dr. Singh—the "red market," the underground organ trade, and Mac's sister, desperately waiting for a kidney.

A chill ran through her, despite the thick heat of the night.

Could it all be connected? The bodies, the strange behavior, the silence.

She didn't answer him. Instead, her eyes drifted to his hand, fingers tapping a rhythm on the wheel—as if the steady beat could distract him from something darker.

Mac noticed her silence. "You think it's all connected, Hunter?"

She held back a gasp. *Could he read her mind?*

His words, casual as they were, sent a wave of doubt surging through her. She shifted uncomfortably in her seat, a prickle of unease creeping up her spine.

"This place," he continued, his voice softer now as they neared Rapture, "is more dangerous than you realize. I've had to treat more than a few of the girls from here at the clinic. Frankie Marciano doesn't exactly run a clean business."

Hunter's gaze snapped back to him, her heartbeat quickening. "You've been treating Marciano's girls?"

"Not by choice," Mac muttered, his voice low. "But when someone comes in, broken, bleeding, you don't ask questions." His knuckles whitened on the steering wheel. The leather squeaked under his tightening grip. "You do what needs to be done."

Do what needs to be done.

The words rumbled more ominously than the thunder outside.

The Volkswagen's engine hummed as Mac slowed the car, pulling into a side street a block away from the club. The neon lights of Rapture glowed faintly in the distance, casting long shadows over the alley. Hunter stared at the looming building, her thoughts spinning.

She couldn't shake the suspicion gnawing at her gut. The way Mac talked about the club, the bodies, the sudden change in his behavior—it all felt too close. Too convenient.

The car stopped. Mac cut the engine, but the tension between them still buzzed in the air, electric and alive.

Hunter turned to face him. "I'm going in alone."

Mac's eyes widened, and for a moment, she saw the faint flicker of surprise, maybe even hurt. He hesitated, then, as if he'd caught himself, the surprise faded. His eyes dropped. When he spoke, his voice was soft. Measured. "You know, maybe you're right. I'm really worried about Rabbit. The storm's almost here. I need to find him."

There was something in the way he said it, something that made Hunter's pulse spike. Like he was avoiding something. She couldn't shake the feeling he was relieved not to have to go in with her.

Her chest tightened as she studied him, watching the way his fingers traced the leather of the steering wheel—as if he was ready to bolt. Hunter nodded slowly, masking her unease, and reached for the door handle.

"I'll be back," she said, stepping out into the drenching rain. Her instincts screamed at her as she glanced back over her shoulder, back at Mac—but the Volkswagen was already moving down the street. She stood on the curb, rain running in rivulets down her face, her skin lit red from the glow of the taillights. She stood and watched until they faded down the street and into the storm.

Hunter turned toward Rapture, squaring her shoulders, the neon lights casting an eerie glow over the entrance.

She wasn't sure who she was walking away from anymore.

Chapter Twenty-Nine

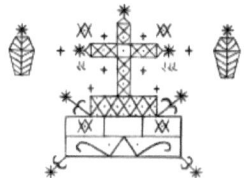

Rabbit's toes squelched with every step as he splashed headlong through the heavy rain that had begun to deluge the city. His Converse had soaked completely through about ten blocks ago.

He probably should have just said the hell with it and headed home, but that meant the possibility of seeing his pop. Rabbit knew from experience that water rolled off your back a heck of a lot easier than the strap of a belt.

But damn, how he wished his bike wasn't trashed!

The clinic wasn't far—he and Eugene had hoofed it even further when they tried to sneak into Jazz Fest that time—but now, as a rude gust of wind sent needles of rain to pelt his face, he realized his bike could have made this trek a lot faster.

He made a right off Clio, colloquially known as

"CL-10"—Rabbit thought half the streets in this town had weird pronunciations—and headed down Oretha Castle Haley Boulevard toward Terpsichore. Finally, he arrived.

"Sonofabitch!" The epithet flew from Rabbit's lips as he slammed his hands into the locked door. He'd come all this way for nothing! He sank against the building, letting the water run over him.

He supposed he could go back to the restaurant, but he doubted Ms. Sabine would let him back in without a note from Doc Steele. And maybe, Rabbit held out the fervent hope, the doc would listen about Eugene—about the horrible thing Rabbit had witnessed at the cemetery.

Eugene was dead.

There wasn't a modicum of doubt in Rabbit's mind. Lingering images of the towering figure with the skeletal face made him shudder. His pulse quickened, and he struggled to catch his breath as his chest tightened.

He needed someone to listen to him!

He whipped back toward the door and pressed his face against the glass. The inside of the clinic was steeped in darkness. He could just make out the shadowy forms of the lobby chairs and the reception desk. All empty.

"Dammit!" he cursed.

Just then, a slight movement caught Rabbit's eye. He cupped his hands around his eyes, trying to block out the griseous light and pelting rain from the outside.

Inside, a piece of the dark peeled away. He couldn't quite make it out. The shadow looked big, but then the dark always had a way of making your fears larger than life, didn't it?

Rabbit leaned in closer, practically pushing through

the glass pane. Maybe it was the doc, he thought. A lot of businesses around town had been closing up, battening down the hatches in light of the storm. But if it was Doc Steele, what was he doing fumbling around in the dark?

"Is the power out?" Rabbit mused aloud. Wouldn't be the first time the wind was strong enough to take out the power lines. But the insistent hum of the nearby streetlamp drew his attention. He squinted through the rain. The drops of water sparkled gold as they fell past the buzzing sodium haze. That light had to be on the same grid as the clinic. Rabbit turned back toward the door.

So, why would someone be in the clinic with the lights off?

Rabbit could count on one hand the number of people he trusted in this life. One of them was Eugene—a knot twisted in Rabbit's gut—but Eugene was dead. He just had to accept that.

Then there was Ms. Sabine. She looked out for him. Granted, she could be damned scary sometimes. She hadn't been too keen when he and Eugene left a pile of fake cockroaches on her desk. There had been so many of them, you could hardly see the stack of bills beneath them.

He and Eugene howled like a couple of monkeys from Audubon Zoo when she let loose that bloodcurdling scream, but the smiles had melted from their faces when she started hacking willy-nilly at the fake insects with a cleaver. You could still see bits and pieces of the plastic carnage around the kitchen if you looked hard enough.

And Doc Steele was alright, too. Rabbit liked listening to his stories about Haiti—his work there, the people. In Rabbit's opinion, the world was a pretty crappy place. It was nice to hear about humans being nice to each other for a change.

"Maybe one day I could do something like that," Rabbit had replied. "I heard you only have to be eighteen to join the Peace Corps, right?"

Rabbit had firmly believed the doc would shoot the idea down, but the doctor's answer had surprised him.

"The work is hard, but it's rewarding."

He had spoken to Rabbit like he was an adult—an equal.

Maybe it was that unexpected respect that the doc had seen him as more than just another "juvenile delinquent," that buoyed Rabbit's bravery just then.

Whatever the impetus, Rabbit screwed up the courage to find out just what was going on at Doc Steele's clinic. He may have failed Eugene, but he would not fail the doc.

Rabbit headed around to the back of the clinic. He cut through the tiny parking lot on the side of the building and was surprised to see Doc Steele's VW occupying one spot.

"Huh," Rabbit mumbled, a bit of tension melting in his thin shoulders. "Guess the doc *is* here."

He watched for a few moments as water rolled off the car's rounded roof and onto the rear. Little wisps of steam rose briefly from the metal before the pouring rain dissolved them to nothing. Rabbit turned and headed for the rear entrance. He found the door slightly ajar. The eyebrow with the recent angry wound rose in surprise.

"Okay," he muttered. "That's a little weird."

He grasped the door handle and pulled it wide.

"Doc?" he called over the patter of rain. Only silence greeted him. He took a hesitant step over the threshold. The rubber of his wet shoes squeaked loudly on the tile floor.

Rabbit looked down. Water puddled at his feet, spreading across the floor and into the shadows beyond. He reached for the light switch on the wall, flicking it to the on position, but everything remained cloaked in darkness.

"Doc Steele?" he called out again, this time with a little less confidence. He heard a sudden rustling coming from the direction of the reception desk, where all the patient files were kept.

"Hello?" Rabbit's voice cracked.

He pulled out his cell phone. Damn! The battery life was crazy low. Still, he needed light. He turned on the phone's flashlight and shone it down the hall before him. It reflected off the wet footprints on the floor.

Only thing was... they weren't his.

Someone stepped out into the quickly dimming beam of his cell phone light.

"What are you doing here?" Rabbit squeaked.

They were the last words he spoke before everything went dark.

Chapter Thirty

Hunter stepped through the doors of Rapture, and the moment she entered, she was hit by the thick haze of cigarette smoke and the pounding bass of the music that reverberated through her body.

The air was heavy, oppressive—the kind that clung to your skin and made every breath feel like you were inhaling the city itself. The club wasn't crowded tonight—just a few scattered patrons, most watching the dancers sway under the dim lights on stage.

Again, what people prioritized as the essentials. Hunter shook her head.

But despite the lack of bodies, the tension in the room was palpable, thick enough to cut through with a knife.

Hunter didn't waste time. Her eyes immediately scanned the space, clocking every detail, every potential threat.

There were Marciano's men—hulking figures standing near the walls, keeping a careful watch on everything that moved. Their eyes flicked toward her as she entered, assessing her, but they didn't make a move. Not yet.

And then there was Frank "Fine Frankie" Marciano himself.

He was seated at a table toward the back, lounging with a casual, almost indifferent air, but even from this distance, Hunter could see the power he exuded. He didn't need to speak or move to command the space—his presence alone was enough to make people fall in line.

Hunter's posture tightened, her senses on high alert as she walked toward him. She wasn't here for a social call, and she knew better than to expect this to go smoothly. As she neared Frank's table, his eyes flicked up to meet hers, cold and calculating, but with a glint of curiosity beneath the surface.

"Detective," Frank greeted her with a slow, deliberate smile. "To what do I owe the pleasure?"

Hunter didn't bother with pleasantries. She took a seat across from him, locking her gaze on his. "I'm here about Peter Scarpetta."

The smile didn't falter, but there was a slight narrowing of Frank's eyes, the smallest shift in his posture as he leaned back in his chair. "Ah, Scarpetta," he mused, drawing out the name. "What's the mook done now?"

Hunter wasn't about to be drawn into his game. "Word on the street is Scarpetta's been organizing private parties here at Rapture. I want to know what you know about it."

Frank raised an eyebrow, clearly amused. "Private parties?" he echoed. "Scarpetta's always been a bit ambitious, but I wasn't aware of any… extracurriculars."

Hunter kept her expression neutral, but she could feel the subtle tension building. "Don't play games, Frank. You know exactly what I'm talking about."

Frank didn't answer immediately. Instead, he studied her, his gaze sweeping over her face as if weighing how far she would push. "And you think that has something to do with me?"

"Why shouldn't I?" Hunter shot back. "You run this place, Frank. Nothing happens here without your say-so."

For the first time, a flicker of something passed across Frank's face—annoyance, perhaps. He leaned forward, just slightly, and the smile disappeared. "Scarpetta may have stepped out of line once or twice, but it was harmless."

"Tell that to Harmony Glazer."

"Who?" Frank's brow furrowed.

"The body on the news? The one they fished out of the Mississippi. She worked here."

A slow laugh burbled in Frank's gut. By the time it made it to his mouth, it was a full-fledged guffaw. He laughed so hard, he could hardly catch his breath as he said, "And you think Pete had something to do with that?" He looked at his guys, who also started chuckling. Frank looked back at Hunter. "That's rich. I mean, that's really rich. Lady, Pete Scarpetta could hardly stand up straight half the time."

"Stood long enough and often enough to mess up

226

his kid."

Frank took a swallow of his single malt. The ice cubes rattled in the glass. "Even a blind squirrel gets a nut now and then." He clunked the heavy-bottomed glass on the table. "But to think that drunk could pull it together long enough to do what happened to that girl…"

His eyes narrowed. "This town is going to hell in a handbasket, Detective. And not just because of this storm." He gestured. "In my organization, when there's a problem, I take care of it." His gaze hardened. "Immediately." His features softened. "Like Scarpetta."

Hunter's gaze sharpened. "What are you suggesting?"

Frank leaned back again, his casual demeanor returning. "Oh, I'm not suggesting anything. But when people in my world start thinking they can run things their way—like Scarpetta, or even that bitch, Sabine Louviere— well, people like that need to be set straight."

Hunter's breath caught, her pulse quickening at the mention of Sabine. It was the first time she'd heard someone outside the precinct link that name with Scarpetta. "What does Sabine have to do with this?"

Frank's smirk returned, though it was colder now. "She's got debts. And like Scarpetta, she thought she could play the game without following the rules."

Hunter filed away the mention of Sabine, but she wasn't done yet. "What about Harmony? Did she 'follow the rules'?"

Frank's expression tightened, just for a fraction of a second, but it was enough for Hunter to see the truth.

He knew Harmony.

"She danced here," Frank admitted, his tone more guarded now. "She wasn't here long enough for me to care about, though. If you're asking if she was part of Scarpetta's little side hustle," he shrugged, "she might've been."

Hunter's jaw clenched. Harmony had been a key part of this puzzle, and now Frank was confirming her involvement in the darker side of Rapture. But before she could press him further, the door to the club swung open again.

Mac.

Hunter's gaze snapped toward the entrance, and there he was—striding through the room, water dripping from his rain-soaked clothes. His white shirt clung to his chest, the fabric sticking to his skin, highlighting the lean, toned muscles underneath.

He looked disheveled, drenched from head to toe, but there was something about the way he moved, the intensity in his blue eyes, that made Hunter's heart skip a beat.

Despite everything—despite her growing suspicions, despite the nagging doubt that had been eating away at her since their post-coital encounter—she couldn't help but notice just how damn sexy he looked.

The rainwater gleamed on his skin, catching the dim light as he shook off droplets from his hair. Her pulse quickened, but she forced herself to focus, to push down the conflicting emotions that churned inside her.

Mac crossed the room toward her and Frank, his expression serious, but there was a flicker of frustration beneath the surface. "Took a bad turn," he said, his voice low but steady. "Flooded street. The Volkswagen sucked up water. I managed to get it to the clinic—checked for Rabbit—but he wasn't there. When I went to start it again, the car stalled. Had to walk back."

Hunter's eyes narrowed, studying him for a moment before turning back to Frank. There was too much happening, too many moving parts, and Mac's sudden appearance only added to the storm brewing inside her. Something didn't feel right, but she couldn't afford to let her guard down.

Not here. Not now.

"Sounds like a rough night," Frank said with a smirk, his gaze flicking between Hunter and Mac. "I'll say this much—you two sure know how to make an entrance."

Hunter ignored the jab, turning her attention back to the task at hand. "Tell me more about Scarpetta. How did you set him straight?"

Frank's eyes darkened, his smile cold and detached. "Let's just say Scarpetta won't be stepping out of line again."

Frank's eyes focused on Mac, narrowing. He tilted his head. "Don't I know you?"

Before Hunter could react, she caught movement out of the corner of her eye. Mac shifted in his seat, his posture uneasy.

"No. I don't think so," Mac replied, subconsciously rubbing a thumb over the scabs on his hand.

"Yeah. I do know you!" Frank wagged his finger. "You're the guy who busted in here the other day and turned Scarpetta's face into hamburger meat."

The bloody knuckles!

Hunter's face whirled toward Mac.

Mac started. Two of Frank's bodyguards, standing in the shadows, noticed the movement, too. Without warning, one of them stepped forward, grabbing Mac's arm roughly.

The tension in the room spiked.

Hunter shot to her feet, her instincts kicking in as her hand moved toward her concealed weapon. "Back off," she warned, her voice sharp and commanding. The atmosphere became electric, the pulse of the music throbbing in the background, adding to the growing intensity.

Frank raised a hand, signaling his men to stand down. "Easy, sweetheart," he said, his smirk widening. "No need to get excited. Your boy just looked a little jumpy."

Hunter's jaw tightened. Her eyes locked on Frank as she slowly lowered her hand. But the moment was far from over. She'd gotten a few answers, but there was still so much she didn't know—so many threads left dangling.

And then there was Sabine. Who was she? And why did Frank speak of her with such disdain?

Mac's sudden tension wasn't lost on her either. He'd been quiet since he arrived, his usual confidence replaced by a skittishness that didn't sit well with her. She couldn't shake the feeling that he was hiding something, and it gnawed at her, making her question everything she thought she knew.

But before she could press Frank further, Mac's phone buzzed.

He glanced at the screen, his expression hardening as he saw who it was. Hunter watched him closely as he answered, stepping slightly away from the table. His voice was low, the tension in his body building as he listened to the voice on the other end of the line. Frankie titled his head, studying her with curiosity as she strained to hear what Mac was saying. She sneered at Frankie, turning away. He just continued staring at her over the rim of his glass.

"You're sure?" A pause. "No, Leroy, that doesn't make sense. Why would she—" Another pause. "Datura? You found it in her stomach?"

Mac's expression darkened, fingers tightening around his phone. He shot a distracted look at Hunter.

"Damn. No, don't put that in your report yet. Just…" Another glance at Hunter. His voice lowered. "Just hold off until I talk to you."

He hung up, rubbing a hand over his face.

Why hold off? Why did the mention of Datura make him so tense?

Datura. Hunter's instincts started firing on all cylinders. Why the hell did that sound so familiar? Her fevered brain struggled, reaching for a connection it couldn't quite make.

Because she knew it by another name…Devil's Trumpet!

It's the same flower Reverend Mother had sitting in a vase in her kitchen. The one *Dante* had brought her from his house!

She opened her mouth, eager to tell Mac what she had remembered, but her instincts flared. Something was wrong.

Mac's posture had shifted—his muscles tensed, his

eyes darting to the floor as he absorbed whatever was being said to him. Hunter couldn't hear the conversation, but she didn't need to. The anxiety etched across Mac's face was enough.

He had hung up, his hand gripping the phone tightly as he returned to the table. Hunter's heart pounded, her mind racing with questions.

"It's about the case." It wasn't a question.

The way Mac's face had paled, the tension in his shoulders—it wasn't just about the case. It was about something else.

Something darker.

Mac met her gaze. But there was a flicker of something in his eyes—something that made Hunter's stomach twist.

She knew now.

He was hiding something.

Chapter Thirty-One

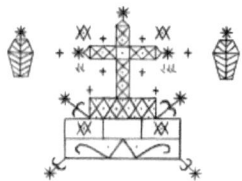

The storm raged like a living thing, slamming the Quarter in furious waves. Wind howled through the alleyways, rattling Rapture's blacked-out windows, driving sheets of rain hard against the tin roof. Outside, Hunter had no doubt the streets were already vanishing beneath swirling, ink-dark floodwaters.

The city was drowning.

Hunter swallowed hard.

So am I.

Inside, cigarette smoke curling in lazy ribbons under the crimson glow of neon. The last of the stragglers huddled in booths and shadows, watching the storm coverage with wary, bloodshot eyes, their drinks untouched. The girls had already cleared the stage, replaced by a few hangers-on still working for last-call cash. The bass-heavy murmur of a slow, bluesy track pulsed through the speakers, low enough that the rain hammering the roof almost swallowed it whole.

Behind the bar, the bartender ran numbers with the focus of a man on borrowed time. Bills snapped in his fingers, the register's dull chime marking every counted stack. His eye darted toward Fine Frankie, who lounged in his usual booth like a man watching his empire burn with a smirk.

Hunter checked her watch.

Time to go.

The bouncer at the door—built like a brick house and probably twice as dumb—checked his phone, muttered a curse, then slid a glance at Frankie's bodyguards, the pair of dead-eyed goons near the exit. One was watching the storm through a crack in the door. The other was watching Mac.

Hunter didn't like it. Didn't like any of this.

She reached for her phone, feeling the weight of eyes on her back.

Something was shifting. The storm wasn't the only thing rolling in.

Frankie exhaled through his nose, slow and deliberate, as he stretched the tension from his spine. The leather booth groaned under his weight as he leaned back, rolling his neck like a man wrapping up a long night at the office—if the office was a smoke-stained den of sin.

He reached for his whiskey, swirling the last amber drop in his glass before knocking it back in one smooth motion. The ice clinked, the empty tumbler landing heavy on the table.

"Well," he drawled, pushing up from the booth,

smoothing out the creases in his suit, "that's it for me. With this mother of a storm, it's time to get the hell outta Dodge."

He flicked a glance at the bartender, who was still tallying up the night's sins in neat stacks of green. Jimmy didn't need to be told twice. He was already tucking the cash away, his hands quick, methodical.

Frankie turned, eyes sweeping over the dancers still milling around, stretching sore ankles, counting tips in the low red glow of the club's lights.

"Go on, girls," he said, flicking his wrist in dismissal. "Get outta here."

They didn't argue. One by one, they grabbed their bags and slipped out the back, their nervous voices drowned into silence by the rising wind before the door slammed shut.

Frankie turned back to Jimmy.

"Lock it up," he ordered, straightening his cuffs. "If the Quarter's still standing tomorrow, we'll open up again."

He turned to Mac and Hunter, a smirk curling the edge of his mouth.

"And you two?" He flicked his eyes between them, as if sizing them up. "Ain't leaving you badges in my joint." Frankie let the silence stretch before giving a lazy shrug. "So, either you walk out that door with me—I'll drop you wherever you want—or you find your own way." His eyes narrowed. "But outside." He hooked his thumb over his shoulder.

Hunter barely spared Frankie a glance as she pulled out her phone, flipping it open with a practiced flick of her wrist.

"We've got our own way," she muttered, already dialing.

The storm roared against the building, rattling the glass, the wind screeching through unseen cracks like a feral thing trying to claw its way inside. The phone rang twice before B.B.'s voice crackled through the line, half irritated, half amused.

"What happened? The Doc's bug float away?"

Hunter exhaled, rolling her shoulders.

"Just come get us."

There was a beat of silence, then a dry chuckle.

"Stay put. I'll be there in ten."

The line went dead before she could say anything else. Classic B.B.—no wasted words, no bullshit.

Hunter slid the phone back into her jacket, shaking off the unease coiling in her gut. Something about the way the night was unraveling didn't sit right. She could feel it— the shift, the way the air thickened like the moment before a gunshot.

And then Mac spoke.

"I'll take a ride."

Hunter's stomach twisted. Her head snapped up. "What?"

Mac shrugged, too casually, like he hadn't just yanked the rug out from under her.

"The water's rising fast. The quicker we get out of here, the better."

Hunter stared at him, pulse thudding against her ribs.

What the hell was he doing?

Across from them, Frankie smirked, slow and

knowing, like a man watching a hand play out exactly the way he expected.

"Not just a pretty face, then, huh?" He nodded approvingly, adjusting the cuffs of his suit. "You're right. Ain't no sense waiting on a damn patrol car in this mess."

Before Hunter could even process a response, Frankie clapped Mac on the back, firm and familiar.

"You know," he mused, eyes sharp with something unreadable, "I could maybe use a guy like you."

Mac didn't react, didn't crack a grin, didn't bat the compliment away. He just stood there, letting Frankie's words settle, letting Hunter's confusion twist into something she didn't like.

The storm rattled the windows again, harder this time, as if the city itself was trying to shake loose the tension building inside Rapture.

Hunter swallowed down the unease crawling up her spine. This wasn't right.

None of this was right.

Hunter's gut twisted, a slow, creeping kind of discomfort that settled deep in her ribs.

Why Mac? Why now?

She could understand Frankie wanting to skip town—men like him thrived on reading the tides, knowing when to stay put and when to vanish before the storm swallowed them whole. But Mac?

Mac didn't move like a man looking for an easy way out. She hadn't known him long, true, but he had never struck her as impulsive. He wasn't reckless. Hailey counted on him too much for him to act that way. And he damn sure wasn't the type to accept a ride from a guy like Frankie.

Frankie wasn't a killer. At least, not proven in any court of law. But he played both sides. Always had.

Hunter knew that. Mac knew that.

But despite that, he was leaving with him.

Hunter's jaw tightened. Mac wouldn't make a decision like this lightly. Unless…

Her stomach sank.

Unless there was a reason he wanted to get out of here before she could press him about Leroy's call.

She ran the conversation back in her head—the way Mac had tensed when he answered his phone, the way his voice had dropped when he told Leroy to hold off on the report.

Now, suddenly, he was fine hopping into a car with Fine Frankie?

The doubt lodged itself in her chest, cold and unwelcome.

Hunter shifted her weight, feeling the eyes of Frankie's bodyguards volley between them. The storm rattled the windows, sending a sharp gust of wind through the door.

Frankie pulled open the door, and the storm answered with a vengeance.

A violent gust of wind and rain slammed inside, drowning out the murmur of the bar, swallowing the last notes of the slow, bluesy track humming from the speakers. The air turned electric, charged with something that had nothing to do with the weather.

Lightning cracked the sky wide open, backlighting Frankie and Mac in stark silhouettes—one man completely at ease, the other unreadable.

Hunter's pulse kicked up.

Before she could second-guess herself, her hand shot out, fingers curling around Mac's arm.

He stilled.

For a brief moment, she looked up at him, searching his face, trying to pin down what she was seeing there—resolve, guilt, something else entirely. His jaw was tight, eyes shadowed by the flickering neon glow.

"Mac."

Her grip tightened just a fraction. She wanted him to say something. To give her a reason to let go.

Instead, he gently pulled away.

No hesitation. No fight. Just a slow, deliberate movement that left her standing there, hand still hovering in empty space.

Frankie smirked like he'd seen this story play out before. He stepped out into the storm first, moving with the easy confidence of a man who knew the city belonged to him, even when it was drowning.

Mac followed.

The door slammed shut behind them, leaving only the echo of their departure and the distant roar of the storm.

Hunter exhaled, slow and controlled, forcing herself to turn back toward the bar.

Mac was going to the M.E.'s office. That's all. That's what he said. No reason to read into it.

Except she didn't quite believe that.

The doubt lingered, pressing against her ribs like a weight that wouldn't shift.

She gritted her teeth, shook off the unease, and leaned against the bar, waiting for B.B.

But her mind wouldn't let go of what had just happened.

Chapter Thirty-Two

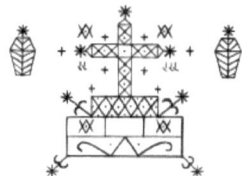

The storm hammered the house—ripping at the siding, pommeling the windows like it wanted to take it apart. Rain battered the roof, a relentless percussion, drumming down in waves that made the entire world sound submerged. Thunder grumbled low in the distance, shaking the walls, an unspoken warning rolling through the night. Every so often, more lightning arced across the sky, turning the sky electric blue.

Inside, however, the house was plunged into near darkness.

The windows had been boarded up earlier that day, thick slabs of plywood nailed tight, sealing the house against the worst of the storm's wrath. Not a sliver of streetlight or lightning reached inside—just the flickering glow of a single candle, stretching its light long and thin against the walls. Shadows shuddered with each gust of wind, shifting, curling, reforming in slow, hypnotic patterns.

Sabine let the silence settle, listening—not just to the storm, but to the spaces between its fury. The wind whistled through unseen cracks, slipping under the doorjamb, cold and restless. The atmosphere weighed heavy. Thick. Waiting.

She liked nights like this.

Nights when the city drowned itself in rain, when the weight of the storm held everything in place. The Quarter would be empty soon—washed clean, quiet, forgotten.

A slow, melancholy tune slipped from her lips, a hummed jazz standard, soft and low. A song from long ago, one that always seemed to surface on nights like this. She didn't remember where she first heard it, only that it had a way of settling into the bones, lingering like perfume on the skin.

She tipped her wine glass slightly, watching the deep red liquid slide along the crystal's curved edge.

Yes. Nights like this were perfect.

She took a slow sip, letting the flavor bloom across her tongue before swallowing, savoring it.

The candlelight caught the rim of the glass, fracturing into deep garnet hues as she turned it in her fingers. Refraction. Perspective. A shift, and everything looks different.

Another rumble of thunder. Another gust of wind. And then—a different sound.

A drip.

Not the rain. Not the storm.

A single, broken rhythm. Soft. Hollow.

Unnatural.

Sabine traced the rim of her wineglass with a single finger, eyes flicking lazily back to the table. An overturned tea glass rested near the half-full pitcher with its tiny flecks floating, swirling in the brown liquid.

A puddle had widened near the mouth of the glass, stretching like an inkblot, crawling over the wood's natural grain. The tea moved slowly, creeping, pooling around the base of the overturned glass.

Another drop slid over the edge.

Drip.

Sabine tilted her head slightly, listening, her lips parting just enough to let a few more notes slip past, the melody soft, whispering through the dark.

Drip.

The candle flickered again, catching the surface of the liquid, making the tea shine a deep amber, almost red in the shifting glow.

Drip.

She watched as the next drop stretched thin, trembled at the edge, then surrendered to gravity.

Drip.

It splashed against the tile, joining the others.

There was something mesmerizing about the way liquid moved when left unchecked. How it sought space, how it filled gaps, how—if left alone—it would spread, slow but unstoppable.

Sabine hummed another note, eyes tracing the path of the spill as it slithered toward the chair.

Something inevitable.

The kitchen chair lay on its side, its legs jutting up at unnatural angles, frozen mid-collapse. The position was almost awkward, almost theatrical—like a body that had crumpled in motion but never quite finished falling.

Sabine studied it for a moment, then let her gaze drift lower.

A single damp shoe print marred the tile nearby, the outline blurred, smudged by movement that had since stilled. A mark left behind. A trace of something undone.

The air inside the house felt… heavy.

The type of weight that lingered in the aftermath of something… irreversible.

Not like the storm outside. That was wild, raging, thoughtless. The pressure inside these walls was different— deliberate, settled, final.

The candle flame wavered. The spill on the table crept another inch.

Another drop fell.

Drip.

The only sounds left were the wind, the rain, the slow, measured breaths of the only other presence in the room.

The candlelight flickered, stretching shadows across the floor—long, distorted, shifting with each unsteady flame.

Beyond the fallen chair, the broad shape of a man lay motionless, sprawled across the tile in unnatural stillness. The dim light caught on his clothes, the fabric slightly rumpled, as though he had been seated just moments before. As though the moment had unraveled too quickly for him to correct it.

Sabine's gaze trailed down the length of him, taking in the details, absorbing them. The slight rise and fall of his chest—shallow, uneven. The smallest flicker of movement in his fingers—a twitch, nothing more.

He wasn't unconscious.

Not exactly.

His limbs remained useless, stretched where they had fallen, his body betraying him in ways it never had before. Strong men were rarely prepared for stillness.

A shift of light. A faint, strained exhale.

His eyes were open. Wide. Fixed on nothing at all.

Sabine tilted her head, watching, thoughtful. There was something trapped there—haunting his frozen expression. What was it?

Not pain. Not anger.

Something worse.

Horror.

Sabine set the wineglass down with careful precision, her fingers releasing it only when she was certain it wouldn't tip. Not hurried. Not sloppy.

Sabine was never sloppy.

She let the moment stretch, listening—not to Dante's breath, not to his presence, but to the storm. The wind rattled the plywood, shaking the walls like a restless spirit. A stronger gust howled through unseen cracks, pressing against the house in protest.

It didn't matter.

Her silk dress rustled as she stood, the fabric catching along the curve of her legs, whispering with each subtle movement. She didn't bother with shoes. There was something about bare feet on cool tile, the grounding sensation of it, the way it made her steps soundless, weightless.

She moved with an effortless grace, weaving around the toppled chair, the widening tea stain, the body that had once been something more.

The candle flickered, its glow stretching long across the floor.

Dante's eyes followed her.

The only thing left for him to control.

Sabine smiled.

She crouched beside him, slow, deliberate, close enough that the warmth of her breath might have brushed his skin.

And then, just for a moment, she simply watched.

Sabine tilted her head, studying him with quiet fascination.

Not concern. Not pity. Just curiosity.

Her eyes flicked over the sharp lines of his face, the tension frozen there, the unspoken questions buried beneath wide, unblinking whites.

There was something captivating about a man stripped of movement. A man who had once carried power in the weight of his presence, now rendered into something else entirely.

Like a specimen under glass.

She lifted a single hand, letting her fingers hover just above his skin, as if deciding whether to bridge the space between them. The hesitation was deliberate. Suspense had its own kind of artistry.

Then, slowly, she lowered her hand.

The edge of her nail—sharp, smooth—dragged

along his jawline, tracing the dark stubble there with an idle sort of precision. A slow, measured path from one side to the other, barely skimming the skin, just enough for him to feel it.

His breathing stuttered. A flicker of a wheeze. A whisper of sound that barely made it past his lips.

Sabine tutted softly, the tip of her nail lingering at the curve of his chin before lifting away.

"So," she murmured, voice slipping between the thunder's distant growl, a whisper just for him. "How'd you like the tea?"

Her fingertip traced across his lips, light, lingering. "It's my own special recipe."

Sabine's gaze drifted lazily toward the boarded-up window, her lips curling at the edges as her eyes landed on the delicate cluster of violet flowers perched on the sill.

The storm's breath rattled the plywood, the wind's mournful howl outside the house like some restless thing seeking entry. But inside, in the glow of flickering candlelight, the blooms stood untouched, their petals soft, pristine, innocent.

Her giggle was light, almost girlish, at odds with the stillness in the room. She stood and drifted over to the kitchen sill. "You know these flowers?" she mused, tilting her head.

She didn't expect an answer.

Dante's chest barely moved, his breath thin, whisper-soft, almost soundless. The only thing he could do was listen.

Sabine sighed, almost wistfully. "Yeah, I know you took some to Reverend Mother." She ran a finger along the stem of one blossom, her touch reverent, almost affectionate. She breathed in the faint citrusy aroma. "Pretty, right?"

She turned back to him, leaned in close enough that he would probably smell her perfume—soft, floral, deceptively sweet.

A whisper of warmth lingered between them, and then another slow, deliberate touch.

Her nail traced down his sternum, unhurried, following the faint rise and fall of his breath, like she was reading something written just beneath his skin.

"Pretty things," she murmured, her voice a gentle chime beneath the storm, "can sometimes be deadly."

She let the words settle before tilting her head, letting her next ones roll off her tongue like a slow caress.

"Datura stramonium."

The name curled into the air, smooth, deliberate, as if it belonged to an old lover, an intimate whisper from another life.

Dante's eyes widened—just a fraction, but enough.

Enough for Sabine to see it.

The smallest shift in already-stretched whites, the faintest flicker of comprehension sinking in. She could see—he understood now.

Too late.

A single tear slipped from the corner of his eye, trailing a slow path down the side of his face before disappearing into the fabric beneath him.

Sabine's gaze followed it with quiet amusement, her expression unreadable. Tears always fascinated her. So much meaning packed into a single drop. Fear. Surrender.

Regret.

His chest gave a shuddering hitch. Not a true breath—not the full rise and fall he so desperately needed. Just a fractured attempt.

Sabine could see it now, the tension under his skin, the desperate will to move—to run—to do anything except what his body had resigned itself to.

But there was no escape.

And that... that was what she enjoyed most.

She exhaled softly, still studying him, her lips curling as if she'd just been reminded of something sweet.

"Some people call it the Devil's Trumpet," she mused, almost dreamily.

Sabine leaned in, slow and deliberate, her breath a warm ghost against his ear.

She could feel the heat of him, the tremor that wasn't really movement at all—just the last desperate flickers of his body fighting a battle already lost.

Her voice dropped lower, slipping into the space between them, an intimate, weightless thing. A whisper meant only for him.

"But it's got another name, too."

Dante's fingers twitched. Once. Twice. The final ounce of his strength spent, leaving nothing but stillness in its wake.

Sabine smiled.

A slow, knowing curve of her lips as she let the words roll from her tongue, savoring them like a final note in a perfectly played melody.

"Some people call it... the zombie cucumber."

Chapter Thirty-Three

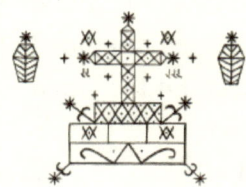

The storm was swallowing the city whole.

Hunter hunched her shoulders against the wind, but it didn't help. Rain drove into her like needles, soaking through layers of fabric, dripping into her collar, plastering strands of hair to her face.

The awning over Rapture barely did a thing to block the downpour—water streamed off the edges in thick sheets, splashing against the flooded pavement beneath her boots. She shifted from foot to foot, scowling at the locked door behind her.

She hadn't stepped outside by choice. The second Frankie and his crew cleared out, the bartender wasted no time flipping the locks, leaving Hunter stranded in the storm. Not even a full minute after Mac had disappeared into the night, she was shoved out like an afterthought, neon lights flickering off as the door sealed behind her.

Fine. I didn't want to be in that damn bar any longer, anyway.

A pair of headlights carved through the dark, cutting across the rain-streaked street like twin blades. The growl of an engine rose above the howl of the wind, and then B.B.'s SUV rolled up to the curb, wipers fighting a losing battle against the relentless downpour. The vehicle rocked slightly as a gust slammed against it, but the moment it stopped, Hunter was already moving.

She stepped forward, boots plunging into floodwater, sending a spray up her shins. It was colder than she expected, seeping straight through the leather, numbing her toes. She clenched her jaw, barely registering it. Her focus was on the SUV.

On getting out of this storm.

And on what came next.

Hunter yanked the door open and threw herself inside, slamming it shut behind her. Air blasted from the vents, fighting against the miasma on the windshield. It didn't do much for the biting cold of the storm that still clung to Hunter's skin, either. She shoved her sleeves up, shaking off excess water, not giving a damn that half of it landed on B.B.

"Hey!" He jerked back, wiping at his arm with a sharp glare. "What in the bayou-loving hell were you doing standing outside in this mess?"

He gestured toward the windshield, where the neon smear of Rapture's sign was already disappearing in the rearview mirror, the last glow of its shuttered doors swallowed by the storm.

"Fine Frankie rolled up the welcome mat," Hunter

muttered, wringing out her cuffs. "Took you long enough." Her voice was tight, clipped. Too much had happened in too little time.

B.B. arched a brow, unimpressed. "You're welcome?" Tires splashing through inches of water pooled along the curb. "City's underwater," he grunted, eyes fixed on the road. "Thought you'd be grateful I showed at all."

B.B. flicked her a look, sharp despite the lazy way he leaned into the wheel. "Something happen in there?"

Hunter exhaled slowly, rolling her shoulders like she could shake off the weight pressing down on them.

She could feel the question sitting between them, expectant.

Something had happened. A lot of somethings. But she wasn't sure how to lay them out, wasn't even sure which ones mattered yet.

Her fingers tapped against the damp fabric of her jeans. She didn't mention Mac leaving with Fine Frankie.

Didn't mention the way her stomach had twisted, watching them step into the storm together.

Didn't mention the way Mac had pulled his arm from her grip without hesitation.

Because she didn't even know what to make of it yet.

Instead, she sighed, stretching her legs out, staring at the windshield wipers battling against the downpour.

"Nothing I didn't already expect," she muttered.
Well, that was a bald-faced lie.

"Scarpetta's in the wind. Frankie wouldn't give him up."

"So, do we think he's our perp?"

Hunter shook her head. "Don't think so. One thing Frankie *did* say is he didn't think Scarpetta had the stones for something like this."

Suddenly, B.B.'s eyes narrowed. "Hey. Where's the doc? Thought he was with you."

An uncomfortable beat passed while Hunter considered her answer. "He got a ride." Hunter averted her eyes from B.B.'s studied stare. She picked at a loose, wet thread on the hem of her shirt. When she finally spoke, she kept her tone measured, steady, like she was just relaying another piece of evidence.

Like she wasn't still trying to figure out why it mattered so much.

"He got a call," she said. "From Leroy. Something about the autopsy on Harmony's torso."

B.B. frowned, shifting in his seat. "And?"

Hunter turned slightly, watching him as she spoke. "Datura."

B.B. blinked. "Come again?"

"It was in her stomach."

The SUV bumped through standing water, tires sending sluggish ripples across the flooded street. B.B. adjusted his grip on the wheel, his mouth pressing into a firm line.

Hunter didn't look away. She was watching for a reaction—any flicker of recognition, any shift in his posture that told her something she didn't already know.

B.B. exhaled through his nose, thoughtful, gaze fixed on the rain-blurred road ahead. "That tracks," he muttered. "Matches up with the tox screen Leroy ran at the outset. Scopolamine."

"Huh?" Hunter scowled.

B.B. grimaced. "So, I might have had a conversation or two with the guy. What was I supposed to do? He was practically holding my Thermos for ransom! Told me scopolamine comes from the same stuff."

Hunter grunted. Her fingers tapped against the door handle, a slow, restless rhythm against the plastic. Something about this wasn't adding up.

B.B. hadn't known about the datura. His reaction had been genuine—surprised, curious, maybe even a little irritated he hadn't been looped in sooner.

But Mac?

Mac had known.

Mac had gotten that call from Leroy. And the first thing he did was tell him to hold off on putting it in the report.

Why?

Her jaw tightened. Leroy wasn't some rookie who needed hand-holding. He knew procedure. Knew when to log findings and when to keep his mouth shut. But Mac had stepped in, pulled rank he didn't actually have.

And then, not even five minutes later—he left.

Not with her. Not with B.B.

With Frankie.

Hunter exhaled sharply, staring out at the sheets of rain hammering against the windshield.

What the hell are you doing, Mac?

Hunter shifted, staring out the rain-streaked window, thoughts pressing down like the storm against the city.

"Dante." The name slipped out, almost without

thought.

B.B. frowned. "Who?"

"Dante Molombe. You know—the guy Sabine mentioned at the station."

B.B.'s expression sharpened as the pieces started clicking into place. "You mean the one she saw with the black garbage bags? Like the ones Harmony's head was found in?"

Hunter exhaled, shaking her head. "Yeah. The bags could just be a coincidence, but there's something else. I saw him the other day. At Reverend Mother's—over in the Marigny? He was acting pretty cagey, all sweaty."

B.B. snorted. "It *is* New Orleans."

"No, it was more than that. It was like he was nervous about something." She leaned forward, elbows on her knees, brain working double-time. "He's a butcher, too, which would make him pretty handy with a blade."

B.B. gave a low whistle. "Keep talking."

"But the thing that's really got my brain working— the thing that makes me think we gotta take a closer look at this guy—"

"Yeah?"

Hunter's stomach twisted. "He brought flowers to Reverend Mother that day."

B.B. raised an eyebrow. "So? He brought flowers. Big whup. Maybe if I'd done that more often, I'd still be married."

Hunter shook her head, pulse ticking at her throat. "Not just any flowers… He brought Devil's Trumpet. Otherwise known as *datura stramonium*."

The words sat heavy between them, the weight of

them pressing in over the noise of the storm.

Hunter swallowed hard. "We need to see if he's home."

Chapter Thirty-Four

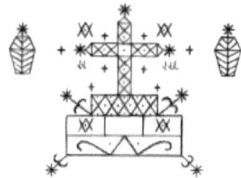

"Looks like we're a little late to the party," B.B. grunted as they arrived at Dante's house.

The trip had taken a lot longer than normal as B.B. monstrous SUV had crawled through the streets of the French Quarter. The vehicle could have made easy work of the standing water. But B.B. abided by the common courtesy most New Orleanians hoped for—prayed for: that drivers would *not* tear through and send damaging waves over the thresholds and into their homes and businesses. Sandbags could only stop so much. Some people weren't even lucky enough to have those.

Hunter could barely make out the crime scene through the lashing rain. Burgundy Street was a mess—floodwater gushing from overburdened drains, trash bins overturned and bobbing like lost buoys, wind-whipped branches clawing at police cruisers parked askew in the street.

Red and blue lights cut through the storm, strobing wildly against the slick pavement, their reflection turning the standing water into a kaleidoscope of chaos.

The SUV rocked as B.B. killed the engine, the wipers groaning one last time before shuddering to a stop. Hunter barely waited for the vehicle to settle before throwing the door open, boots splashing into the flood creeping up the curb.

"Jesus," B.B. muttered as he climbed out, yanking his hood up. "Crime scene in a hurricane. Love this job."

The moment she saw it, her stomach twisted. The black vinyl bag, slick and glistening under the punishing rain, was carried out by two officers, their boots sinking into the saturated grass as they moved stiffly toward the waiting coroner's van. The zipper had been drawn all the way up—nothing visible, nothing to identify, just a shape beneath the plastic. A body who had been alive hours ago, now reduced to something faceless. Nameless. Hunter's pulse thrummed, thunder echoing the sensation in her chest.

B.B. inhaled sharply beside her. "Well, shit." He rocked back on his heels, watching the officers maneuver the body bag over the flooded pavement. "Guess Dante's not gonna answer any questions."

Hunter didn't respond. She was still watching. Still processing. Because something about this didn't sit right.

Crime scene tape flailed against the wrought-iron fence, the wind snapping it like a live wire. Hunter ducked beneath it, rain-soaked fingers gripping the wet plastic for balance as she waded forward.

The small house—pink clapboard and sagging

porch—looked even more fragile against the storm. Its shutters rattled, threatening to tear loose, and water cascaded off the roof in steady sheets. The officers guarding the perimeter looked miserable, huddled in rain gear that did little to protect them from the elements.

"Despré!" One of them, a uniformed sergeant with a five o'clock shadow darkened by rain, scowled at her approach. "You better have a damn good reason for being here."

"I do," Hunter called back, brushing wet strands of hair out of her eyes. "What's the official story?"

The sergeant sighed, rubbing rain from his chin. "Looks like a murder-suicide. Got a signed confession, and the scene backs it up." He jerked a thumb toward the front door, where more officers were moving in and out. "Dante Molombe killed the missing kid inside, then offed himself. Poison."

B.B. frowned, arms crossed. "Poison?"

"That's what it looks like. Medical Examiner's already confirming preliminary tox screen. Some kind of plant toxin—datura or some shit."

Hunter and B.B. exchanged a look. Datura. The same toxin found in Harmony's system. The same flowers Dante had brought to Reverend Mother's.

Hunter's jaw tightened. "Where's the note?"

"Inside. Signed by Dante himself."

Something cold slid down Hunter's spine that had nothing to do with the rain.

This was too neat. Too easy.

Movement to her left drew Hunter's attention, and suddenly, she was enveloped in warmth, despite the cold storm.

Reverend Mother.

The older woman wrapped Hunter in an embrace, her broad palm pressing against the back of Hunter's soaked head, pulling her in like a grieving mother clutching a lost child. Her robes were wet, clinging to her form, but she didn't seem to notice. Her body trembled with something deeper than the storm.

"Oh, child," she murmured, voice thick with sorrow. "Ain't it the most awful thing? I was just telling Sister Rose I can't believe it. I just can't believe it."

Tears shone in her dark brown eyes, catching the crime scene lights like fractured glass.

"Dante's dead?" Hunter's voice came out raw, unsteady.

Reverend Mother nodded so hard her soaked red head wrap bobbed. "Poison." Her broad face grew stern as her voice rose over the howl of the wind. "But they got it wrong. I'm telling you, there ain't no way Dante did to that boy what they're saying. Not to them poor others neither."

Reverend Mother hesitated, then her lips tightened. "The young one. The boy that went missing. They say…" She exhaled shakily, lowering her voice like she feared the wind might carry her words too far. "They say he was all cut up. Torn apart. Like some kind of animal did it."

B.B. swore under his breath.

"And they're blaming Dante?" Hunter pressed.

Reverend Mother sniffed up her resolve and folded her arms. "They saying he left a note. Confessing to killing that poor girl, too. Saying it was all him." Her lips pressed together. "But I know better."

"Reverend Mother…" Hunter exhaled, choosing her words carefully. "I get that this is hard, but if they have evidence—"

"You listen to me, and you listen to me good, Hunter Despré." Reverend Mother's voice dropped to a near growl, her thick finger jabbing toward Hunter's chest. "I am telling you Dante wouldn't hurt a fly and he didn't write no note."

"How can you be so sure?"

The older woman's expression darkened. "Because Dante couldn't read or write."

A powerful gust ripped through the street, lifting the crime scene tape in a violent arc. Hunter barely had time to brace before debris smacked against the house, a loose shutter breaking free and clattering down the steps. But it wasn't the noise that made her stomach drop—it was the mailbox.

It wrenched free from the porch post, dangling by a single rusted screw. The nameplate beneath it twisted, its last tether breaking loose. The wind whipped it through the air, its sharp metal edge slicing Hunter's cheek before the plate clanged on the wet cement. She winced, bringing her hand to her face just as her eyes landed on the lettering.

S. Louviere.

Hunter stared. Her palm dropped. She hardly noticed the trickle of blood running down her face as the storm howled around her, police radio chatter buzzing at the edge of her consciousness. All she could hear was her own pulse hammering against her ribs.

Louviere.

That name had been thrown around before.

Suspicious. Unattached to anything concrete.

But now it was here. At Dante's house.

And Dante was dead.

B.B. stepped up beside her, rain dripping from his brow. He looked at the cut on her face with fatherly concern. "Damn. You should have the paramedic take a look at that."

Hunter, still fixated on the nameplate, shrugged him off. "I'm fine!"

"Okay, okay. But don't expect me to play nurse later when it comes up infected with all this storm crap floating around, oozing pus, and…"

Hunter froze. Her gaze shot to B.B. "Wait… what did you say?"

"I said it's going to get infected if you don't let somebody take care of it.

"No, no, no! About the nurse." Hunter shook her head.

B.B. scowled. "I said I'm not gonna play nurse?"

"Nurse." She let her brain toss the word around, staring into space. Sabine was a nurse. A nurse practitioner. She would likely know her way around a blade.

"Yeah," B.B. continued, oblivious to the thoughts rattling around in Hunter's head. "And, last time I checked, you can't get a face transplant—even for one as ugly as yours." B.B. snorted despite the driving rain.

Transplant!

Hunter's brain exploded into action as she started piecing all the random bits together. Her eyes darted to B.B.'s hand, where he held the dangling keys to his SUV.

"I'm sorry!" she yelled over the storm, though, in

her heart, she wasn't certain exactly who, or what, she was apologizing for anymore.

Chapter Thirty-Five

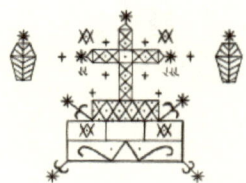

The SUV skidded through the flooded streets, tires struggling for traction against the rising water. Wind screamed, yanking at the vehicle like unseen hands trying to rip it from the road. The storm howled around her, rain hammering the windshield in thick, blinding sheets, but Hunter barely registered it.

Her pulse slammed against her ribs. Her hands were slick against the wheel—sweat, rain, or both, she couldn't tell.

Her mind was a war zone.

Transplant. Sabine. Mac. The red market.

Everything was colliding at once, a rapid-fire assault of memories and gut-churning connections that made her want to scream.

Mac needed a kidney for Hailey.

Sabine was in debt to Fine Frankie.

Harmony. Eugene. Rabbit? They all had something in common. They weren't just killed…

…*they were harvested.*

Hunter swallowed hard, her stomach twisting, bile rising in the back of her throat.

She didn't want to believe it.

She refused to believe it.

But she had been wrong before.

A violent gust of wind slammed into the SUV, nearly shoving her sideways into the flooded median. The wheel wrenched in her hands, the tires momentarily losing their grip. The tail end of the vehicle fishtailed dangerously before she yanked it back under control.

She gritted her teeth, forcing herself to focus.

The clinic.

She had to get to the clinic. Had to see it for herself.

Because if she was right—if she was right—then Mac wasn't just desperate.

He was dangerous.

A blinding flash of lightning split the sky, illuminating the street ahead in a ghostly white glow. For a brief, flickering instant, she swore she saw a tall, shadowed figure in the rearview mirror.

A top hat. A skeletal grin.

The Baron.

Her blood turned to ice.

A thunderous crack of lightning followed instantly, as if the sky itself had bellowed a warning. Hunter's breath hitched, her fingers tightening so hard on the wheel her knuckles ached.

She blinked, and he was gone.

The SUV bucked hard as it plunged into a pothole. The impact jarred her spine. She barely flinched.

The streets were turning into rivers.

Hurricane Marisol had arrived in full force, wind screaming through the abandoned French Quarter like a banshee, rain coming down in violent sheets.

Most of the city had already evacuated.

But Hunter wasn't running.

She was chasing something.

Her tires carved through swirling floodwaters as she sped toward the Oretha Castle Hailey Free Clinic, knuckles white against the wheel.

If there was even a chance that Mac was involved in this...

No.

No, she wasn't going to finish that thought.

She just needed answers.

Then her phone rang.

The shrill buzz cut through the wail of the storm, the name flashing across the screen: B.B.

Hunter swore under her breath but hit "accept" without slowing down.

"You have about three seconds to tell me why you stole my damn truck, Despré!" B.B. barked over the line, his voice half-drowned by the sound of pounding rain and dispatch chatter.

Hunter clenched her jaw, wipers struggling against the downpour. "I borrowed it."

"The hell you did!"

B.B.'s voice crackled with fury. "The captain is breathing down my neck, the mayor's about to have a stroke, and meanwhile, my goddamn SUV is tearing through the worst flooding in the city with a madwoman behind the wheel! I thought my exes were crazy!"

Hunter ignored the dig, gripping the wheel tighter, squinting through the slanting rain at the flashing red and blue barricades ahead, half-submerged in the rising floodwaters.

"Turn the hell around," B.B. snapped. "Now. They're locking everything down. The city's about to go to hell in a handbasket. Get your ass and my divorce settlement out of town—NOW."

"I can't."

"You sure as hell can."

Hunter exhaled sharply. "I need to get to the clinic."

B.B. paused.

She could hear the shift in his breathing, the weight of it.

He wasn't just pissed off anymore.

Now he was listening.

"Why?" His voice dropped a notch, more controlled now, but no less dangerous.

Hunter hesitated.

Because I think Mac might be a killer.

Because I don't know who to trust.

Because I have to be sure.

The words clawed at the back of her throat, but she couldn't say them.

Wouldn't.

Instead, she stared ahead, past the storm, past the rising waters, past the barricades.

Because I'm not leaving this city until I know the

truth.

The wind howled. Rain lashed against the windshield in violent sheets.

B.B. let out a slow, frustrated exhale.

"You're the dumbest smart person I know."

Hunter almost smiled. Almost.

Then B.B.'s voice hardened.

"Fine. But if you get yourself killed, I'm telling everyone it was your own damn fault."

She heard him grumble his last words just before she disconnected.

"This... this is why I'm never getting married again."

Hunter didn't hesitate.

She hit the gas.

*****

Hunter was finally listening.

The Baron had been speaking, and she was finally receiving the message loud and clear.

The *ghede* of the dead had been forcing her to remember that horrible night—the night of her sister's tragic death—for a reason.

Serafina had been born without pigment. She had a genetically inherited disorder characterized by a lack of pigmentation in the hair, skin, and eyes.

Zeru zeru.

Papa had called her by the Tanzanian name for such people.

The name that meant "ghost."

But the name was not the only thing Papa had brought from Tanzania.

He had brought something else.

A sickness.

A perverted belief that the body parts of such people held magical properties.

Wealthy business owners and politicians were willing to pay top dollar for the blood of a *zeru zeru* to bring power.Or fat from the abdomen for luck. Severed hands buried under the door of a business were believed to bring customers.

They were not a wealthy family.

Perhaps that's what drove their father to commit such a heinous crime against his own daughter.

Hunter had woken in the night, startled by a disturbing vision.

She had stumbled into the courtyard and found her father, standing over her mutilated sister, cleaver dripping blood.

She screamed.

He ran, and she screamed.

She fell to her sister's side and gathered what was left of her small body in her arms.

The Baron had awoken her—called to her in her dreams. He had been trying to tell her.

Desperate people would risk just about anything.

And Mac was desperate.

The question was…

Was he the only one?

She had to get to the clinic.

And she had to beat the storm.

Chapter Thirty-Six

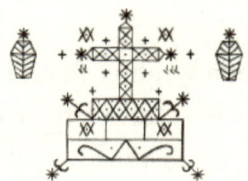

The area around the Oretha Castle Hailey Free Clinic was starkly empty. The silence was eerie—no cars, no lights, no voices. A post-apocalyptic void. Just the howling wind and the relentless battering of rain.

Nearly everyone had listened this time. The city had taken the mandatory evacuation order seriously.

Everyone except me.

Hunter jumped the curb and yanked the SUV into park, water sloshing up the tires. She shoved the door open, the force of the wind nearly ripping it from her grip.

Rain sheeted down her face, sharp and stinging. The hurricane was here. Full force. The clinic's darkened windows loomed ahead, streaked with water, glass rattling from the relentless wind.

She tugged on the locked door.

Nothing.

Her pulse slammed against her ribs. No time to pick it.

She bent her elbow, braced against the pain, and rammed her arm straight through the glass.

A violent shatter.

Shards hit the ground, tinkling like wind chimes. Wind and rain howled through the broken door, but Hunter didn't hesitate. She reached inside, turned the lock, and shoved her way inside.

The clinic was pitch black.

The generators were dead. No power.

Hunter shook herself off, rainwater pooling at her feet.

She yanked the flashlight from her coat, flicked it on, and moved.

The metal filing cabinets loomed behind the desk.

A place that should be filled with hope and healing now felt like a morgue.

Hunter hopped the counter and yanked the first drawer open. Old-school patient files. No computers here.

She flipped through the tabs, her fingers numb and shaking.

Harmony Glazer. The same rare blood type as Hailey.

Her throat tightened.

Mac hadn't claimed to recognize her. But something B.B. had said gnawed at her.

A struggling single mom, barely getting by.

Hunter scanned the file.

Then Eugene Watson. O-Negative. The universal donor.

An emancipated minor, who no adult would likely miss.

Then Rabbit. Also, O-Neg.

And a lost boy whose father could have cared less.

One after another.

Her stomach clenched.

They hadn't just been random victims. They'd been selected. Picked for a reason. People polite society didn't notice.

Her pulse roared in her ears. It was true.

Mac needed a kidney for Hailey.

A free clinic was the perfect hunting ground. Patients down on their luck, no insurance, no families. Who would miss them?

Hunter's throat constricted.

She had chased this truth through hell and back.

And now that she had it, she wished she was wrong.

The floor creaked.

A shadow moved.

Hunter's blood turned to ice.

She whipped around, gun raised.

A voice in the dark. Calm. Controlled.

"Find what you were looking for?"

Hunter's flashlight beam slammed into the figure.

Mac.

Soaked to the bone. Expression unreadable.

His dark eyes flicked to the open files in her hands. A slow, terrible realization dawned.

His jaw tightened.

"What the hell are you doing, Hunter?"

Hunter's breath came hard.

"I could ask you the same thing."

Mac took a step forward.

Hunter snapped the gun up higher. "Don't."

He froze. Hands slowly lifted. "You think I killed them."

Hunter swallowed hard. The words hung between them like a live wire. His eyes darted to the files. Then back to her. Something dark flashed in them.

Pain.

A pain that cracked something deep inside Hunter.

She forced steel into her voice. "Harmony. Eugene. Rabbit. All of them, Mac. They were all potential donors for Hailey."

Mac's face paled.

Hunter's voice grew raw. "Tell me it's not true."

Mac exhaled sharply. His voice was low. Dangerous.

"You think I picked them out of my own damn clinic?"

Hunter swallowed. The storm outside raged, screaming through broken glass.

"You tell me."

Mac's jaw flexed. Then his expression shifted. Harder. Colder.

"You really think I'm some sort of Frankenstein? Becoming some sort of monster just to save one life?"

"Not just one life." Her stomach clenched. "Your little sister's life. The only family you have left."

He laughed, but there was no mirth in it. "And what? You think I did these terrible acts where? Here?"

She shrugged, nodding towards the locked door—

the one she had seen him direct her away from the first time she set foot in the clinic. The door whose key she suspected she saw dangling from the rearview mirror of his VW, away from easy access. The door she had originally dismissed as nothing more than a supply closet. "I don't know. What's behind the locked door, Doc?"

Mac blinked. Once. Twice.

She whispered, "Is that where you cut them open, Mac? In that room?"

Then something in him broke.

His shoulders slumped. A slow, disbelieving shake of his head.

Then, wordlessly, he reached beneath his shirt—and pulled out the key.

Hunter barely breathed as he moved past her, boots scuffing against the floor.

The door.

The one she had dismissed. The one she was now convinced was the place where Mac had butchered them. The key turned. The lock clicked. Mac pushed the door open. And Hunter's entire world shattered.

Not a murder room.

Not blood.

Not horrors beyond her worst fears.

A soft, glowing sanctuary.

The room smelled of sage and candle wax, warm and heady, nothing like the antiseptic tang she'd braced for. The flickering light threw soft shadows over the *veves* carved into the table, the beads carefully laid in patterns only Mac understood. The walls held no horrors. No blood. No death.

Only faith.

The gun in her hand suddenly felt like it weighed a thousand pounds. Her stomach lurched. Her hands shook so violently, she almost dropped the flashlight. She had wasted so much time. Chased the wrong ghost. Doubted the wrong man.

Mac's voice was quiet. Rough. "This is where I come to pray for Hailey."

Hunter couldn't move. Mac's eyes met hers. And she saw everything. Not a killer, or a monster. Just a man clinging to hope.

And she had doubted him.

Her legs nearly gave out… and then they did. Hunter fell to the ground in front of an icon of the Black Madonna.

A stack of files slapped the ground in front of her.

"Look!" Mac's voice was torn, guttural above her. Hunter weakly pushed the files away. Mac leaped forward, squatting down, and pulled them open. "No! Really look!" He shoved Harmony's file in her face. "Yes, all these patients could have been donors, but you want to know something else? Not a single one of them was viable. Even if they had done it the right way. And Harmony? She might have been a perfect match for Hailey. Don't think for a second it didn't cross my mind when I did the exam of her body. But she had an infection that rendered her organs useless for somebody like Hailey."

The first fat tear welled in the corner of Hunter's eye.

Mac continued seething. "Eugene Watson. Great kid, but he had diabetes. Scratch him." Hunter tried to look away, but Mac grabbed her face, making her see the truth. She didn't fight him.

She couldn't.

"Rabbit? Rabbit was on so many anti-depressants to deal with his dad—I would have donated him my *life* if it had been possible."

"I was hunting the wrong person," she whispered.

Mac said nothing. Didn't have to. Hunter's hands shook.

Sabine.

Sabine had access to patient files. Sabine owed Fine Frankie. Sabine was the one running the operation. Sabine.

Not Mac.

Her breath hitched. She had wasted so much time. Mac's phone rang.

Raj.

Mac lifted it to his ear. His entire body stiffened. "No. No. Raj—don't let my sister die."

The words slammed into Hunter's gut like a bullet. Her stomach dropped.

"Hailey's not responding," Mac whispered, voice hoarse. "She needs a transplant. Now."

Hunter's heart pounded. "What can we do?"

Mac looked up at her, raw and desperate. "Pray," he whispered. "Pray that you'll help me save my sister's life."

The storm screamed around them.

Hunter looked at Mac. At the man she had doubted. At the man who had never stopped fighting for his sister— even when the world turned against him. Even when she turned against him. The weight of her mistake would haunt her. But right now, it didn't matter. Right now, only one thing did.

She grabbed her coat. "Let's go."

Chapter Thirty-Seven

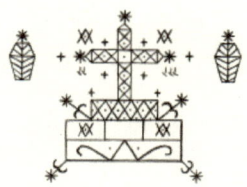

Wind screamed through the broken city, howling like a demon. The streets were black rivers, the floodwaters swallowing everything in their path.

Hunter couldn't breathe.

She was soaked, shaking, teeth chattering, her pulse a ragged drumbeat in her skull. Mac's hands were locked white-knuckle on the wheel, his jaw set like stone, but the SUV was fighting them. Water clawed at the tires, shoving them sideways with every turn.

"We're not gonna make it," she rasped, barely audible over the howling wind.

"We'll make it," Mac growled.

A power line snapped ahead, the cable whipping like a live snake, vomiting blue sparks into the flood.

Mac wrenched the wheel. The SUV hydroplaned—the tires losing grip, momentum whipping them into a spin.

Hunter's head cracked against the window. Stars exploded behind her eyes.

"Hold on!" Mac barked.

The hospital loomed ahead—a beacon of weak, flickering light in the drowned city. It was right there. So close.

Then—the wave hit.

A massive wall of black water came surging around the corner, a liquid battering ram obliterating everything in its path.

Hunter sucked in a breath—but it was too late. The SUV lifted off the ground. Tires spun uselessly in open air. The car pitched, rolled. The windshield exploded. Water rushed in like an open mouth.

Hunter's world flipped upside down.

She lurched for the door handle, but the flood sucked her under.

Chapter Thirty-Eight

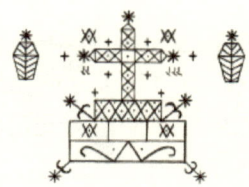

Cold.

A crushing, all-consuming cold.

It punched into her chest, stealing her air, paralyzing her limbs.

Hunter kicked blindly, but she couldn't tell which way was up.

The water was too black. Too deep.

Something snagged her arm. Debris. Metal. A piece of the SUV sinking fast.

Her lungs screamed. Her chest burned. She struggled, but the current dragged her deeper.

She was going to die here.

No.

NO!

She thrashed harder, reaching for anything. Then she felt hands. Hands gripping her jacket.

Mac.

His arms locked around her, pulling her up, up, up...

Hunter burst through the surface, gasping—choking.

Mac kicked furiously, one arm around her, fighting the current.

"Come on, Hunter," he snarled. "Breathe!"

Her lungs convulsed. She coughed—vomited water—sucked in burning, beautiful air.

Mac's grip tightened. His voice was raw. Desperate.

"You don't get to die on me," he ground out. "You hear me? Not tonight."

The storm raged around them. The hospital was still ahead. So close. But the water wasn't done with them yet.

The current dragged them toward the wreckage of a collapsed building, twisted rebar and shattered glass jutting out like jagged teeth.

Hunter's arms felt useless. Mac was fighting for both of them. She tried to kick, tried to help—but her body was sluggish, leaden, drained.

"Stay with me," Mac gritted, teeth chattering from the cold. "Almost there."

Lightning ripped the sky apart. For a split second, Hunter saw the entrance to the hospital, the storm-swollen stairs leading up to safety. Mac saw it, too. He gave one last push.

With a final, inhuman effort, he surged toward the steps, the current fighting him every inch of the way. His feet found purchase.

Hunter felt the moment the water went from a sucking abyss to knee-deep, and Mac half-dragged, half-carried her up the steps of the medical center. She coughed, staggered, fell against Mac's shoulder as they shoved through the hospital doors, leaving the storm screaming behind them.

The halls were dim, powered by failing generators, the building half-abandoned. Dr. Singh was waiting.

His gaze flicked over them—drenched, bleeding, shaking. Then to Mac. Then to her.

"Is this the donor?"

Mac nodded, voice raw. "She's the match."

Singh's brows shot up. "The detective?"

Mac grabbed his wrist, his voice ragged. "She has Rh-null blood, Singh. The rarest in the world. She can save her."

A flicker of shock—then understanding.

"This way," Singh said, already moving.

Hunter stopped thinking. Her legs carried her forward, through the swinging doors, past the operating room lights. Serafina had died in her arms.

Not this time.

She wasn't losing this one.

Chapter Thirty-Nine

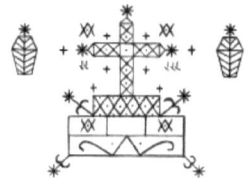

Darkness crawled in.

It was slow. Thick. Honey-thick.

Hunter felt it drag her down, like hands wrapping around her ankles, pulling her into the deep.

Above, voices blurred. The surgeons moved around her, their words like water swirling down a drain.

"Anesthesia's going in—Hunter, count backward from ten."

Ten.

She tried to speak. Tried to ask Mac if Hailey was okay.

Nine.

The lights flickered.

Eight.

She heard someone swear. A nurse's voice, sharp and tense.

Seven.

The room shuddered.

Then, the power cut out.

Chapter Forty

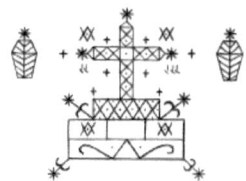

Hunter's mind fractured.

She was no longer in the operating room.

She was standing in floodwater, knee-deep, her reflection shimmering in the dark liquid.

A red glow bled through the sky. And then...a whisper. A chuckle. A gloved hand reaching down, plucking a cigar from nowhere and lighting it with a snap of his fingers.

"Well, now," the Baron said, grinning widely. "Ain't this interestin'."

Hunter tried to turn, tried to move—but her body felt slow, drugged, useless.

"You..." She swallowed thickly. "You're not real."

The Baron just laughed. "You're dreamin', sugar. But that don't make it any less real."

He took a drag, exhaling smoke that turned into

writing shadows. The storm howled around them, the floodwaters rising.

Hunter struggled to stay standing. "I don't have time for this."

"That so?" The Baron adjusted his crooked top hat, tapping the brim. "Then wake up."

She blinked.

And suddenly, Mac was there. Except—he wasn't standing. He was slumped against a hospital wall, blood blooming across his chest. And standing over him...

Sabine. A scalpel in her fist. Her wiry, wet hair plastered against her face, her lips curled in a snarl.

Hunter sucked in a breath. "No."

The Baron tipped his hat. "Tick-tock, cher."

Chapter Forty-One

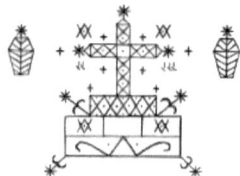

Hunter gasped. Her lungs burned. Reality slammed into her like a fist. She was back on the operating table.

The room was dark—only emergency lights glowed faintly overhead. The storm raged beyond the walls. She heard the shouts of doctors scrambling to restart the power.

She turned her head just enough to see Hailey on the table beside her. Still. Unmoving. Unconscious. But Mac—Mac was out there.

And she had just seen him die.

Hunter's fingers twitched. *Move.*

She clenched her jaw, fighting through the fog, the anesthesia drowning her body.

MOVE.

Her arms wouldn't obey. Her legs felt like they didn't exist. But she forced herself to roll off the table.

Her body collapsed to the floor, her limbs sluggish,

useless. She gagged, coughed, her stomach twisting violently.

A nurse shouted from the other room. Hunter staggered forward. The hallway tilted beneath her feet. The Baron's whisper curled in her ear.

"Tick-tock."

The hallway lights flickered, casting long, eerie shadows as Hunter staggered into the hall, the world spinning. Then…

"You really are one of a kind, Doc Steele," Sabine's voice purred from the dark.

Hunter saw Mac whirl.

Just like her vision.

Sabine was there, stepping forward, soaked to the bone, a scalpel gleaming red in her grip beneath the emergency lights.

Hunter staggered into the hall, the world spinning.

"Sabine—" Mac started.

She smirked. "Oh, relax, baby," she cooed, twirling the blade. "This won't take long."

Hunter lunged. Her body was too slow. Sabine's scalpel arced. Mac twisted—but not fast enough. The blade sank into his chest.

Hunter's vision blurred with white-hot fury. She threw herself forward, knocking into Sabine. Sabine let out a sharp laugh. But then—she froze.

Sabine's breath hitched. Her eyes locked on something over Mac's shoulder. Hunter didn't look. She already knew what had caught Sabine's shocked gaze.

Sabine saw *him*.

The Baron had tipped his hat.

Sabine's face contorted in horror. She stumbled back, back, back—and plunged through the window.

Hunter's breath ripped from her chest.

She lunged toward Mac and grabbed at him, pressing her hands against the wound. "Mac—Mac, stay with me, stay—"

Mac let out a laugh.

Hunter froze.

Mac's fingers curled around the scalpel's handle. And pulled it free.

Hunter braced for blood. For the wound to gush.

But... *nothing.*

Mac let out a shaky exhale. His fingers brushed the torn remains of his gris-gris bag.

"I'll be a sonofabitch," Hunter breathed.

Mac looked down at the charm. His lips curved into a wry grin. "Just have a little faith."

Hunter collapsed against him. The storm screamed outside.

The Baron's whisper echoed in her ear. *"I told ya, cher. Ain't nothin' ever really gone."*

She squeezed her eyes shut.

The power glared to life as the generators kicked back on. Singh and the nurses rushed into the hallway, staring with confusion at the wind-whipped curtains flapping near the broken window.

Singh rushed to Hunter's side. "Are you okay?"

Hunter gripped the doctor's arm. "Hailey... tell me it's not too late to save Hailey."

Mac looked imploringly at his friend.

Raj's face stayed serious, but he smiled. "If we get

you back in there now, she still has a chance."

Hunter turned to look at Mac.

"Go," he said, still trying to catch his breath. "It'll be okay."

"How?" she asked, almost begging. "How do you know?"

He smiled tiredly and wiggled the gris-gris bag.

Singh and the nurses helped her to her feet and back toward the operating room.

Hailey was alive. Mac was alive. And for the first time in her life…

Hunter let herself believe.

Epilogue

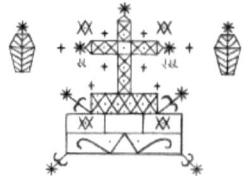

The sun bore down through thick humidity, turning the morning into a sauna. The squeal of tires and the protesting screech of brakes cut through the sleepy Sunday stillness.

Mac could feel his cervical vertebrae dislocating one by one.

"Hey," Hunter piped up from the cramped back seat of the Volkswagen, smirking. "You're the one who let her drive."

Mac groaned, rubbing his temples. "What was I supposed to do? She threatened to tell Reverend Mother on me."

Hunter pursed her lips, tapped a finger to her cheek in mock consideration, and then shot Hailey a wink in the rearview mirror. "Yeah. She's got you there."

Hailey grinned, completely unrepentant, her hands

still firmly gripping the steering wheel.

Looking at her now, six months later, you'd never know she had almost died. Her skin was warm with color again, her eyes bright, her laughter easy. Even her hair had regained its fullness and luster—though Mac still threatened to shave it every time she annoyed him. The operation had been a *miracle*, even in the middle of a hurricane.

A damn miracle.

Mac fervently wished he'd paid for driving lessons instead of dance classes. His sister's lead foot was going to give him a permanent case of whiplash. Yet somehow, she still parallel parked the car without running over any pedestrians, so he chalked it up to a good day.

The trio stepped out onto the steps of the cathedral just as Reverend Mother emerged, hands on her hips. "I was beginning to think y'all done got lost," she chided. Then, without warning, she wrapped them all up in one of her famous, bone-crushing hugs.

Mac tried—and failed—not to grunt.

Reverend Mother held Hailey back for a moment, eyeing her appraisingly. Then she nodded. "You still got some of that fire in you?"

Hailey grinned, standing taller. "You bet I do."

Reverend Mother slung an arm around her shoulders and led her toward the cathedral. "Come on, child. I'll show you how to make that scrawny docent cluck like a chicken."

"Really?" Hailey's eyes widened as the two disappeared inside.

Mac looked a little nervous. Hunter laughed.

The city had started rebuilding almost as soon as the floodwaters receded. A year later, the scars were still there—but so was the resilience.

Some things, however, hadn't survived the storm.

Sabine's body had been found crumpled in a dumpster below the shattered hospital window. A freak accident, the authorities said. Just another casualty of the storm.

But Hunter and Mac knew better.

So did the Baron.

B.B. hadn't bought the official report either. He'd dug deeper, pulling Sabine's phone records, tracing her web of connections. Calls to Dubai. Abu Dhabi. Riyadh. Contacts in the United Arab Emirates—people willing to pay top dollar for her "wares."

Turned out Sabine had run a tight operation. She had lured people in with the promise of easy cash, desperate souls barely scraping by. Then she'd made them disappear, leaving just enough of a gruesome calling card to send law enforcement chasing the wrong story.

The symbols carved into the victims' foreheads? The Baron's *veves*?

Smoke and mirrors.

Sabine had used superstition as a smokescreen, making the deaths look ritualistic when they were really just cold-blooded, calculated, and profitable.

She had everyone fooled.

Until she didn't.

And now?

She was just another ghost in the storm.

Dante had made things interesting—performing the

ritual in the cemetery and taking Eugene's body out to the swamp. But his heart was in the right place. As a true believer, he feared the Baron would not accept Eugene's desecrated body. So, when he had stumbled on Eugene's body in the bags behind the double, he had tried to appease the *ghede* the only way he knew how.

"What I don't get is why he didn't report it?" Mac had mused one morning over coffee.

Hunter had shrugged. "Dante wasn't exactly in this country legally. He was desperate to avoid any entanglements with local law enforcement."

"Okay," Mac had agreed. "But if he suspected Sabine was behind it, why would he have stayed at the double?"

"He might not have had a choice," Hunter had replied solemnly. "Harmony, Eugene, Rabbit, Dante… they were faced with impossible choices. One's most people couldn't even begin to fathom. They did the best with what life handed to them. But to most people they encountered on this planet, they were…. forgettable." An earnest look came over Hunter's features. "But not if I have anything to say about it."

Scarpetta had been found, too—or what was left of him.

Whether the hurricane had taken him or Fine Frankie's goons had done the job, no one cared enough to ask questions.

B.B., meanwhile, had somehow managed to both meet a woman and file for divorce within the same year.

"Best hurricane evacuation I ever had," he'd grumbled, flipping through legal paperwork. "Though next time, remind me not to marry a girl whose ex works for the IRS."

Mac had laughed so hard he nearly fell off his chair.

The cathedral doors loomed ahead. Mac hesitated.

He still wasn't much for church.

Never had been. Faith was one thing. Walls… well, that was a different story.

But some things were different now.

Like Hailey being alive. Like Hunter still standing by his side. Like the gris-gris bag tucked safely inside his coat pocket, the torn fabric stitched back together but worn thin from use.

"Come on, Doc," Hunter murmured. "You don't wanna keep the good sister waiting."

Mac shot her a sideways look. "I don't suppose you believe she's really gonna make that docent cluck like a chicken?"

Hunter smirked.

"I don't know." She tilted her head, the faintest ghost of a grin playing on her lips. "Depends on what you believe."

The wind whispered through the narrow alleyways of the city, curling around them like a knowing hand.

Mac swore, just for a second, that he heard a chuckle—low, deep, laced with smoke and mischief.

The Baron.

Mac shook his head, lips twitching as he followed Hunter up the steps.

"Yeah," he murmured, more to himself than anyone else.

"Guess it does."

Keep Reading...If You Dare

From the author of *The Devil She Knows* comes a chilling new standalone psychological thriller set in the haunted heart of New Orleans.

Different case. Different characters. Same shadows.

Step into a city where the ghosts don't stay buried—and neither does the truth.

THE JUDAS CRADLE
A Southern Noir Psychological Thriller

by

M.T. Falgoust

The bar was dark enough to hide in. I liked that about it—how the lights flickered in a way that made everything seem hazy, like the world itself couldn't make up its mind whether it wanted to stay solid or fade into the background.

The place smelled of old wood and stale beer, with a hint of desperation clinging to the walls, and it was just quiet enough that you could hear the ice shift in your drink if you were paying attention.

I wasn't paying attention.

I ran my finger around the rim of the glass, the whiskey inside glowing amber like it held the last remnants of the sun. I hadn't touched it yet, but it called to me, whispering promises of numbness, of forgetting, even if just for a little while.

But forgetting never lasts long.

The noise of the city outside was muffled, almost as if New Orleans was drowning, just like me. Even the humidity felt like it was wrapping its thick, sticky fingers around my neck, pushing me deeper into the darkness I'd carried for years.

My sister Emily's face floated in the glass—laughing, always laughing—but that laughter had long turned into an echo. A ghost.

I swirled the whiskey, trying to chase her image away, but it lingered, like a bad memory that refused to leave. And that's what Emily was now, wasn't she? A bad memory. The one I couldn't shake, no matter how much I tried.

I'd spent years looking for her, convinced she wasn't dead, but the truth hung there like the stink of the bar. She was gone, and I'd never been able to save her.

"Another?" the bartender asked, pulling me out of my head. I glanced up, blinking against the dim light that barely illuminated his face. He was a faceless figure, one I'd seen too many times to count, standing behind too many bars.

I shook my head, but it wasn't for him. It was for me. For the part of me that wanted to sink into oblivion and never come back. "No," I muttered, my voice gravelly from the whiskey I hadn't yet drunk. "I'm good."

A lie.

The truth was, I was far from good. I was drowning in a past I couldn't escape, with ghosts I couldn't exorcize. Emily was just one of them.

I tossed back the drink anyway, the liquid burning its way down my throat, searing a path straight to my chest. It didn't warm me. It never did. I thought about another, about sinking back into the numbness, but I knew it wouldn't last. It never did.

Emily's face flashed behind my eyes again. The day she disappeared. She was wearing that stupid pink dress—

stained with dirt from the backyard, but still grinning like the world couldn't touch her. Like I could protect her. I couldn't. I hadn't.

I pushed the glass away, the sound of it scraping against the wood echoing louder than it should have. The bartender didn't say anything. He never did. He knew the look of a man who was trying to out-drink his past. The phone in my pocket buzzed, and for a second, I considered letting it ring. What could be so urgent at this hour that it couldn't wait? But my hand moved on instinct, fishing it out before my brain had a chance to protest.

"Yeah?" I rasped.

It was Charles, my partner. His voice came through the line, sharp and clear, cutting through the fog in my brain. "We've got a case. You're gonna want to see this."

I exhaled, rubbing my face. There was a weight to his words, something grim lurking beneath them, the kind of tone you get when it's more than just another body on the streets.

The city always had bodies—too many for any one man to handle—but this sounded different. This sounded bad. I hesitated. The ghosts of my sister's laughter still clung to me, reminding me of all the things I couldn't fix, of all the people I couldn't save. But I stood anyway. Because what else could I do?

"I'm on my way," I said, already moving toward the door.

Outside, the city hit me like a punch. The heat was oppressive, heavy with moisture that wrapped around my skin, suffocating. Neon lights flickered in the distance, casting a sickly glow over the streets. The air tasted of salt and rot, like something had been festering just beneath the surface for too long. It matched the knot in my gut. The past always did that to me, especially when it involved Emily.

I climbed into my car, the leather armrest sticking to my skin. The dashboard light flickered on, bathing the inside of the car in a green glow that made me feel like I was in a bad dream. Maybe I was. Maybe I'd been in one for years.

As I pulled away from the curb, the city blurred by, shadows slipping in and out of the corners of my vision. New Orleans at night was like that—alive with ghosts, the ones that you could see and the ones you couldn't. And my ghosts?

They were always waiting for me.

*****

As I drove through the narrow streets of New Orleans, the city's pulse beat in the distance—muffled jazz from the French Quarter, the laughter of tourists who didn't know better. But the deeper you went, the more the Crescent City showed its true face. The neon glow of Bourbon Street dimmed to flickering streetlights, casting long shadows over cracked sidewalks. Here, the charm faded into something darker, something more real. The kind of real that kept you up at night.

I kept the window down, letting the thick, humid air roll in, even though it felt like breathing through wet cotton. My fingers drummed against the steering wheel, the weight of Charles's call hanging in the air like a storm cloud. He wouldn't have called if it wasn't serious. Not at this hour. And not with that tone.

I couldn't shake the feeling that this case— whatever it was—would be another notch in the endless tally of things I couldn't control. Couldn't fix. Couldn't save. Emily's face flashed again behind my eyes, her smile that last day, the sound of her bare feet on the kitchen floor, quick and light as she ran from the house. The memory twisted, warping, as it always did. Her footsteps faded, replaced by a scream.

No. I shook my head, gripping the wheel tighter, forcing myself back to the present.

The past was a dark, sticky thing, always creeping in when I wasn't looking. But this wasn't about Emily. Not tonight. I turned down a side street, the tires crunching over gravel.

The warehouse loomed ahead—abandoned, decaying. The city had forgotten about this place long ago, and now it was just another part of New Orleans that had gone to rot, like so many other things in this town.

But tonight, it had a purpose again.

Charles's squad car was parked just outside, lights off. That meant it was bad. I killed the engine and stepped out, the door creaking louder than it should have in the silence.

The smell hit me first—like rust and old water, mingled with something metallic that I knew all too well.

Blood.

Charles met me halfway across the gravel lot. He was wearing that look he always did when we were walking into something we couldn't unsee. His face was set, but the tension in his jaw told me everything I needed to know before he even opened his mouth. "This one's... different, James," he said, his voice low. "Real different."

I nodded, my stomach tightening. Different meant it was going to be the kind of scene that stuck with you. The kind that etched itself behind your eyelids so that every time you closed your eyes, it was there, waiting for you.

"Who found it?" I asked, keeping my tone flat—professional. The part of me that was still sober enough to function took over.

"Couple of kids trying to break in. Got more than they bargained for." He shook his head, rubbing the back of his neck like he was trying to shake off the image already burned there.

"Let's see it," I said, walking toward the warehouse.

My boots crunched over broken glass, each step pulling me deeper into the darkness of the place. The door was hanging off its hinges, one of the metal panels barely holding on. Inside, the air was stale and thick, laced with the unmistakable copper tang of blood. I followed Charles's flashlight beam as it cut through the gloom, casting eerie shadows along the walls.

Then I saw it.

The body was suspended in the middle of the room, strung up like some grotesque marionette, arms splayed wide and head slumped forward. Blood had pooled beneath him, soaking into the concrete floor, thick and sticky. But it wasn't just the blood. It was the way the body was positioned, the unnatural twist of the limbs—the way the man's chest had been carved open with a precision that made my stomach turn. His face was bruised—swollen—

but it wasn't the kind of bruises you get from a fistfight.

No, this was different.

I stepped closer, the sound of my breathing loud in my ears. A low buzzing filled my head, a familiar hum that always came when I saw something like this. But this wasn't like anything I'd ever seen before.

"That's not all," Charles said quietly, pointing to the man's chest. His light shifted, revealing a jagged line of letters carved into the dead man's skin.

A message. Written in blood.

The first sacrifice.

I stared at the words, my mind working to make sense of what I was seeing.

Sacrifice.

The word echoed in my head, dredging up memories I'd long buried. "What the hell is this?" I asked, my voice barely above a whisper.

Charles shook his head, his face pale in the dim light. "I don't know, but this isn't some random killing. Whoever did this… they're sending a message."

My chest tightened, the familiar weight of dread settling in. I could feel it in the air—the shift. This wasn't just another murder. This was something deeper, something darker. And somehow, I knew it was only the beginning.

As I stood there, staring at the bloodied corpse hanging in the middle of the room, I couldn't shake the feeling that the past was clawing its way back to the surface. Emily's laughter echoed in my mind, and I knew, deep down, that whatever this was—it was tied to me. To her. To everything I'd tried to forget. I took a deep breath, my hands balling into fists at my sides.

The ghosts were back. And this time, they weren't going to let me go.

Want More?

Be the first to uncover the secrets behind *The Judas Cradle*.
Join the author's inner circle for:
- Early access to exclusive content
- A subscriber-only redacted case file from *The Judas Cradle*
- Behind-the-scenes extras
- Launch announcements & preorder alerts

Scan the QR code below to join instantly.

Or visit https://mtfalgoustauthor.kit.com/832fcc23b4

Redacted files. Bonus content. One killer story.

Acknowledgements

This story was sparked in part by *Blood, Bones and Organs: The Gruesome Red Market*, an unforgettable NPR article by journalist Scott Carney. The brutal reality behind the piece haunted me—and ultimately helped shape the dark heartbeat of this book. You can read it here: https://bit.ly/judas-cradle-inspo.

To the city of New Orleans—my hometown and forever muse—thank you for your ghosts, your secrets, and your shadows.

And most of all, to you, dear reader…

If this story kept you turning pages, made you question what's real, or left you unsettled in all the right ways… please consider leaving a review. Your words help stories like this find their way into the hands of other readers who crave the dark.

Some stories whisper their way into your life. Others come screaming.

This one refused to stay quiet.

About the Author

I weave dark tapestries of suspense, action, and chilling fiction—stories where shadows move when no one is looking, danger lurks in the most unexpected places, and the line between hero and villain is razor thin.

As an award-winning author with a fascination for the macabre, I don't just tell stories—I orchestrate nightmares that linger long after the final page is turned.

When not writing, I'm chasing mysteries, exploring forgotten corners of the world, and diving into obscure history. Because in my world, the truth is always stranger (and far more terrifying) than fiction.

More Thrills from M.T. Falgoust

The Eye of the Storm: A.R.I.E.S. Files #1

Clive Cussler Adventure Writers Award Honoree

"Had me on the edge of my seat one minute and laughing out loud the next!"

Dirk Cussler, NYT Bestselling Author of Dirk Pitt Look for it at your favorite bookstore or online.
"Make a sandwich with an extra snack and don't bother looking for a bookmark! You'll want the sandwich but won't need the bookmark."

★★★★★ Amazon Customer

"Wonderfully fast-paced, so hold on tight!"

★★★★★ Diane Kathryn Plopa, Author of *Free Will*

Look for it at your favorite bookstore or online.